FIELD, FOREST AND FARM

This edition published 2025
by Living Book Press
Copyright © Living Book Press, 2025

ISBN: 978-1-76153-389-1 (hardcover)
         978-1-76153-390-7 (softcover)

First published in 1919.

This edition is based on the 1919 printing by The Century Co.

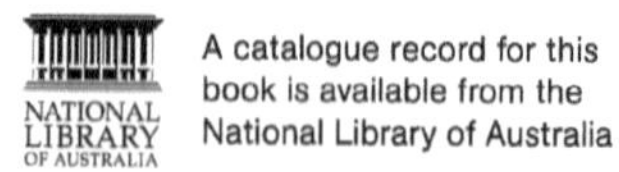

A catalogue record for this book is available from the National Library of Australia

Field, Forest and Farm

by

Jean-Henri Fabre

Contents

CHAPTER I

THE STAFF OF LIFE

WITH HIS nephews as willing companions and eager listeners, Uncle Paul continued his walks and talks in the pleasant summer afternoons.

"Bread is made of flour," he began, "and flour is wheat reduced to powder under the millstone. What an interesting mechanism that is, the flour-mill, driven by water, by the wind, sometimes by steam! What wearisome effort, what waste of time, if we had not this invention and were forced to do its work of grinding by sheer strength of arm!

"I must tell you that in ancient times, for want of knowing how to grind wheat, people had to content themselves with crushing it between two stones after parching it a little over the fire. The coarse meal thus obtained was cooked in water to a sort of porridge and eaten with no further preparation. Bread was unknown.

"Later the plan was hit upon of kneading the meal with water and of cooking the dough between two hot stones. Thus was obtained a crude sort of biscuit, about as thick as your finger, stodgy and hard, and mixed with charcoal and ashes. It was preferable to the porridge, the insipid paste, of the earlier time, but far inferior to the poorest bread of to-day. To make a long story short, by trial after trial success was at last attained in the making of bread like ours. It became necessary then, without possessing

anything to compare with our mills, to grind wheat in large quantities.

"Flour was obtained by triturating the wheat in a hollowed stone with a pestle. This latter was sometimes light enough to be operated directly by hand; sometimes, to produce quicker results, it was so large and heavy that it had to be turned in its stone mortar with the help of a long bar. Such was the first mill. With appliances of this sort I leave you to imagine how long a time was required for the production of a single handful of flour. For bread enough to feed one person at one meal, wretched slaves were kept toiling from morning till night and from night till morning in turning the pestle."

"What cruel masters they must have had!" exclaimed Emile.

"Yes, the slaves were harnessed to the bar like beasts of burden; and when, weakened with fatigue, they did not go fast enough, a rawhide was applied to their bare shoulders. These unfortunate millers were poor wretches taken in war and afterward sold in the market with the same indifference with which a drover sells his cattle. Such, then, were the hardships that led the way to the modern mill which to-day, with a few turns of its water-wheel, and to the cheerful accompaniment of its *tick-tack*, can make flour enough for a whole family.

"But let us leave the mill and turn our attention to the following interesting experiment. Take a handful of flour and with a little water make it into dough. This done, knead the dough with your fingers over a large plate while an assistant moistens it continually with water from a pitcher. Keep the dough well in hand and continue kneading it, flattening it out and gathering it together again, turning it over and over under the fine stream of water poured from above.

"Examine carefully the water that passes over the dough and washes it. It falls into the plate as white as milk, showing that it carries with it something from the flour. This something will finally settle at the bottom of the liquid, and we shall find it to be a substance not unlike the starch used for starching linen. In fact, it is starch, or fecula, as the chemists call it—neither more nor less. The starch used in the laundry is obtained in considerable quantities by similar means: dough is washed and the whitened water, left undisturbed, deposits a layer of starch which has only to be gathered together and dried.[1]

"So much, then, is made clear: flour contains starch, but it contains something else also. There is a limit beyond which the washed dough yields no more starch; it is useless to knead it, the water falls colorless into the plate. What remains in one's hands after this prolonged washing is a soft, gluey substance, having something of the elastic quality of rubber. Grayish in color, it has a rather pronounced odor. When dried in the sun, it becomes hard and translucent like horn. It is called gluten from its gluelike character, its viscosity.

1   Laundry starch is now obtained chiefly from rice and from pulse.—*Translator.*

"Now this substance, so unattractive in appearance, all soft and sticky and getting clogged between the fingers—this gluten, in short—do you know what it is? Don't try to dispute me, for what I am going to tell you is the exact truth. In its composition gluten does not differ from flesh. It is vegetable flesh, capable of becoming animal flesh by the simple process of digestion, without any material loss or gain. Therefore it is gluten, first and foremost, that gives to bread its great nutritive value.

"Of all the cereals, wheat contains the most gluten, with rye holding second place. Maize and rice, as well as

RYE

chestnuts and potatoes, are wholly lacking in this ingredient; and for that reason flour made from them, rich though it be in starch, is not at all the kind of flour for bread. This will explain to you the superiority of wheat over all other farinaceous grains.

"Wheat, the only cereal that can give us white bread, that superior bread which nevertheless is not always to your taste unless spread with a little butter, does not grow in all countries. Open your atlas and run over with your finger the countries bordering on the Mediterranean; your travels will embrace the principal regions where wheat flourishes. Farther north it is too cold for the successful culture of the precious cereal; farther south it is too warm.

"But that is not all. In the privileged regions not every district is adapted to this incomparable crop: wheat needs the mild

B ARLEY

temperature and fertile soil of the plains, not the harsh climate and dry slopes of the mountains. Let us consider France in particular. Its plains produce excellent wheat, but not enough to feed the entire population; therefore in the hilly and cooler regions, where this cereal cannot be raised, recourse is had in the first place to rye, which yields a bread that is compact, brown, and heavy, but on the whole preferable to any other except, of course, wheat. This rye bread is the customary food of the country in the greater number of our departments.

"The raising of rye becomes in its turn impossible in regions too cold and too sterile. There then remains, as a last resort, barley, the hardiest of cereals, which is found in the mountains until we reach the neighborhood of perpetual snow, and can be raised even in the frigid climate of the extreme North.

"You ought to taste the miserable bread made from barley in order to find our bread good—or, I might better say, in order to find it an exquisite dainty even without butter or jam. Barley bread is full of long bristles that stick in the throat; it contains more bran than flour; it is bitter, stodgy, and of a disagreeable odor. Oh, what sorry stuff! And yet many have to be content with it, and are only glad if they can get enough of it.

"In the greater part of the world wheat,

R ICE

widely distributed by commerce, furnishes bread only for the tables of the rich. The rest of the population knows nothing, as a rule, of this article of food, has never so much as seen it, and at most has only heard of it as a rare curiosity. In place of bread the people eat here one thing, there another, according to the country. Asia has rice, Africa millet, America maize. In India and China the people have hardly anything to eat but rice boiled in water with a little salt. Half the entire world has practically the same diet.

"The plant that produces rice has a stalk resembling that of wheat, but instead of ending in an upright ear it bears a cluster of feeble and pendent branches, all loaded with seeds. The leaves are narrow and ribbon-shaped, rough to the touch. This plant is aquatic. In order to flourish, it must send down its roots into the submerged mud and spread its foliage, excepting the tip, in the flood. Marshy shallows, inundated a part of the year, are adapted to its cultivation."

"But what do they do where there are no such marshes?" asked Louis.

"When such marshes are lacking, the ingenious Chinaman floods the lowlands with water from some near-by stream until the ground is all soft and muddy. He then draws off the water through a series of little canals, and works the mud with a light plow drawn by a buffalo, a kind of ox with a long beard hanging from its chin and a mane waving on its back.

"The seed once sown in the furrows and the young plants started, the water from the stream is again made to flood the fields, where it remains until harvest time. Then for the second time it is drawn off, and the reaper, sickle in hand and with the black mud up to his knees, cuts down the rice-laden tops of the stalks.

"Maize, or Indian corn, is the staple food of South America, as rice is that of Asia. Many call it Turkish wheat, a name doubly inappropriate, for in the first place this grain is not indigenous to Turkey, but to America, and in the second place it has nothing in common with the wheat from which bread is made. From America its cultivation has spread to our part of the globe.

"The ear of maize is very large and is composed of full, rounded kernels, yellow and shiny, closely packed in regular rows. Like rice, maize furnishes a fine flour of pleasing appearance but lacking in one essential: it contains no gluten. Hence the utter impossibility of using either rice or maize for making bread, despite the good appearance of the flour made from them.

"Nevertheless maize is a very wholesome article of food, and one of great value in the country, where the appetite is sharpened by open air and hard work. Only it is not in the form of bread that it best yields its nourishment, but rather in that of porridge, or boiled meal and water."

CHAPTER II

THE HISTORY OF TOBACCO

"**B**EFORE TAKING the form of the powder which the user of snuff pushes up into his nose to tickle his nostrils and promote sneezing, before being rolled into the cigar or reduced to that crisp, moss-like substance which the smoker stuffs into his pipe, tobacco has had a previous existence as a plant bearing this same name. A stalk about one meter in height, large, clammy leaves of a strong odor, bright red flowers each shaped like a narrow funnel and expanding into the five points of a star at the orifice, dry capsules filled with innumerable little seeds—there you have the tobacco plant.

"Only the leaves are used, and these only after undergoing certain processes that intensify their natural properties and cause them to lose their green color. Rolled into compact little cylinders, they become cigars; cut very fine, they take the form of smoking tobacco. Reduced to powder, they furnish what is known as snuff.

"America, the same land to which we owe the potato, also gave us tobacco. When, almost four centuries ago, Christopher Columbus discovered the new world, one of the first landings he made was on

TOBACCO PLANT

the large island of Cuba. Apprehensive of danger in the forests from the savage tribes on every side, Columbus sent scouts ahead to reconnoitre the country.

"The sailors forming this party encountered on the way, to their extreme surprise, numerous Indians, both men and women, holding each a sort of lighted fire-brand between the teeth and inhaling the smoke. These fire-brands, called 'tabagos,' were made of a plant rolled up in a dry leaf. There, then, were the first smokers and the first cigars recorded in history.

"The natives of Cuba and the neighboring islands had, we infer, been addicted to smoking for a long time, probably for centuries, when the Europeans first appeared among them. They had their rolls of dry leaves, or tabagos, and their smoking appliances of soft stone or baked clay, appliances called by us 'pipes' and by them 'calumets.' Tobacco, in fact, played a prominent part in their medicine, their superstitious observances, and their political assemblies.

"Consulted as to future events, the soothsayer first of all inhaled the smoke of several tabagos, while the other persons present, seated in a circle, vied with one another in the energy of their smoking, their ultimate object being to enwrap themselves in a dense cloud. Then from the midst of this cloud the soothsayer, his imagination wrought to a high pitch by the fumes of the tobacco, delivered his oracles in unwonted terms that made the hearers believe they were listening to the voice of God.

"A like ceremony was observed in the assemblies held for discussing public affairs. Seated on a stone and inhaling the smoke from his calumet, the orator who was about to take the floor waited in passive silence while the chiefs of the nation approached him, one at a time, to blow into his face plenteous puffs from their pipes and to commend to him the interests of the tribe. These fumigations concluded, the orator abandoned himself to his eloquence amid the enthusiastic acclaim of the assembly.

"Seeing the islanders smoking, Columbus's companions wished to try this singular custom for themselves. To the gratification of this desire the Indian lent his ready assistance: he showed them how the tabago is rolled, and how the calumet is filled and lighted. Though history is silent on the subject, it is clear that the first sailor to undertake the inhalation must have been seized with that fearful nausea which no novice in smoking can escape. A stomach of any delicacy would have been forever repelled; the harsh gullet of the mariner found a certain charm in the thing when once the trying experiences of initiation were over.

"The taste for smoking was so soon acquired that, on their return to Spain, the companions of Columbus very quickly extended this Indian custom in their own country. Before long, too, there was discovered a new way to use tobacco: some one conceived the idea of reducing the leaf to a dry powder and stuffing it into the nostrils, sniffing with each pinch of the powdered substance. The Indian had discovered smoking tobacco; the European in his turn invented snuff.

"Spain and Portugal numbered their smokers and snuff-takers by the thousand when, in 1560, tobacco made its first appearance in France. Nicot, French ambassador at Lisbon, sent as an object of curiosity to his sovereign queen, Catherine de Médicis, some seeds of the fashionable plant and a box of tobacco in powdered form. Charmed with this gift, the queen quickly contracted the habit of taking snuff. To please her, tobacco was cultivated, and snuff-takers soon became numerous in all the provinces. It was said that a certain great personage of the period took as much as three ounces daily. He certainly must have had his nose well tanned.

"From one nation to another the use of tobacco gradually spread, but not without serious opposition. The Turks are to-day passionately addicted to smoking, extremely fond of their long pipes; yet hear what sort of a reception they at first gave to tobacco. Against smokers and snuff-takers their emperor, Amurat, issued an edict severe to the point of cruelty. Every delinquent was condemned to receive fifty strokes with the rod on the soles of his feet."

"That ought to have driven tobacco out of the country in short order," remarked Jules.

"That was merely a warning to first offenders," returned his uncle. "For a second offense the luckless person caught in the act had his nose cut off. It was a radical measure to discourage the snuff-taker: no more nose, no more snuff. But the smokers, after this horrible mutilation, persisted in their smoking.

"A king of Persia devised what he thought would cure even this habit: every one caught with a pipe in his mouth had his upper lip cut off. At the same time, of course, every nose proved guilty of snuff-taking fell under the executioner's knife. But the atrocious edict of the Persian king proved as futile as that of the Turkish emperor. Despite all the noses struck off, all the lips cut away, all the feet made to tingle under the rod, the use of tobacco still continued to spread. These fruitless severities had to be abandoned.

"Other regulations sprang up here and there, less cruel, but sufficiently fruitful in fines, imprisonments, vexations of all sorts. Still nothing was of any avail; smokers and snuff-takers remained incorrigible. Finally, taking wiser counsel, the government authorities conceived a plan for making this passion, which no severity had been able to subdue, yield them large revenues. The government itself became exclusive vender of the very article it had at first proscribed with such rigor. France alone derives a yearly revenue of almost three hundred million francs from the sale of tobacco."

CHAPTER III

THE ORIGIN OF FERTILE SOIL

"FERTILE OR arable soil," resumed Uncle Paul, "constitutes only the surface layer of earth, that which is worked by the farmer's implements and yields nutriment to the roots of plants and promotes their development. In one place you will see bare rocks and utter barrenness; in another you find fertile soil to a depth of an inch or two, scantily carpeted with grass; and again, in a third, you come upon rich earth so deep as to maintain abundant vegetation. But nowhere does this fertile layer have an indefinite thickness: at a depth never very considerable a subsoil having the qualities of the neighboring mountains is sure to be found. How then has there come to be formed this layer of earth whence is derived all the nutriment required by plants, animals, and men?

"Undermined all winter, and even the whole year round on high mountains, by the ice that forms in their slightest fissures, rocks of all kinds break into small fragments, divide into grains of sand, fall into dust, and furnish the powdery mineral matter which the rain washes away and deposits in the valleys. This as a rule is the origin of broken stones, sand, clay, and fertile soil. Ice by its expansive force has detached them from the tops of mountains and the waters have swept them away and carried them further. One can form an idea of the action of ice in crumbling rocks to make soil of them and enrich the valleys, by examining the surface of a hard road at the moment of thawing.

Firm underfoot before freezing, this surface loses its firmness after a thaw and is pushed up here and there in little finely-powdered clods. At the moment of freezing, the humidity with which the soil was impregnated turned into ice which, increasing in volume, reduced to fine particles the surface layer of the road. When the thaw comes, these particles which the ice no longer holds together form first mud, then dust. In exactly this manner arable land was formed by the disintegration of rocks of all kinds, which were reduced to particles by the action of frost.

But soil suitable for agriculture contains not only powdery mineral matter, but also a little mold from the decomposition of vegetable matter. To give you an idea of the causes which from the very earliest times have little by little fertilized this rock-dust with vegetable mold, let us take the following example.

Geography has taught you what a volcano is. It is a mountain whose summit is hollowed out in an immense funnel-shaped excavation called a crater. From time to time the ground trembles near a volcano and formidable noises similar to the rolling of thunder and the booming of cannon are heard from the depths of the mountain. The crater throws up into the air a lofty column of smoke, dark by day, fiery red at night. All at once the mountain is rent and vomits up through the crevices a stream of fire, a current of melted rock, or lava. Finally the volcano quiets down; the source of the terrible flood dries up. The streams of lava harden and cease running; and after a lapse of time which may be years they become quite cold. Now what is to become of this enormous bed of black stone similar in character to the slag from a forge? What will this sheet of lava covering an area of several square miles produce?

"This desolate, blasted expanse seems destined never to be clothed with verdure. But in any such assumption one would be mistaken. After centuries and centuries a vigorous growth of oaks, beeches, and other large trees will have taken root there. In fact, you will see that air, rain, snow, and, above all, frost attack in turn the hard surface of the lava, detach fine particles from it, and slowly produce a little dust at its expense. On this dust there will spring into being certain strange and hardy plants, those white or yellow patches, those vegetable incrustations, calculated to live on the surface of stone and known as lichens. These lichens fasten themselves to the lava, gnaw it still more, and in dying leave a little mold formed from their decaying remains. On this precious mold, lodged in some cavity of the lava, there is now a growth of mosses which perish in their turn and increase the quantity of fertilizing material. Next come ferns, which require a richer soil, and after that a few tufts of grass; then some brambles, some meager shrubs; and thus with each succeeding year the fertile soil is added to from the new remnants of lava and mold left by the preceding generation of plants that have gone to decay. It is in this way that gradually a lava-bed finally becomes covered with a forest.

"Our own arable land had a similar origin. Sterile rocks, hard as they are, contributed the mineral part by being reduced to dust through the combined action of water, air, and frost; and the successive generations of plant-life, beginning with the simplest, furnished the mold.

"Notice how admirably, in the processes of nature, the smallest of created beings perform their part and contribute as best they can to the general harmony. To produce fertile soil there is needed something more than the frosts and thaws that crumble the hardest rock: there is need of plants hardy enough to live on this sterile soil, such as tough grasses, mosses, lichens, which gnaw the stone. It is through the medium of these rudimentary plants, so pitiful in appearance and yet so hardy, that the dust of the rocks is enriched with mold and converted into a soil capable of bearing other and more delicate plants.

"It is not in cultivated fields that you will find those thick carpets of mosses and lichens, valiant disintegrators of stone; it is on the mountain-tops that they can be seen at their work of crusting over the smooth rock in order to convert it into fertile soil. It is from these heights that this fertile soil has descended, little by little, washed down by the rain, until it has fertilized the valleys. This work is going on all the time; in hilly regions plants of the lowest order are constantly adding to the extent of arable land. The little threads of rain-water that furrow these regions carry away with them some of this humus and bear it to the plains below.

"What a worthy subject for our thoughtful study is this formation of arable soil by these legions of inferior plants, obscure workers indefatigably crumbling the rock! What immense results obtained by the simplest means!"

CHAPTER IV

DIFFERENT KINDS OF SOIL

"Four substances, mingled in very variable proportions, enter into the composition of fertile soil, or arable land, namely: sand or silica, clay, limestone, and humus, or vegetable mold. Each one of these ingredients separately would make but very poor soil, quite unsuited for agriculture; but united, mixed together, they fulfill the conditions necessary to fertility. Arable land generally contains all four, with the predominance sometimes of one, sometimes of another. The soil takes the name of its most abundant constituent. Thus have arisen the names, silicious soil, argillaceous soil, calcareous soil, and humous soil, to designate the fertile lands dominated respectively by sand, clay, limestone, and humus. Compound terms are also used. For example, when it is said of a certain soil that it is argillo-calcareous, it is meant that clay and limestone are its chief constituents.

"Sand consists of particles, more or less minute, of very hard rock, sometimes opaque, sometimes as transparent as glass, and always easily recognizable by its property of emitting sparks when struck with steel. Flint and white pebbles belong to this kind of rock, which is called silex, silica, or quartz. These three expressions mean about the same. Sandy soils have little consistency, are easily permeated by water, and freely absorb the sun's heat, which makes them very subject to drought.

"The name of granite is given to a rock composed chiefly of silica and which forms whole mountains, as in central France and in Brittany. The soil formed by the gradual disintegration of this rock is sometimes called granite soil. It is not very good for agriculture. Chestnut trees prosper in it, as well as certain wild plants characteristic of this kind of land. The principal ones are the various species of heather and the purple digitalis. Heather, with its dainty little pink blossoms, carpets in richest abundance the poorest of sandy soils. The purple digitalis is a large-leaved plant whose flowers, red on the outside, striped with purple and white inside, are arranged in a long and magnificent distaff reaching almost to the height of a man. The flowers are in the shape of long tun-bellied bells or, rather, glove-fingers; hence the plant is sometimes called foxglove, sometimes lady's fingers.

"The soil composed of substances thrown up by volcanoes is also sandy, and is called volcanic soil. It is generally black and sometimes very fertile.

"Sandy-clay soil is found in the valleys of great rivers. It is the most fruitful and the easiest to cultivate. Such are the soils of the Rhone valley, the valley of the Loire, and that of the Seine. It is still more fertile if it is flooded by the stream at high water. Then the river deposits a rich slime composed of clay and organic matter washed down by the current.

"The soil of heathy or shrubby land is composed of fine sand and of humus from the decayed leaves of heather and other plants. It is only used for flower gardens, and furnishes an example of what might be called sand-and-humus soil.

"Clay is a soil which, when moistened with water and thoroughly kneaded, becomes a soft and tenacious dough, suitable for molding into any desired shape. When perfectly pure it is white, and is known as kaolin, a rare substance of which porcelain is made. Plastic clays are those that are unctuous to the touch, forming with water a yielding mass that hardens with firing. They are used in making pottery. Smectite, or fuller's earth, is a clay of very different character, not pliable when moistened, but very absorbent of grease and hence used by fullers for cleansing cloth of the oil left on it in weaving. Ochres are clays colored either red or yellow by iron-rust. They are used in coarse painting. Red chalk belongs to this class of clays. Marl is a mixture in variable proportions of clay and limestone. According to which constituent predominates, it is called argillaceous or calcareous. Subjected to the action of air and moisture, marl becomes flaky and crumbles to dust. Marl is used in agriculture to improve the soil.

"A clay soil is quite the opposite of a sandy soil: water makes it swell and converts it into a sticky paste which clings tenaciously to farming implements. Once wet, it is cold, that is to say it dries very slowly. A spade can only divide it into dense clods slow to crumble in the air and not fit for receiving seed. The farmer must be careful to drain off the water and break up the ground by working it before and during frosts. It is improved by mixing with it sand, coal-ashes, and lime. Wheat flourishes better in a clayey soil than in any other kind.

"Clayey soils are recognized by their vegetation. The wild plants peculiar to this kind of soil are colt's-foot and danewort. Colt's-foot is also called horse-foot from the shape of its leaves, the outline of which reminds one of a horse's hoof. The leaves are white underneath. The flowers are yellow like little marigolds, and they appear at the beginning of spring before the leaves. Danewort is a kind of herbaceous elder of about half the height of a man. Its small white flowers are succeeded by berries full of a violet-red juice."

CHAPTER V

DIFFERENT KINDS OF SOIL
(Continued)

"Limestone is the rock from which lime is obtained. It is composed of carbonic acid and lime. To obtain the latter, the limestone is subjected to intense heat in a furnace or lime-kiln. The carbonic acid escapes, is dissipated in the air, and only the lime remains. In arable land limestone is found rather often in smaller or larger pieces, but more frequently as a fine powder which the eye can scarcely distinguish from the other constituents, especially clay. The water of rivers and other streams almost always contains a small proportion of dissolved limestone. Thence comes the thin layer of stone that accumulates little by little on the inner surface of bottles, coating the glass. Some waters contain enough of this dissolved limestone to deposit a mineral crust on objects immersed in them, as mosses and aquatic plants, and to obstruct their aqueducts. The clearest water, in which no foreign substance can be seen, absolutely none, nevertheless contains dissolved limestone, just as sweetened water contains invisible sugar. In drinking a glass of water we drink a little stone at the same time. Our body, in order to grow strong and increase in size, needs considerable calcareous matter for the formation of bones, which are to us what its solid framework is to a building. This material, so necessary to us, is not created by us; we obtain it from our food and drink. Water plays its part in furnishing this limestone, which it furnishes also to plants; they all contain a greater or less proportion of this mineral matter.

"Calcareous soils are whitish from their chief constituent, chalk. Entirely sterile when the proportion of limestone is excessive, they are tolerably productive when clay is added. They are especially suitable for vineyards and for raising lucerne, sainfoin, and clover. Champagne and the south of France offer examples of this kind of soil. Its principal varieties are chalky soil, which is nearly sterile, containing as much as ninety-five per cent of chalk, and marly soil which is composed of clay and chalk.

"The plant-life characteristic of calcareous soils comprises the box-tree, whose compact and fine-grained wood is so esteemed by turners; the wild cornel, whose red, olive-shaped fruit is one of the best-liked autumn products that nature offers us; and the alkekengi, or winter cherry, whose yellow berries are used for coloring butter. These berries are encased in a large, gorgeously red membranous bag.

"Wood, leaves, herbage, left a long time in contact with air and moisture, undergo a slow combustion; in other words, they rot. The result of this decomposition is a brown substance called humus or vegetable mold. The heart of old hollow willows is converted into humus; it is the same with leaves that fall from the trees and rot on the ground. Humus from the remains of earlier generations of plant-life nourishes the plant-life of to-day, and this in turn will become mold from which future plants will spring. It is in this way that vegetation is maintained in places not cultivated by man. Humus, then, is nature's manure. Where it is allowed to form freely, vegetation never loses its vigor, using over and over again the same material, which takes alternately the two forms of plant and humus. But hay from the field is stored in the hay-loft, and the annual harvest of wheat is taken to the granary. Thus the land is robbed of the mold that would be formed naturally by the rotting of this hay and wheat; therefore we must give back to it, under some form or other, this mold that has been taken away, since otherwise the soil will become less and less productive until finally it is quite sterile. This restitution is made in the form of animal manure, which is a sort of humus produced by digestive processes instead of by natural decay.

"Humus plays a twofold part in the soil. First, it mellows the land, or in other words makes it more easily permeable by air and water. Secondly, by the slow combustion taking place in the humus there is constantly being liberated a small quantity of carbonic acid gas, which is taken up by the adjacent roots. Agriculture can succeed only in so far as the soil contains humus. Wheat requires nearly eight per cent, oats and rye only two per cent. In poor, sandy soils, to increase the amount of vegetable mold, it is customary to plow certain green crops under, as the farmers express it; that is, the surface soil is turned over and the growing crop intended for manuring purposes is buried and left to decay in the ground. That is what is done when the plowman turns under a field of growing grass or a stretch of clover. When it is proposed to improve a piece of land by this process, it is the practice to begin by raising a crop (which will later be turned under) that derives the greater part of its nourishment from the air, since the soil in this instance cannot of itself furnish this nourishment. Among the plants satisfying these conditions are buckwheat, clover, lupine, beans, vetches, lucerne, and sainfoin.

"Soils rich in humus have for their chief constituent the brown substance that results from the decaying of leaves and other vegetable matter. Turf land stands first as rich in humus. Turf is a dark, spongy substance that forms in moist lowlands from the accumulation of vegetable refuse, especially mosses. Turf, or peat, as it is also called, is used for fuel. To turn such a soil to account, it must first be made wholesome by drainage, it must be mellowed by paring and burning and by the addition of sand and marl, and a proportion of lime must be mixed in to hasten the decomposition of all vegetable matter. Turf lands are recognized by their *sphagnei*, great mosses that grow with their roots in the water; and by their flax-like sedges, from the tops of which hang beautiful tufts of down having the softness and whiteness of the finest silk."

CHAPTER VI

POTASH AND PHOSPHORUS

"LET US burn a plant, no matter what kind. The first effect of the heat is to produce carbon, which, mixed with other substances, constituted the plant. If combustion continues, this carbon is dissipated in the air in the form of carbonic acid gas, and there remains an earthy residue which we call ashes. Here then are two kinds of material, carbon and ashes, which without exception enter into all plant-life. The plant did not create them, did not make them out of nothing, since it is impossible to obtain something from nothing. It must, then, have derived them from some source. We shall take up before long the subject of coal and its origin, and shall find that it comes chiefly from the atmosphere, whence the leaves obtain carbonic acid gas, which they decompose under the action of the sun's rays, retaining the carbon and throwing off the air in a condition fit for breathing. The vegetation of the entire earth thus finds its principal nutriment in the atmosphere, an inexhaustible and increasingly abundant reservoir, because the respiration of animals, putrefaction, and combustion are continually giving forth as much carbonic acid gas as the combined plant-life of the earth can consume. To maintain the fertility of his fields, therefore, the farmer need not give a thought to the subject of carbon; with no assistance from him his growing crops find in the air all the carbonic acid gas they require. There remains for our consideration, then, the residue left after combustion, the ashes in fact, a mixture of various substances of which we will now examine the most important.

"Let us put a few handfuls of ashes to boil in a pot of water. After boiling a little while we will let the contents cool. The ashes settle to the bottom and the liquid at the top becomes clear. Well, we shall find this liquid emitting a peculiar odor, exactly like that which comes from the lye obtained by passing water through a barrel of ashes. We shall also find that it has an acrid, almost burning taste. This smell of lye, this acrid taste were not in the water at first; they come from the ashes, which have yielded a certain constituent to the water.

"Hence we see that ashes must contain at least two substances of different kinds, of which the principal one cannot dissolve in water, but settles at the bottom as an earthy deposit, while the other, forming but a very small part of the whole, dissolves easily in water and gives it its properties, especially its odor and its acrid taste.

"If we wish to obtain this latter element by itself, we can very easily do so. All that is necessary is to put the clear liquid into a pot over the fire and boil it until all the water has evaporated. There will be left a very small quantity of whitish matter resembling table salt. But despite its appearance it is not table salt by any means; far from it, as we shall quickly discover from its unbearable taste. It is known as potash, and it is what makes lye so good for cleaning linen. Furthermore, of the various components of ashes it is the one most essential to vegetation. Every tree, every shrub, every plant, even to the smallest blade of grass, contains a certain proportion of it, sometimes larger, sometimes smaller, according to the kind of plant-life, and therefore must find it in the soil in order to thrive. Let us add that in growing plants potash is not as the action of fire leaves it after the plants have been reduced to ashes. In nature it is combined with other substances which free it from that burning acridity. In the same way carbon, when combined with other elements, loses its blackness and hardness; in fact, it is no longer common coal.

"What else is there in ashes? A short account of the matter will tell us. In 1669 there lived in Hamburg, Germany, a learned old man named Brandt, whose head was a little turned and who sought to turn common metals into gold. From old iron, rusty nails, and worn-out kettles, he hoped to produce the precious metal. But he did not succeed in his endeavors, nor was it destined that he should succeed, for the simple reason that the thing is impossible. Never is one metal changed into another. When he was about at the end of his resources he took it into his head to conceive a crowning absurdity. He imagined that in urine would be found the ingredient capable of turning all metals into gold. Behold him, then, boiling urine, evaporating it, and cooking the disgusting sediment, first with this, then with that, until at last one evening he saw something shining in his phials. It was not gold, but something more useful: it was phosphorus, which to-day gives us fire. Don't make fun of old Brandt and his foolish cooking: in seeking the impossible he made one of the most important discoveries. To him we owe the sulphur match, that precious source of light and fire so easily and quickly used.

"If you examine a sulphur match you will see that the inflammable tip contains two substances: sulphur, laid on to the wood, and another substance added to the sulphur. This last is phosphorus, colored with a blue, red, or brown powder, according to the caprice of the manufacturer. Phosphorus by itself is slightly yellow in color and translucent like wax. Its name means 'light-bearer.' When rubbed gently between the fingers in the dark, it does indeed give out a pale gleam. At the same time there is a smell of garlic; it is the odor of phosphorus. This substance is excessively inflammable: with very little heat or with slight friction against a hard surface, it catches fire. Hence its use in the manufacture of matches.

"Phosphorus is a horribly poisonous substance. By melting a little of it in grease a poison can be obtained that will destroy rats and mice. Crusts of bread are smeared with this composition and exposed in places frequented by these animals. A nibble is enough to ensure speedy death. Hence you perceive that because of their poisonous nature matches are to be handled with extreme care. Contact with food might produce the gravest consequences."

CHAPTER VII

PHOSPHATES AND NITROGEN

"PHOSPHORUS, WHICH is a dangerous poison, as we have seen, is nevertheless found in abundance in the bodies of all animals. It occurs in the urine, whence Brandt was the first to extract it; it is found still more plentifully in the bones, and from thence it is now obtained. There is some in meat, in milk, and in cheese; also in plants, notably cereals; hence flour and bread contain it. But do not be alarmed: we shall not die of poison like the rats that have nibbled crusts smeared with grease and phosphorus."

"But why not," asked Emile, "if we eat it as the rats do?"

"I will try to explain," replied his uncle. "When two or more substances are mixed together, they lose their original properties, while the new substance obtained by their combination is found to possess new properties having nothing in common with the old ones. Thus carbon, when combined with the air that we breathe, becomes an invisible gas, subtle, and unfit for breathing. In like manner lime, burning to the taste, is converted by union with carbonic acid gas into chalk, a calcareous stone void of taste. Furthermore, poisonous substances, deadly in a very small dose, may become harmless and even enter into the composition of our food when they are combined with other substances. Thus it is with phosphorus. What, then, is united with phosphorus in the form in which it ceases to be poisonous and enters into the composition of meat and flour? That is what we will now consider.

"When phosphorus is burned it produces a thick white smoke, of which you can get some idea by striking a number of matches all at once. This white smoke with the slightest trace of humidity is reducible to an extraordinarily acid liquid called phosphoric acid. Since this compound results from the combustion of phosphorus, just as carbonic acid is the result of the combustion of carbon, it must and in fact does contain the air without which no combustion can take place. Phosphoric acid is no longer inflammable, however much it may be heated; being itself the product of combustion, it cannot burn again. But if there is no danger of its catching fire, phosphoric acid is nevertheless dangerous on account of its intense acidity, which makes it violently corrosive in its action on flesh. If mixed with lime, however, this formidable compound loses its injurious properties and is changed into a white substance without the least taste or the slightest poisonous effect. This substance is called phosphate of lime. Burnt phosphorus and lime, thus united, furnish the greater part of the mineral matter found in bones. Put a bone into the fire: the grease and juices that permeate its substance will be burnt up and the bone will lose a part of its weight and become friable and perfectly white. Well, this bone, calcined in the fire for a long time, is composed chiefly of phosphate of lime. It contains phosphorus, the most combustible of substances, and yet is itself absolutely incombustible; it contains one of the most poisonous substances, and yet is itself quite harmless; into its composition there has entered an ingredient possessing atrocious acidity, and yet the compound itself has no taste. Similarly combined and equally harmless, phosphorus is found in meat, milk, cereals, in flour and bread.

"A cow can furnish each week about 70 liters of milk containing 460 grams of phosphate. This phosphate comes from hay, which obtains it from the soil. But as the soil contains only a moderate quantity of it, and the hay continually takes it away, the supply will at last become exhausted and the milk will become poorer and less abundant. If a kilogram of powdered bones, containing about the same quantity of phosphate as the 70 liters of milk, is spread over the pasture, it will make good the weekly loss in phosphate that the soil undergoes in the production of the cow's milk. Hence the efficacy of powdered bones on exhausted pasture land.

"Phosphoric acid combined with other substances is found in all our agricultural products, and hence the phosphate from bones has a very marked effect on our crops. Harvests have been doubled as if by magic through the use of powdered bones. A kilogram of this powder contains enough phosphoric acid for the growth of a hundred kilograms of wheat. Despite their great value as a fertilizer, bones will never be thus used except to a limited extent, because they are not abundant enough and also because they are much in demand in various arts and manufactures. Fortunately in some localities phosphate of lime is found in certain coarse pebbles called nodules or coprolites. These precious stones are carefully collected and ground to powder in a mill. Then, in order to make the substance more soluble in damp soil, and thus better fitted for the nutrition of plants, it is sprayed with an extremely corrosive liquid called sulphuric acid or, more commonly, oil of vitriol. In this way is obtained the superphosphate of lime which manufacture gives to agriculture as one of the most powerful of fertilizers, especially for the raising of grain.

"We were wondering a little while ago what substances could

be contained in the ashes of a burnt plant, and we have now found potash to be one of them. Moreover, since all vegetation must have phosphate in order to thrive, this also ought to be found in the ashes, phosphate being indestructible by heat. And, in fact, after the incineration of any vegetable matter whatever, as a bundle of hay or a handful of grain, the delicate processes of science can always recover this compound of phosphorus; and they further find lime, iron in the form of rust, the silicious component of pebbles, and divers other substances of less interest.

"To finish this difficult but very important subject of the nutrition of plants, I must say a few words about ammonia. This word does not tell you anything since it is a new word to you. But I will make its meaning clear to you by a familiar illustration.

"You must have noticed the strong, penetrating odor prevalent in ill-kept water-closets; and you have also perceived the same odor when soiled garments are cleaned with a certain liquid that looks like clear water. Well, this odor, so pungent that it almost produces the effect of fine needles thrust up into the nostrils and brings tears to the eyes, is the odor of ammonia.

"Ammonia is an invisible gas capable of being taken up in large quantities by water, the mixture being known as *aqua ammoniæ*, or water of ammonia. Combined with other substances ammonia loses its pungent odor and forms compounds which are among the most effective fertilizers. These compounds furnish vegetation with one of its essential ingredients called nitrogen. By itself nitrogen is an odorless and colorless gas. In this state it forms four-fifths of the volume of ordinary air, the air we breathe. The other fifth is composed of a second gas called oxygen, also colorless and odorless. It is oxygen that our lungs demand when we breathe, and it is oxygen that is necessary when we wish to burn anything. It is this alone that plays its invaluable part in the combustion of certain substances in our blood and in the generation of natural heat; it is this that in the process of combustion releases carbon, phosphorus, sulphur, and other combustibles, to combine with them and produce a compound known as carbonic acid gas in the case of burnt carbon, phosphoric acid in the case of phosphorus. In fact, to it belong the properties that we have until now attributed to the atmosphere as a whole. As for nitrogen, it has no other purpose in the atmosphere than to moderate by its presence the too violent energies of oxygen; it plays there the part of the water that we put into too strong wine.

"All vegetation requires nitrogen. Wheat, for example, must have it to develop the grain in the ear; peas, beans, lentils demand it in order to fill out their pods; the pasture and the hay-field need it if they are to furnish the nutriment that the sheep and the cow will transform into milk. But plants cannot take this nitrogen from the air, where it is so abundant; it must be served up to them after a certain necessary preparation. We ourselves need phosphorus, since it enters into the composition of our bones; we need carbon still more, the principal fuel used in maintaining the heat of the body. But are we to eat the charcoal that the charcoal-burner manufactures in his furnace, and the phosphorus used in the making of matches? Certainly not. The first would be a frightful mouthful, the second an atrocious poison. We must have them prepared in a suitable way, such as they are found in bread, milk, meat, fruits, vegetables. In the same manner plant-life requires nitrogen, not as it occurs in the atmosphere, but as it exists in certain combinations, of which the most notable are the compounds of ammonia. This explains to us the highly beneficial effect of manure on our crops. Manure is composed of the bedding used in stables and the animal excrement with which it has become mixed and impregnated. Now this excrementitious matter, especially urine, yields ammonia in decomposing, as is proved by the odor arising from latrines in hot weather and so powerfully affecting the eyes and nose. Thus manure may be said to hold ammonia compounds in storage, and from them plants derive their nitrogen, as also many other ingredients.

"Let us summarize these details. In the nutrition of plants four substances are of prime importance. First, carbonic acid gas, which yields carbon, the most widely diffused of all the elements (but which we need not dwell upon here), since plants take it chiefly from the atmosphere, to which it is supplied unceasingly. After carbonic acid come potash, phosphoric acid, and nitrogen, all of which the roots extract from the soil, where it occurs in some compound or other. These are the ingredients that the soil, if it is to remain fertile, must have given back to it as fast as they are exhausted by the crops. Such is the part played by fertilizers, without which the soil becomes exhausted and ceases to produce."

CHAPTER VIII

VEGETATION AND THE ATMOSPHERE

"THE CARBONIC acid gas produced simply by the breathing of the great human family amounts every year to about 160,000,000,000 cubic meters, which represents 86,270,000,000 kilograms of burnt carbon. Piled up, this carbon would form a mountain one league round at its base and between four hundred and five hundred meters high. So much carbon is required by man to maintain his natural heat. All of us together eat this mountain of carbon in our food and in the course of the year dissipate it all in the air, a breathful at a time; after which we immediately begin the dissipation of another mountain of carbon. How many mountains of carbon, then, since the world was created, must mankind have exhaled into the atmosphere!

"We must take account, too, of the animals, which, collectively, those of the land and those of the sea, use up a big mountain of combustible matter. They are much more numerous than we; they inhabit the entire globe, both continents and seas. What a quantity of carbon it must take to sustain the life of our planet! And to think that it all goes forth into the air, as a deadly gas, of which a few breaths would cause death!

"Nor is that all. Fermentation, as in grape-juice and rising dough, and putrefaction, as in decaying manure, produce carbonic acid gas. And it needs only a light layer of manure to cause a cultivated field to give forth between one hundred and two hundred cubic meters of carbonic acid gas per day for each hectare.

"The wood, coal, and charcoal burnt in our houses, and especially the quantities consumed in the great furnaces of factories—are not they also returned to the atmosphere in the form of harmful gas? Just think of the amount of carbonic acid gas vomited into the atmosphere by a factory furnace into which coal is poured by the carload! Think also of the volcanoes, gigantic natural chimneys which in a single eruption throw up such quantities of gas that furnaces offer no comparison. It is very clear: the atmosphere is constantly receiving carbonic acid gas in torrents that defy computation. And yet animal life has nothing to fear for the present or for the future, since the atmosphere, though continually being poisoned with carbonic acid gas, is at the same time always being purged of it.

"And what is the purgative agent commissioned by Providence to maintain the salubrity of the atmosphere? It is vegetation, my friends, vegetation, which feeds on carbonic acid gas to prevent our perishing and turns it into the bread of life for our sustenance. This deadly gas, which absorbs into itself all sorts of putrefaction, is the choicest of nourishment for plant-life; and thus out of the bosom of death the blade of grass builds up new life.

"A leaf is riddled with an infinite number of excessively minute orifices, each encircled by two lips which give it the appearance of a half-open mouth. They are called *stomata*. On a single leaf of the linden more than a million can be counted, but so small are they as to be quite invisible without a magnifying-glass. This picture shows you how they look under a microscope. Well, through these orifices the plant breathes, not pure air such as we breathe, but poisoned air, fatal to an animal

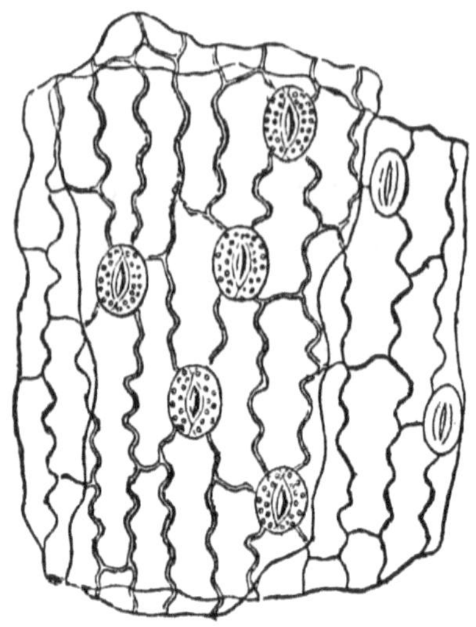

STOMATA ON A LINDEN LEAF

but wholesome for a plant. It inhales through its myriads of millions of stomata the carbonic acid gas diffused through the atmosphere; it admits this gas into the inner substance of its leaves, and there, under the sun's rays, a marvelous process follows. Stimulated by the light, the leaves operate upon the deadly gas and take from it all its carbon. They unburn (the word is not in the dictionary, more's the pity, for it gives the right idea)—they unburn the burnt carbon, undo what combustion had done, separate the carbon from the air with which it is bound up; in a word, they decompose the carbonic acid gas.

"And do not think it any easy thing to unburn a burnt substance, to restore to their original condition two substances united by fire. Scientists would need all the ingenious means and powerful drugs they possess to extract carbon from carbonic acid gas. This task, which would tax the utmost resources of the man of science, leaves accomplish noiselessly, without effort, even instantaneously, and with the sole requirement that they shall have the aid of the sun.

"But if sunlight fails, the plant can do nothing with the carbonic acid gas, the chief item in its diet. It then pines away with hunger, shoots up as if in quest of the missing sunshine, while its bark and leaves turn pale and lose their green color. Finally it dies. This sickly state induced by the absence of light is called etiolation. It is artificially produced in gardening for the purpose of obtaining tenderer vegetables and of lessening or even entirely removing the too strong and unpleasant taste of some plants. In this way some salad greens are bound with a rush so that the heart, deprived of the sun's rays, may become tender and white; and thus, too, celery is banked up and left to whiten, since otherwise its taste would be unbearable. If we cover grass with a tile or hide a plant under a pot turned upside down, we shall after a few days of this enforced darkness find the foliage all sickly and yellow.

"When, on the other hand, the plant receives the sun's rays without hindrance, the carbonic acid gas is decomposed in no time, the carbon and the air separate, and each resumes its original properties. Freed of its carbon, the air becomes what it was before this admixture: it becomes pure air, fit to maintain both fire and life. In this state it is restored to the atmosphere by the stomata to be used again in combustion and respiration. It entered the plant as a fatal gas, it leaves it as a vivifying gas. It will return some day with a new charge of carbon, which it will deposit in the plant, and then, restored to purity once more, it will recommence its atmospheric round. A swarm of bees goes and comes, from the hive to the fields and from the fields to the hives, on one trip lightened and eager for booty and on the other heavily laden with honey and returning to the comb on wearied wing. In the same way air on coming to the leaves is charged with carbon from an animal's body, a burning firebrand, or decaying matter; it gives it to the plant and departs for a fresh supply.

"It is thus that the atmosphere preserves its salubrity despite the immense torrents of carbonic acid that are cast into it. The plant lives on deadly gas. Under the action of the sun's light it decomposes the gas into carbon, which it keeps for building up its own substance, and breathable air, which it returns to the atmosphere. From this carbon combined with other substances come wood, sugar, starch, flour, gum, resin, oil, in fact every kind of vegetable product. Animal and plant are of mutual assistance, the animal producing carbonic acid gas, which nourishes the plant, and the plant changing this deadly gas into air fit to breathe and into food. Thus our dependence on plants is twofold: they purify the atmosphere and they give us food."

CHAPTER IX

LIME

To make mortar with which masonry is held in place it is customary to use lime. In a sort of trough lined with sand are placed lumps of stone having a calcined appearance, and on these stones water is poured. In a few moments the pile becomes heated to high temperature, cracks and splits and finally crumbles into dust, at the same time absorbing the water, which disappears little by little as it is taken up by the solid matter or vaporized by the heat. More water is added to reduce it all to paste, which is finally mixed with sand. The product of the mixture is mortar. Such is the process often witnessed by Emile and Jules, who are always surprised, that stone, by having water poured on to it, should become hot and turn the water into jets of steam. "Lime," Uncle Paul explained to them, "is obtained from a widely diffused stone called limestone or, in more learned language, carbonate of lime. The process is of the simplest sort. It consists of heating the stone in kilns built in the open air in the vicinity of both limestone and fuel, so as to avoid the expense of transportation in the manufacture of a product that it is desirable to furnish at a low price.

"A lime-kiln is about three meters high, and is lined with fire-proof brick. An opening at the bottom serves for taking out the lime when the firing has continued long enough. In filling the kiln it is the usual practice to begin by laying large pieces of limestone so as to form a sort of rude vault over the fireplace, and on this vault are piled smaller fragments until the entire cavity is filled. The fuel used may be fagots, brushwood, turf, or coal. After the firing has gone on long enough, operations are suspended and the lime is withdrawn by breaking down the vault supporting the entire mass, which crumbles and comes crowding out at the lower opening, whence it is usually removed.

"Another method still followed in some localities and of more ancient origin consists of filling the kiln with alternate layers of fuel and limestone. The whole rests on a bed of fagots that serves for starting the fire. As soon as the fire has spread throughout the mass, the opening at the top is closed with pieces of sod in order to make the combustion slower and more even."

"Nothing could be simpler," said Jules, "than lime-making. Now I should like to know what effect the heat of the kiln has on the limestone. How does it happen that stone turns into lime by passing through fire?"

"Limestone," answered his uncle, "contains two different substances: first, lime, and then an invisible substance, impalpable as air itself, in fact, a gas, carbonic acid gas. The name of carbonate of lime given to the limestone denotes precisely this combination. As it is when taken from the ground, the stone contains the two substances closely united, so incorporated indeed as no longer to have the qualities characterizing them when apart. Heat destroys this union: the lime stays in the kiln, and the carbonic acid gas is dissipated in the atmosphere with the smoke from the burnt fuel. After this liberation of the gas the lime is left in its pure state, no longer masked by the presence of another substance, but just as it is needed by the mason for making mortar."

"Then all that the fire does," queried Jules, "is just to break apart the limestone and drive out the carbonic acid gas that it contained?"

"What takes place in the lime-kiln," replied his uncle, "is nothing but the separation of the lime and the gas. Now let us turn our attention to the mortar. When lime is watered, it gets very hot, swells, cracks open, and crumbles into a fine powder like flour. The heat that is generated comes from the violence with which the two substances rush together. Before absorbing water lime is called quicklime; after this absorption, which has reduced it to powder, it is called slaked lime. This slaked lime is reduced to a paste with water, and then well mixed and kneaded with sand. The result is the mortar used in laying stone and brick in order to hold the courses firmly together and give solidity to the building.

"There is one thing I advise you to note, if you have not already done so, since it will explain to you the part played by mortar in masonry. Look at the water that for several days has covered a bed of lime slaked by the masons. You will see floating on the surface small transparent particles resembling ice. Well, these tiny fragments of crust are nothing but stone like that from which the lime was obtained; in a word, they are limestone or carbonate of lime. To make stone of that kind two substances are necessary, as I have just told you: lime and carbonic acid gas. The lime is furnished by the water, in which it must be present in solution, since the water covers a thick bed of this material; and as to the carbonic acid gas, it is furnished by the air, where it is always to be found, though in small quantities. Lime, then, has this peculiarity, that it slowly incorporates the small amount of carbonic acid gas present in the atmosphere, and so once more becomes the limestone that it was before.

"A similar process goes on in mortar: the lime takes back

from the atmosphere the gas that it had lost in the heat of the lime-kiln, and little by little becomes stone again. The sand mixed with it serves to disintegrate the lime, which thus more easily absorbs the air necessary for its conversion into limestone. When the mortar has fully resumed the form of limestone the courses of masonry are so strongly bound one to another that the stones themselves sometimes break rather than give way.

"What is known as fat lime is lime that develops great heat when brought into contact with water, and also increases considerably in volume, forming with the water a thick, cohesive paste. On the other hand, poor lime develops but little heat, disintegrates slowly, and increases scarcely any in volume. The first kind comes from nearly pure limestone and can be mixed with a large proportion of sand, thus making a great quantity of mortar. The second kind is obtained from limestone having various foreign substances and will admit of but a small admixture of sand, thus yielding less mortar than the other. Both have the property of hardening in the air by the absorption of carbonic acid gas which converts them into limestone.

"There is a third variety of lime called hydraulic lime, which has the peculiar merit of being able to harden under water. It is made from a limestone containing a certain proportion of clay. Hydraulic mortar is used for the masonry of bridges, canals, cisterns, foundations, vaults, in fact for all stone and brick work under water or in damp soil."

CHAPTER X

LIME IN AGRICULTURE

"TO BE fertile a soil must contain limestone, sand, and clay, besides the organic substances coming from humus and fertilizers. Now it may be that nature has not endowed the soil with a sufficient quantity or with any of these three constituents. Then the character of the soil must be corrected by giving it what it lacks. That is what is called improving the land. Thus a soil that is too sandy is improved by the addition of limestone and clay; one that is too compact, too clayey, is improved by adding sand and, still more, by adding limestone. Mineral substances thus added to the soil to correct it are called correctives. These substances coöperate also in the nutrition of plants, and from this point of view may be regarded as mineral fertilizers.

"One of the most valuable of correctives is lime, which is indispensable to soils lacking limestone, indispensable also to the nutrition of nearly all our cultivated vegetables. It acts in various ways. First, it energetically attacks vegetable substances, decomposing them and converting them into humus. A pile of leaves that would take long months to rot becomes in a short time a mass of humus when mixed with lime. Hence its great utility in fields overgrown with weeds, and in newly cleared land—in short, wherever there are old stumps, piles of leaves, remnants of wood, and patches of heather, which need to be decomposed. With the help of lime all these herbaceous or woody substances are quickly converted into humus, with which the soil becomes enriched to the great advantage of future crops.

"In the second place, lime corrects or neutralizes the acidity peculiar to certain soils, as is proved by the following experiment. Let us mix some vinegar, no matter how strong, with a little lime. In a short time the smell and acid taste of the vinegar will have disappeared. Now wherever masses of vegetable refuse, such as leaves, mosses, rushes, old stumps, are undergoing decay, there are produced certain sour-tasting substances or, in other words, acids, which are invariably harmful to agriculture. This generation of acid occurs notably in turfy soils, which have an excessive acidity favorable to the growth of coarse rushes and sedges that are valueless to us, and at the same time this acid is highly injurious to all our cultivated plants. Lime, therefore, which is sure to correct this acidity, works wonders in marshy lands, damp meadows, and turfy soils. We are warned of the need of lime by the appearance of ferns, heather, sedge or reed-grass, rushes, mosses and sphagnei.

"Thirdly, when once mixed with the soil, lime speedily resumes the form it wore before passing through the lime-kiln; that is to say, it becomes limestone, but in the shape of fine powder. This return to the limestone condition is brought about by union with the carbonic acid gas coming from the atmosphere or thrown off by the substances decaying in the ground. Under this new form lime continues to play a useful part by supplying the calcareous ingredient to soil that lacked it, and also by preventing the clay from becoming too cohesive, too impervious to air and water.

"The addition of lime to the soil should take place at the end of summer, when the ground is dry. Little heaps of quicklime, each containing about twenty kilograms, are placed at intervals of five meters and covered with a few spadefuls of earth. In a short time the moisture in the atmosphere reduces the lime to a fine powder, which is then spread evenly with a shovel and covered with earth—an operation involving no severe labor.

"Lime should never be applied with seed. Mere contact with it would burn the young shoots. Neither should it be mixed with manure before it is used, since the immediate result would be a total loss of great quantities of ammonia, thrown off in gaseous form; and ammonia, as I have explained, is one of the richest of fertilizers. Lime and manure, therefore, should be used separately.

"Soils rich in turf, clay, or granite are the ones on which lime acts most beneficially. Because of the important results attained by the use of lime, its manufacture for purely agricultural purposes by certain expeditious and effective methods is customary in many places. Thus in Mayenne, where this application of lime has converted tracts of uncultivated clayey land into rich pastures or into wheat fields of exceptional fertility, lime is made in enormous kilns a dozen meters high and supported by the cliff that furnishes the limestone and sometimes the fuel also.

"All animal matter makes excellent fertilizer. Of this class are old woolen rags, stray bits of leather, fragments of horn, dried blood from slaughter-houses, and flesh not fit for human consumption. All these substances are rich in nitrogen and phosphates, and if mixed with farm manure they add greatly to its value. Lime furnishes us the means of utilizing one of these substances, flesh, in the best way possible.

"Dead bodies of animals, heedlessly left for dogs and crows and magpies to devour, should be cut up in pieces and then buried with a mixture of earth and quicklime. This attacks the flesh and quickly decomposes it, so that in a few months' time there would be available a deposit of the most powerful fertilizer instead of a useless, disease-breeding carcass. As to the bones, resistant to the action of lime, they are burned to render them more friable, and then reduced to powder. This bone-dust, mixed with the fertilizer furnished by the decayed flesh, will contribute to grain-field or pasture a rich supply of phosphorus. To uses of this sort the farmer should put all horses and mules that have had to be killed, as well as all large farm animals that have died of disease."

CHAPTER XI

PLASTER OF PARIS

"THOUGH LESS important than lime, plaster of Paris is nevertheless much used in building, especially for ceilings, molded chimney-pieces, and in the filling of cracks and cavities. It is a white powder which is made into a paste by adding water, prepared a little at a time and only as fast as needed."

"I've seen them do it," Emile interposed; "the workman takes a few handfuls of that powder out of a bag, and then he mixes it with a little water in his trough with a trowel. He scrapes the paste all together in his hand and uses it immediately, before making any more. Why don't they mix all the plaster at once, as they do with lime when they make mortar?"

"Plaster is not all prepared beforehand for the reason that it hardens very quickly, turns to stone, and is then unfit for use. Accordingly, to have it in a suitable state of softness, it must be prepared at the moment of using."

"And what do they make that powder of that turns to stone when it is mixed with water?"

"Plaster is made from a stone called gypsum, which, always the same as to its nature, varies much in appearance according to its state of purity. Sometimes it is a shapeless rock, whitish and more or less grained; sometimes a fine fibrous mass with a silky luster; or, again, a substance as transparent as glass and splitting into very thin scales which show, here and there, the superb colors of the rainbow. Struck by their beauty, workmen engaged in quarrying gypsum have given the name of 'Jesus-stone' to these brilliant laminæ. Also, from their brilliance and their cheapness, they are called 'donkey's mirrors.' In ancient times these beautiful sheets of transparent gypsum were used as window-panes.

"Impure gypsum, in the form of shapeless rock, is used for ordinary plaster, while pure gypsum, which comes in glass-like sheets or in blocks of a silky appearance, is used for fine plaster, as in all sorts of molding. The stone from which plaster is obtained occurs in abundance in several departments of France, where it forms hills and even whole mountains, as for example in the departments of the Seine, the Mouths of the Rhone, and Vaucluse. For conversion into the usual plaster of Paris this stone must be subjected to a moderate heat. To this end it is the practice to build with gypsum blocks a row of small vaults, and on these vaults to pile fragments of smaller size. Then the firing is done by burning fagots and brushwood under these vaults."

"And is it carbonic acid gas this time, too, that is driven out by the heat, as in the manufacture of lime?" asked Jules.

"No, my friend: gypsum does not contain any carbonic acid gas. It is made of lime, as in limestone, but united with sulphuric acid, which heat is powerless to drive out. Besides this it contains water, which forms a fifth of the total weight of the stone. This water, and nothing further, escapes under the action of heat. With this expelled the gypsum is turned to plaster.

"But this latter has a strong tendency to take on again the moisture parted with in the kiln, and thus to become once more what it was in the beginning—primitive stone. It is this peculiarity that renders gypsum suitable for plaster. Moistened in the trough, the powdery matter quickly incorporates the water that is thus restored to it, and the whole hardens into a block having the solidity of gypsum that has not yet passed through the kiln. Lime turns to stone by being permeated with carbonic acid gas, which restores it to its limestone state. Plaster becomes stone by absorbing water, which brings it back to the state of gypsum. The transformation of lime is slow, of plaster very rapid.

"As soon as it comes from the kiln plaster is ground under vertical millstones and then sifted. The powder must be kept in a very dry place, since it contracts moisture easily and then will not harden or set, as they say, when mixed with water. You will perceive clearly enough that after being more or loss impregnated with moisture plaster cannot have the same tendency to absorb the water necessary to change it into a solid mass; the substance being already somewhat soaked will not show the same thirst when the time comes for using it. All damp and, still more, all wet plaster is of no further use.

"Statues, busts, medallions, and various other ornamental objects are made by casting with fine plaster of Paris. This is prepared from the purest gypsum, those beautiful transparent scales I told you about a little while ago. It is heated in ovens similar to those used by bakers, and cut off from contact with the burning fuel, so as to preserve its whiteness. The powder, which looks like fine flour, is mixed with water and reduced to a smooth paste, which is then poured into molds. When the plaster has set, the mold, which is in several pieces, all joined together, is taken apart and the finished cast withdrawn."

CHAPTER XII

PLASTER OF PARIS IN AGRICULTURE

"IN AGRICULTURE plaster of Paris has by no means the importance of lime; nevertheless it produces excellent results on clover, sainfoin, and lucerne. It is used in the spring for sprinkling the young leaves when they are still damp with the morning dew. Still, foggy weather is the most favorable for this work. Plaster also acts well on rape, flax, buckwheat, and tobacco, but has no effect on cereals.

"The intelligent farmer puts plaster of Paris to still another use. In every dunghill there is always going on a slow combustion, or fermentation, giving forth ammonia in vaporous form; and this ammonia escapes into the air as a total loss, whereas it ought to be retained as far as possible in the manure, since the compounds of ammonia constitute the source whence plants obtain nitrogen. Therefore to prevent this waste, plaster is sprinkled over the dunghill. Sometimes, too, it is sprinkled over each layer of manure as the pile rises. The plaster absorbs the ammoniac vapors, gives them a little of its sulphuric acid, and converts them into a compound, sulphate of ammonia, which is proof against vaporization. Hence we say that plaster of Paris fixes ammonia, that is to say prevents its being dissipated.

"To illustrate the fertilizing effect of plaster of Paris on lucerne, the following incident is related. Franklin, one of the chief glories of the United States of North America, aware of the great fertilizing power of plaster, wished to extend the agricultural use of this substance among his fellow-citizens; but they, clinging to old customs, would not listen to him. To convince them, Franklin spread plaster over a field of lucerne by the side of the most frequented road leading out of Philadelphia, but spread it in such a way as to form letters and words. The lucerne grew all over the field, but much taller, greener, and thicker where the plaster had been applied, so that the passers-by read in the field of lucerne these words traced in gigantic letters: 'Plaster of Paris was applied here.' The ingenious expedient was a great success and plaster was very soon adopted in agriculture."

"The doubters must have been convinced," said Jules, "on seeing those big green letters rising above the rest of the lucerne. Did not Franklin do some other remarkable things? I remember the name; I have seen it several times in books."

"Yes," replied his uncle, "Franklin became by his learning, one of the most remarkable men of his time. Among other things, we owe to him the invention of the lightning-conductor, that tall pointed iron rod erected on the roofs of buildings to protect them from the thunderbolt. It was he who first had the superb audacity to evoke the lightning from the midst of the thunder-clouds, to direct it according to his wishes, and to bring it to his feet that he might study its nature. One stormy day in 1752 he went out into the country near Philadelphia in company with his young son who carried a kite made out of a silk handkerchief tied at the four corners to glass rods. A pointed piece of metal terminated the apparatus. A long hemp cord, with a shorter cord of silk tied to the lower end, was fastened to the kite, which was then sent up toward a black thundercloud. At first nothing happened to confirm the previsions of the American sage, and he was beginning to despair of success when there came a shower of rain and with it a flash of lightning. The wet cord proved a better conductor than when dry. Without thinking of the danger he ran, and transported with joy at having brought within his reach that which causes thunder, Franklin put his finger near the cord and made little spurts of fire dart out, lighted brandy from these sparks out of the sky, and only brought his perilous experiment to an end when he had fully determined the origin and nature of thunder and lightning. This was the way he studied the mystery at close quarters, discovered its nature, and finally succeeded in protecting buildings by means of a pointed iron rod.

"Benjamin Franklin was born in Boston, North America, in 1706. He was the youngest[2] of seventeen children. Hence, as his father was a poor tallow-chandler and soap-boiler, he could not acquire at home anything beyond a knowledge of reading, writing, and arithmetic. At ten years of age he was taken from school and set to performing small tasks about the house. He cut candle-wicks and poured the tallow into the molds, waited on customers in his father's shop, and ran errands. His work brought him in a few pence which he did not yet know how to spend judiciously. He tells us the following little story on this subject, which we may all profit by.

" 'One day,' says he, 'finding myself the possessor of a hand-ful of coppers, I ran out to buy some toys, when a little boy of about my own age happened to pass that way with a whistle in his hand. Delighted with the sound of the whistle, I proposed to my comrade to exchange all my money for his musical instru-ment. To this he very willingly agreed. Elated with my purchase, which I thought very fine, I returned home, where I continued whistling to my great joy, but to the great displeasure of the ears

---

2   The author is not quite accurate here. Franklin was, as he tells us, "the young-est son, and the youngest child but two."—*Translator.*

of my family. I told them of the magnificent exchange I had just made. My brothers and sisters made fun of me, saying that for the price I had paid I might have bought dozens of such whistles at the toy-shop. Only then did it occur to me what fine things I might have bought with my money, and I began to cry with vexation. Chagrin at the exchange I had made now caused me more pain than the whistle had before given me pleasure. This little incident made an impression on me that has never been effaced and has been of service to me on more than one occasion. Ever since, whenever I am tempted to buy some useless thing, I say to myself, "Do not pay too much for your whistle"; and so I save my money.' "

CHAPTER XIII

NATURAL FERTILIZERS—GUANO

"PLANT-LIFE FINDS a part of its sustenance provided by nature in the atmosphere; it finds carbonic acid gas, whence it derives the carbon it requires; but the care and ingenuity of man have to supplement these natural resources by providing fertilizers.

"One of the chief of these fertilizers, farm manure, is furnished by the bedding and excrement of animals. To obtain an excellent dressing of this sort it is customary to use for bedding, as far as possible, the straw from grain, since this, being composed of hollow stalks, is capable of holding considerable moisture. But, as in certain cases straw would hardly be able to absorb all the fluid matter, it is well to make a trench in the stable and thus carry off the excess of liquid to a reservoir outside, where another heap of straw or similar material is in readiness to receive it. Then, at a distance from all rain-spouts and gutters, and in the shade of trees, a substantial layer of clay is spread on the ground, and on this is erected the pile of manure. All around it is dug a little trench which conducts the brown liquid that oozes from the manure, and that is known as liquid manure, into a hole large enough to admit of the use of a bucket in drawing out the liquid.

"Liquid manure is composed of the fluid matter with which the bedding is steeped, and it holds in solution a great part of the nutritive constituents of the manure. Agriculture knows no richer fertilizer. Hence care should be taken not to let it go to waste in neighboring ditches or soak into the ground. That is why the pile is placed on a layer of clay, which keeps the liquid manure from soaking into the ground where it would be wasted; and it is also the reason for digging a trench to receive this fluid matter and conduct it to the hole. When this hole is full the liquid manure is drawn out with a bucket and thrown back on to the dung-hill.

"Nor is that the whole of the story. A slow combustion will soon begin throughout the pile of manure; its mass will ferment and become heated, and as a consequence the nitrogenous constituents will decompose and will liberate ammonia, which will escape into the air and be lost if the fermentation is excessive. It is to avoid too rapid a heating that the manure-pile is placed in the shade and not under the direct rays of the sun. Moreover, the liquid manure thrown on to the heap from time to time also moderates the fermenting process.

"Compare this careful method with the practice on most farms, where the manure is heaped up without any precaution, without shelter from the sun, unprotected from the drenching rains, which wash away the soluble constituents. Think of those rivulets of liquid manure trickling away in this direction and that, and collecting here and there in puddles of infection. See how all the inmates of the poultry-yard scratch at the heap, turning over and scattering its contents, and thus causing the ammonia to escape into the atmosphere. Can such a dung-hill be as valuable as one that is attended to properly?

"Liquid manure being the richest part of the whole pile, care should be taken not to let escape what the bedding does not absorb. It should be first diluted with water and then

COMMON GULL, OR MEW-GULL

applied to the growing crops. When it is desired for use in non-liquid form, it should be mixed with enough earth to absorb it, and the result is an excellent fertilizer.

"In summer it is not unusual to enclose with hurdles a piece of land soon to be cultivated, and into this enclosure a flock of sheep is driven to pass the night under the care of the shepherd in his movable hut, and with the protection of trusty dogs well able to cope with any marauding wolves. The next night the flock is quartered in another spot, and so on until the entire field has thus served, a little at a time, as stable for the flock. The purpose of this procedure is to utilize the excrement, both solid and liquid, left behind by the flock. In one night a sheep can fertilize a square meter of surface. This method of fertilizing is very effective because of the complete absorption of the fluid matter by the soil.

"Off the coast of Peru in South America are several small islands which form a common rendezvous for great numbers of sea-birds. Birds that frequent the sea are all notorious for their insatiable appetite. Constantly in search of fish, which they live on, they spend the day exploring the surface of the waters at immense distance from land. Nature has endowed them with prodigious flying power. To these indefatigable rovers an aërial promenade of some hundreds of leagues before dinner is a mere nothing. Scattered during the day in all directions in quest of prey, they reach the islets in the evening to spend the night, arriving in flocks so dense as to darken the sky. Being well fed, thanks to their foraging excursions, they cover the ground at night with a thick layer of excrement. And as this has been going on century after century ever since the world was made, these deposits, piled one on another, have at last become massive beds twenty or thirty meters thick, and so hard, so compact, that to break them it is necessary to use a pick or a petard, just as one would in quarrying stone. Workmen operate this dung mine, and vessels from all parts of the world fetch cargoes of this valuable material, which is called guano. This enormous mass of dung, which has by the lapse of ages been turned into a sort of whitish loam, gives Peru an annual revenue amounting to sixty millions of francs.

"Guano is the strongest fertilizer known to agriculture. It is scattered broadcast over the field when vegetation is starting, and for the best results a rather damp time is chosen for this work in order that the moisture may convey to the roots of the plants, by gradual infiltration, the soluble constituents of the fertilizer. The action of guano on vegetation is of the promptest, most powerful sort."

CHAPTER XIV

THE STALK OF THE PLANT

"THE STALK is the common support of the plant's various parts. It is called annual or herbaceous when it lives only one year, as in the potato, spinach, parsley, and all forms of vegetation that from their soft structure belong to the class of herbs. Ligneous is the name given to the stalk when, designed to live for a greater or less number of years, it is made of strong woody fibers, such as we find in the trunks of trees.

"Let us make a clean cut through any tree-trunk, that of an oak for example. We shall find it divided into three parts: in the center the pith or marrow, very slightly developed; around the marrow the wood proper; and, finally, on the outside, the bark. A closer examination shows that the wood is formed of concentric layers which are indicated in the cross-section by a series of circles having the marrow for a common center. These layers are called ligneous zones or, since one is formed every year, annual layers. During the summer there is a downward flow, throughout the tree, of a peculiar liquid, the descending sap, which constitutes the fluid nourishment of the tree. This liquid runs between the wood and the bark and becomes, little by little in its course, on one side a layer of wood which attaches itself to the outer surface of the preceding year's layer, and on the other side a thin sheet of bark which is added to the inner surface of the bark already formed.

"Thus each year both bark and wood form a new layer; but this added layer is applied in opposite ways in the two instances,—outside on the wood, inside on the bark. The wood thus encircled from year to year by new layers increases in age toward the center and becomes younger and younger toward the cir- cumference, whereas the bark, lined

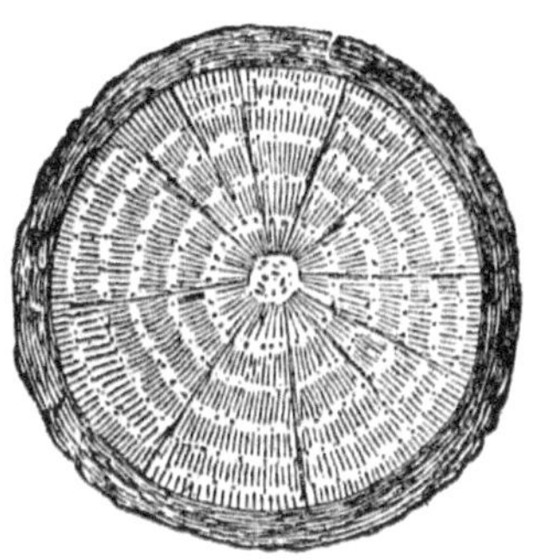

CROSS SECTION OF
TREE TRUNK

every year with a fresh sheet, shows its youth on the inside and its age on the outside. The first buries inside the trunk its decrepit and dead layers; the second thrusts its old layers outside, where they crack and fall off in large scales. This aging process is simultaneous on the outside and in the center of the tree-trunk; but between the wood and the bark life is always at work, creating fresh accretions.

"Here are some experimental proofs of this annual formation of a ligneous layer. A strip of bark is removed from the trunk of a tree, and on the wood thus laid bare is fastened a thin sheet of metal. The bark is then replaced and bound with ligatures so that the wound may heal. We will suppose ten years have passed. The bark is raised again at the same place. The metal sheet is no longer visible; to find it you must bore deep into the wood. Now, if you count the ligneous layers removed before reaching the metal sheet, you will find precisely ten, just the number of years that have passed.

"A number of observations like the following are famil- iar: Some foresters cut down a beech bearing on its trunk the date 1750. The same inscription was found again in the inner substance of the wood, but to reach it they had to cut through fifty-five layers on which no mark whatever appeared. If now, we add 55 to 1750 we obtain precisely the year when the tree was felled, or 1805. The inscription carved on the trunk in the year 1750 had passed through the bark and reached the layer of wood that was then outermost. Since that event fifty-five years had passed and new layers, exactly the same in number, had grown over the first.

"Thus a tree is composed of a succession of woody sheaths, the outer ones enveloping the inner. The stem or trunk contains them all; the branches, according to their age, contain more or fewer. Each one represents a single year's growth. The woody sheath of the present year occupies the exterior of the trunk, immediately under the bark; those of former years occupy the interior, and the nearer they are to the center the older they are. The layers of future years will come one at a time and take their places over preceding layers, so that what is now the outermost layer will in its turn be found embedded in the body of the trunk.

"Of all these ligneous zones of unequal age the most important to-day is the outside one; its destruction would cause the death of the tree, since through it the nutritive juices of the earth reach the buds, leaves, and young branches. In their time the interior layers, one by one, when they formed the surface, rendered the same service to the buds of their day; but now that these buds have become branches the inner layers have only a secondary office, or even none at all. Those nearest the outside still have some aptness for work and help the layer of the year to carry the juices from the earth to the branches. As to the innermost ones, they have lost all activity; their wood is hard, dried up, encrusted with inert matter. In their decrepitude these interior layers are incapable of service in the work of vegetation; the most they can do is by the support of their firm woody structure to give solidity to the whole. Thus the tree's activity decreases from the outside toward the center. On the surface are youth, vigor, labor; in the center old age, ruin, repose."

CHAPTER XV

THE ROOT

"THE STALK or trunk is the upward-growing part of the plant, and needs air and light. The root, on the contrary, is the downward-growing part, and it needs soil and darkness. The extreme ends of the root's various subdivisions are always growing, always young, of delicate structure, and for that reason admirably fitted for imbibing, very much as a fine sponge would do, the liquids with which the soil is impregnated. Because of their facility in absorbing moisture these ever-growing tip-ends are called spongioles. The spongioles terminate the rootlets, that is to say the final subdivisions of the root, subdivisions known as root-hairs on account of their resemblance to real hair.

"The root takes various forms, which are all reducible to two fundamental types. Sometimes it consists of a main body or tap-root, which sends out branches as it bores deeper into the soil. This designation, tap-root, is a common and familiar term. Sometimes the root assumes the form of a tuft, a bunch of rootlets, simple or branching, which, springing from the same point, continue to grow at a nearly equal rate and on an equal footing as to importance. Roots of this sort are commonly known as fibrous roots.

"As a general rule, the growth of the root keeps pace with that of the stem or trunk. Thus the oak, elm, maple, beech, and all our large trees have a vigorous, deep-growing root as anchorage for

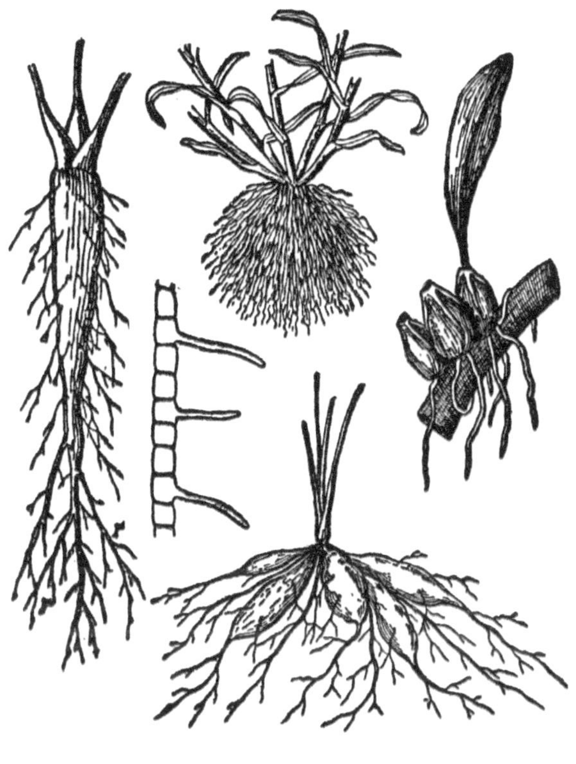

ROOTS

the enormous superstructure, to brace it firmly against the wind. But there is no lack of lowly herbage that has roots quite out of proportion to the other parts,—veritable tap-roots of greater size and vigor than many a plant of far greater aërial development can boast. To this class belong the mallow, carrot, and radish. Lucerne has for support to its meager foliage a root that bores two or three meters into the ground.

"An agricultural practice of supreme interest is based, at least partly, on the excessive development of certain roots. The plant is a laboratory where life converts into nutritive matter the manure from our stables and poultry-yards. A cart-load of dung becomes at the farmer's pleasure, after passing through one sort of plant or another, a crop of peas or beans, a basket of fruit, or a loaf of bread. Hence this fertilizer is a very precious thing which nothing can replace and which must be utilized to the very utmost. The nourishment of us all depends on it. Enriched with this fertilizer, the soil produces, we will say, a first harvest of wheat. But wheat with its bunch of short and fine roots, has drawn only upon the upper layer of fertilizing material, leaving intact all that the rain has dissolved and carried down into the lower layers. It has performed its mission admirably, it is true; it has made a clean sweep and converted into wheat all the fertilizer contained in the layer of soil accessible to its roots, so that if wheat were sown a second time no harvest would be obtained. The soil, then, is exhausted on the surface, but in its underlying strata it is still rich. Well, what crop shall we choose for the utilization of these lower strata and the production of still further supplies of food? It cannot be barley, oats, or rye, since their little fibrous roots would find nothing to glean in the surface soil after the first crop of wheat. But it will be lucerne, since this plant will send down its roots, each as thick as your finger, to the depth of one, two, or even three meters, if need be, and give back the fertilizer in the form of forage, which, with the help of the animal that feeds on it, will be converted into nutritious meat, valuable dairy products, excellent wool, or, at the very least, animal power for draft service or other work. This succession of two or more different kinds of crops for the utmost utilization of a given area of prepared soil is called rotation of crops, of which there will be more to say later.

"Deep roots, so admirably adapted to the utilization of the lower strata of the soil, become in other circumstances a source of serious difficulty. Suppose a tree is to be transplanted. Its long tap-root will make the operation difficult and hazardous. You must dig deep, both in pulling it out and in replanting it; and then you must be careful not to injure the root, for it is all in one piece and if it does not take hold and grow the sapling will die. In this case it would be much to the tree's advantage to have fibrous roots running down only to a slight depth; it could then be pulled up easily, and if some roots perished in the operation enough would be left intact to insure the success of the transplanting.

"This result can be obtained: it is no difficult matter to make the tree lose its tap-root and acquire, not a regular bundle of roots of even length; but a short and much ramified root that possesses the advantages of the bunch of small roots without having its shape. Thus in nurseries where young trees remain for some years before being transplanted, after two years' growth a spade is passed under the surface of the soil to cut off the main root, which would in time become a deep tap-root. The stump that remains then branches out horizontally without going deeper. Another way is to pave the nursery bed with tiles. The tap-root of the young tree pushes downward until it reaches this barrier, where it is straightway forced to stop growing in depth and compelled to send out lateral branches.

"The kind of root we have thus far been talking about is primordial, original; every plant has it on emerging from the seed; it appears as soon as the seed germinates. But many plants have other roots that develop at different points of the stem, replacing the original root when that dies, or at least coming to its aid if it continues to live. They are called adventitious roots, and they play a highly important part, notably in certain horticultural operations such as propagating by slips and layers, which we will talk about later.

"Besides these two operations, the object of which is to multiply the plant, it is customary to prompt the growth of adventitious roots either for the purpose of fixing the plant more firmly in the ground or in order to increase its yield. The best way to attain this result is to bank up the earth at the base of the stalk. This process is sometimes called earthing up. The buried portion soon sends out a great number of roots. Indian corn, for example, if left to itself is too poorly rooted to resist wind and rain, which beat it down. In order to give it greater stability the farmer earths up the corn. In the earth banked up at the base of the stalk bundles of adventitious roots form and furnish the plant a firmer support.

"Wheat stalks bear on their lower ends buds which, according to circumstances, perish to the detriment of the harvest or develop into roots and promote the growth of more ears of grain. Let us suppose wheat has been sown in the autumn. In that cold and rainy season vegetation is slow, the stalk grows but little, and the various buds remain very close together almost on a level with the ground. But if they are favored by having damp soil near them, these buds send forth adventitious roots which nourish them directly and promote a fullness of growth that the ordinary root by itself could not have secured. Thus stimulated by nourishment, these buds develop into so many wheat-stalks, each one ending at a later period in an ear of grain. But if wheat is sown in the spring, its rapid growth under the influence of mild weather brings the buds too high for them to send out roots. The stalk then remains single. In the first case from one grain of wheat sown there springs a cluster of stalks producing as many ears; in the second case the harvest is reduced to its lowest terms: from one grain of wheat one stalk, one ear. Hence this development of the lower buds of cereals is of the greatest importance. To obtain it, or, in agricultural terms, to make the wheat send up suckers, the lower buds must send down adventitious roots, as they will do if they are brought into contact with the soil. To this end, shortly after germination a wooden roller is passed over the field, and this roller, without bruising the young stalks, pushes them deeper into the ground."

CHAPTER XVI

BUDS

"LET US take a branch of lilac or any shrub. In the angle formed by each leaf and the branch that bears it, an angle called the axil of the leaf, we shall see a little round body enveloped in brown scales. That is a bud or, as it is also named, an eye.

"Buds make their appearance at fixed points, and it is the rule for one to form in the axil of each leaf; it is also the rule for the tip-end of the branch to bear one. Those situated in the axils of the leaves are called axillary buds, and those that are found on the ends of branches, terminal buds. They are not all equally vigorous, the strongest being at the top of the branch, the weakest at the bottom. The lower leaves even shelter such small ones in their axils that only the closest scrutiny will reveal them. These diminutive buds often perish without developing unless artificially encouraged to do so. On a lilac branch it is easy to note these differences of size from bud to bud.

"Both terminal and axillary buds are divided into two classes. In developing some sprout up and produce only leaves; these are called leaf buds. When fully developed they become shoots or scions, and finally branches. Others push upward but little and bear only flowers or leaves and flowers simultaneously. They are called flower buds, or simply buds. It is very easy to distinguish one kind from the other on our fruit-trees, the leaf buds being long and pointed, the flower buds round and thicker.

"All summer long the leaf buds grow in the axils of the leaves; they are gaining strength to go through the winter. Cold weather comes and the leaves fall, but the buds remain in their place, firmly implanted on a ledge of the bark, or a sort of little cushion, situated just above the scar left by the falling of the adjacent leaf. To withstand the rigors of cold and dampness, which would be fatal to them, winter clothing is indispensable. It consists of a warm inner envelope of flock and down, and a strong outer casing of well varnished scales. Let us examine for instance the bud of a chestnut-tree. Within we shall find a sort of wadding enswathing its delicate little leaves, while on the outside a solid cuirass of scales, arranged with the regularity of tiles on a roof, wraps it closely. Furthermore, to keep out all dampness, the separate pieces of this scale armor are coated with a resinous cement which now resembles dried varnish, but softens in the spring to let the bud open. Then the scales, no longer stuck together, separate, all sticky, and the first leaves unfold covered with a velvety red down. Nearly all buds, at the time of their spring travail, present in different degrees this stickiness resulting from the softening of their resinous coating. I will mention especially the buds of the ash, alder, and, above all, the poplar, which when pressed between the fingers emit an abundant yellow glue, of bitter taste. This substance is diligently gathered by the bees, which use it to make their bee-glue, that is to say the cement with which they stop the fissures and rough-coat the walls of their hive before constructing the combs. Under its modest appearance the bud is a veritable masterpiece: its varnish excludes dampness; its scales protect it from harmful atmospheric influences; its lining of flock, wadding, downy red hair, keeps out the cold.

"The scales form the most important part of the bud's winter clothing. They are nothing more nor less than tiny leaves hardened and toughened, in short so modified as to serve the purpose of protection. The leaves immediately under them and constituting the heart of the bud have the usual form. They are all small, pale, delicate, and arranged in a marvelously methodical manner so as to take up the least possible room and at the same time to be contained, all of them, despite their considerable number, within the narrow limits of their cradle. It is surprising what a quantity of material a bud can make room for under its sheath of scales in a space so small that we should find it difficult to pack away there a single hemp-seed; and yet it holds leaves by the dozen or a whole bunch of flowers. The bunch enclosed in a lilac bud numbers a hundred and more blossoms. And all this is contained in that narrow cell, with no tearing or bruising of any portion of it. If the various parts of a bud were disconnected, one by one, if the delicate arrangement were once undone, what fingers would be clever enough to put it together again? The principal leaves lend themselves to a thousand different modes of arrangement in order to occupy the least space possible. They take in the bud the form of a cornet; or they roll themselves up in a scroll, sometimes from one edge only, sometimes from both; or they fold up lengthwise or crosswise; or they may roll up into little balls, or crumple up, or fold like a fan."

CHAPTER XVII

ADVENTITIOUS BUDS

"BUDS SUCH as we have been considering appear in the spring and then spend the summer in gaining strength, after which they remain stationary and as if wrapped in deep sleep all through the winter. The following spring they wake up and grow into branches or blossom into flowers. It is plainly to be seen that these dormant buds, as arboriculture calls them in its picturesque language, must, in order to withstand the summer heat and the winter's cold, be clothed so as not to be parched by the sun or killed by the frost. They are all in fact covered with a wrapping of scales, and for that reason are called scaly buds. Buds of this class are found in the lilac, chestnut, pear, apple, cherry, poplar, and in fact nearly all the trees of our country.

But if a tree can wait and devote a whole year to the development of its buds, which are clothed in a sheath of scales because of this waiting, there are a multitude of plants that have only a limited time at their disposal: they live only a year, and hence are called annuals. Such are the potato, carrot, pumpkin, and a great many more. In a few months or days they must hastily develop their buds. These, not having to pass through the winter, are never enveloped in protecting scales: they are naked buds. As soon as they appear they elongate, unfold their leaves, and become branches taking part in the work of the whole. Very soon, in the axils of their leaves, other buds make their appearance and behave like their predecessors; that is to say, they develop quickly into branches which in their turn produce other buds. And so on indefinitely until winter puts a stop to this scaffold of branches and kills the whole plant. Thus annuals ramify rapidly. In one year they produce several generations of branches implanted one on another, sometimes more, sometimes fewer, according to their species and their degree of vigor. Their buds, designed for immediate development, are always naked. On the contrary, those forms of vegetation that have a long life, such as trees, ramify slowly; they have only one generation of branches a year, and their buds, destined to live through the winter, are scaly.

Certain examples of plant-life have both kinds of buds. Such, for instance, are the peach-tree and the grape-vine. At the end of winter the vine-shoot bears scaly buds lined with flock, and the peach branches scaly buds coated with varnish. Both belong to the class of dormant buds: they have slept all winter in their sheaths of fur and scales. In the spring they develop into branches according to the general rule; but at the same time there appear in the axils of the leaves other buds without any protecting covering, and these develop immediately into branches. Thus the grape-vine and the peach-tree beget two generations in one year: the first, the issue of the scaly buds that have endured the winter; the second, naked buds formed in the spring and developing very soon after their formation. The branches arising from these latter finally give birth to scaly buds, which sleep through the winter and reproduce the same order of things the following year.

"Both axillary and terminal buds are in the normal order of plant-life: they appear in all forms of vegetation that live several years. But when the plant is in danger, when by some accident the regular buds are lacking or insufficient, others spring into being here and there at haphazard, even on the root if necessary, to restore a languishing vitality and put the plant once more in a flourishing condition. These accidental buds are to the part of the plant above the ground what adventitious roots are to the part below the ground: the menace of the moment calls them into existence at any endangered point. The edges of the wound caused by the lopping off of a branch, the part of a tree-trunk constricted by a band, portions of the bark injured by contusion, these are the points where they appear by preference. They are called adventitious buds, but their structure does not differ from that of normal buds.

"Adventitious buds lend themselves to valuable uses. Suppose a number of young saplings to be planted at proper intervals in the ground. If they are then left to themselves these saplings grow each into a single trunk and form collectively a wood or forest. But it may be of advantage to replace each of these single trunks by a group of several trunks. In that case the young plantation is cut down to the level of the ground, and around the edge of each cross-section there presently spring a number of adventitious buds which shoot up into an equal number of stems, so that each sapling that would have developed only one trunk is transformed into a stump from which start numerous sprouts or suckers, all of the same age and strength. Then instead of a wood or forest we have a growth of underbrush, or a copse. When the suckers have acquired the desired size, a fresh cutting back lays them low and induces a still denser growth of shoots by multiplying the number of wounds. It is thus that from a single stock, repeatedly cut back and as often reinvigorated by the growth of adventitious buds, a quantity of wood is obtained exceeding that produced by the free and solitary development of one tree.

"Spared by the axe, the poplar rises in a majestic obelisk of verdure. The willow, so ungraceful in appearance along the banks of our ditches, with its shapeless top bristling with shoots sticking out in all directions, is, in its natural state, a tree of rare elegance on account of the suppleness of its branches and the fineness of its foliage. Considered as a thing of beauty, it certainly has nothing to gain by man's interference with its mode of growth. But, alas, productivity does not always go hand in hand with beauty; and if it is desired to make these two trees, the poplar and the willow, produce a great mass of branches and fire-wood, decapitation, repeated periodically, transforms them into pollards, seamed with scars, gaping with bleeding wounds, disfigured with bruises, but at the same time contending against all this hard usage by a never-failing growth of adventitious buds which constantly replace with increasing prodigality the brushwood that has fallen victim to the axe.

"To finish the subject of adventitious buds—buds that persist in multiplying even when the parent stock languishes, and that withstand destruction until utter exhaustion has set in—let us recall for a moment certain weeds such as dog's-tooth grass, cockspur grass, and other grasses that are so hard to keep out of our garden paths unless we do something more than merely rake the surface of the ground. You may have taken infinite pains, we will say, to clean the paths, and have left them immaculate, or at least you think so. But you are mistaken. In a few days the grass has all come back in richer tufts than ever. The reason is plain enough now: your raking simply cut back the stems, leaving wounds that immediately covered themselves with adventitious buds, which quickly sent up new stalks. Thus, instead of destroying, you have multiplied. The only way to clear the ground of weeds is to pull them up by the roots; that done, you may consider the job well done."

CHAPTER XVIII

BULBS AND BULBLETS

"**A**FTER ATTAINING the requisite degree of strength the buds of certain plants leave the parent stalk and, if we may so express it, emigrate; that is to say, they detach themselves and take root in the earth, to draw nourishment directly therefrom. Now it is evident that a bud designed for independent development cannot have precisely the structure of one destined never to leave the parent stem. To satisfy its first needs before roots capable of nourishing it have been sent down into the soil, it must of necessity have a certain prepared store of nutriment. Therefore every bud that emigrates carries a supply of food with it.

"There is cultivated in gardens a pretty little lily native to high mountains, bearing orange-colored blossoms, and known as the bulbiferous lily. Here is a piece of the stalk with its buds situated in the axils of the leaves. These buds must pass through the winter and develop the following spring. They are covered with succulent scales, very thick, tender, and fleshy, good for nourishment as well as for protection. This store of provisions makes the bud quite plump. Toward the end of summer some of these buds leave the mother plant; they fall at the slightest wind, scatter on the ground, and are henceforth given over to their own resources. If the season is a wet one, many of them, still in place at the axils of the leaves, send out one or two little roots that hang in the air as if trying to reach the ground. Before October arrives all the buds have fallen. Then the mother stalk dies. Soon the autumn winds and rains cover the scattered buds with dead leaves and mold. Under this shelter they swell all winter from the juices of their scales, plunge their roots into the ground little by little, and, behold, in the spring each one displays its first green leaf, continues henceforth its independent growth, and finally becomes a plant like the original lily.

"The fleshy, scaly buds destined to develop independently of the mother stalk are called bulblets. No plant known to agriculture could furnish us so striking an example of bud-emigration as the bulbiferous lily; but in our kitchen gardens we have garlic, which acts in almost the same way. Take a whole head of garlic. On the outside are dry, white wrappings. Strip these off and underneath you will find large buds which can easily be detached one by one. Then come more white wrappings followed by new buds, so that the entire head is a package of alternate wrappings and buds.

"These wrappings are the dried-up lower portions of the old leaves of the plant, leaves blanched where the soil covered them, and where they still remain, and formerly green where exposed to the air, though that part is now lacking. In the axils of these leaves buds have formed according to the general rule; only, as they are destined to develop by themselves, they have stored up supplies in their thickened scales, and that is what makes them unusually large. Split one of them lengthwise. Under a tough sheath you will find an enormous 

fleshy mass forming almost the whole of the bud. That is the storehouse. With such supplies of food the bud is well able to take care of itself. And, in fact, when a market-gardener wishes to raise a crop of garlic, he does not have recourse to the seed; that would take too long. He turns his attention to the buds; that is to say, he plants in the ground, one by one, the bulblets of which the heads of garlic are composed. Each of these bulblets, sustained at first by its own reserves of food, puts forth roots and leaves and becomes a complete garlic plant.

"From the bulblet to the bulb, from garlic to an onion, there is but a single step. Let us split an onion in two from top to bottom. We shall find it composed of a succession of fleshy scales compactly fitted together. In the heart of this cluster of succulent scales, which are nothing but leaves so modified as to form a food-storehouse, are found other leaves of normal shape and green color. An onion, then, is a bud provisioned for an independent life by the conversion of its outside leaves into fleshy scales; and it is called a bulb, not a bulblet, because of its size, the latter term being the diminutive form of 'bulb.' Bulb and bulblet differ merely in size: the bulb is larger, the bulblet smaller, and that is all.

"Every one has noticed that an onion hanging on the wall ready at hand for the cook, is awakened to life in the course of the winter by the heat of the room, and from within its envelope of red scales puts forth a beautiful green shoot that seems to protest against the rigors of the season and reminds us of the sweet pleasures of spring. As it develops, its fleshy scales wrinkle, soften, become flabby, and finally fall off in decay to serve as fertilizer for the young plant. Sooner or later, however, its store of provision being exhausted, the shoot perishes unless placed in earth. There we have a striking example of a bud that develops independently by means of its own accumulated supplies. The leek is also a bulb, but very slender in shape. Like the onion, it consists of a cluster of lower leaf-parts sheathed one inside another. Among ornamental plants having bulbs are the lily, the tulip, and the hyacinth."

CHAPTER XIX

TUBERS—STARCH

"THERE ARE buds that, though called to an independent existence, do not, before separating from the mother plant, store up provisions nor thicken their scales; but the plant itself is charged with feeding them. When it is intended that the stem or branch shall itself maintain the buds it bears, then, instead of coming out into the open air where it would speedily cover itself with foliage and flowers, it remains underground and has for leaves only rudimentary scales. It grows so corpulent and deformed as to cease to bear the name of branch and to take instead that of tuber. As soon as necessary supplies have been stored up, the tuber detaches itself from the mother plant, and thenceforth the buds it bears find in it abundant nourishment for their separate existence. A tuber, then, is an underground branch swollen with nutritive material and having undeveloped scales in place of leaves, and it is also dotted here and there with buds which it must feed.

"Let us now look at a potato. What do we see on the surface? Certain small cavities or eyes; that is to say, so many buds, for these eyes develop into branches if the potato is placed in favorable conditions. On old potatoes, late in the season, the buds are seen to send forth sprouts which need only a little sunshine to turn green and become stalks. Agriculture makes good use of this peculiarity: to propagate the plant it is customary to put into the ground, not the seeds, which would yield no harvest before the lapse of several years, but the tubers, which produce abundantly the same year. Or else the potato is cut into pieces and each piece, planted in the ground, sends up a new plant on condition that it has at least one eye; if it has none it rots without producing anything.

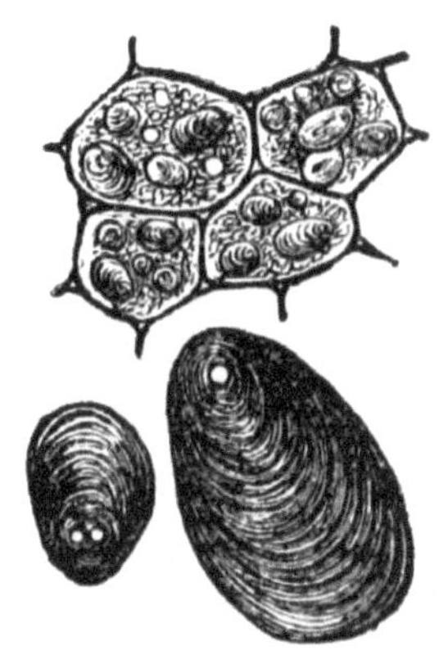

STARCH GRAINS
OF POTATO

"Furthermore, you can see on the eyes tiny little scales, which are leaves modified to adapt them to an underground life, leaves with the same right to the name as the tough scales of an ordinary bud. Since it has leaves and buds the potato is therefore a branch. Should there remain any lingering doubts on this subject, it might be added that by earthing up the plant, that is to say by heaping soil around the stalk, the young branches thus buried can be converted into potato-bearers; and it might also be added that in rainy and cloudy seasons it is not rare to see some of the ordinary branches thicken and swell up in the open air, and thus produce potatoes more or less perfect. Accordingly the potato is to be regarded as an underground branch swollen with nourishment—in short, a tuber.

"Many other plants produce similar branches that grow under ground. In this number is the Jerusalem artichoke, the tubers of which have buds arranged two by two on opposite swellings, from front to back and from right to left in turn, exactly as are leaves and buds on the stem.

"The potato feeds it buds on a farinaceous substance called fecula or, in less learned language, starch. It is the very material that makes the vegetable so rich in nutriment for us. We turn to our own account what the plant has stored up for its young shoots. Starch is contained in the extremely small cavities with which the flesh of the tuber is all riddled. These cavities are called cells. They are microscopic sacs made of a fine membrane and having no opening. Crammed full of starch grains and crowded one against another, they compose the fleshy substance of the potato. But these cavities are so small that a person would strain his eyes in vain in any attempt to see them in the cross-section of a potato. A magnifying glass is necessary. So minute are the cells that in a piece of potato no larger than a pin's head there is room for dozens and dozens of them. This picture shows you, but much larger than in nature, a potato cell with the grains of starch it encloses."

"How beautifully," exclaimed Emile, "those grains of starch are arranged in their little cubby-hole! They might be taken for a nest of eggs. And you say there are heaps and heaps of these little starch cells?"

"Yes, my boy; in a medium-sized potato they could be counted by millions and millions."

"It must be rather a curious sight to look at a little piece of potato through a powerful magnifying-glass."

"It is indeed one of the most curious sights, this countless multitude of starch grains, all the same shape, all white as snow, gathered together by tens, dozens, scores, and even more, in their delicate little box-like cells.

"Let us perform an experiment not beyond our means; let us remove the starch from a potato. All we need to do is to tear open the cells in order to liberate the starch grains, and then filter them out. Watch me do it. With a kitchen grater I reduce the potato to pulp and thus tear the cells open. Now I put the pulp on a piece of linen over a large glass and pour a little water through it with one hand while with the other I keep stirring the pulp. The grains of starch from the ruptured cells are washed away by the water and carried through the meshes of the fabric, while the remnants of the cell-walls, being too large to pass through, stay behind in the filter.

"Thus I obtain a glassful of turbid water. Look at it under a bright sun. In the water a multitude of white satiny specks are falling like so much snow and piling up on the bottom. In a few moments the deposit has settled. I then throw away the clear water above it and have left a powdery substance, magnificently white, which if pressed between the fingers creaks like fine sand. It is the starch of the potato, and is made up of such fine grains that it would take from one hundred and fifty to two hundred to equal the head of a pin in size. Nevertheless these grains, minute though they are, have a very complicated structure, each one of them being composed of a large number of tiny leaflets folded one over another. The picture I showed you just now will serve to give you an idea of these superposed leaflets that go to make, all together, a single grain. Now if some of this starch is boiled in a little water, the successive leaflets of the grain open and separate, and the whole becomes an unctuous jelly far exceeding in volume that of the starch used."

To prove this assertion, Uncle Paul proceeded to heat in a little water the starch taken from the potato, and soon the powdery matter was reduced to a beautiful pellucid jelly.

CHAPTER XX

USES OF STARCH

"THAT JELLY," remarked Jules, "looks just like the paste that I make with laundry starch. Your potato starch there in the bottom of the glass has exactly the same appearance as starch dissolved in cold water for ironing clothes."

"That close resemblance," replied his uncle, "is explained by the fact that potato starch and laundry starch are at bottom the same thing. Both substances are chemically known as fecula; but laundry starch is made from cereals, particularly wheat, while fecula, properly speaking, comes either from potatoes or from various grains and roots.

"Like the starch of the potato, laundry starch is in the form of superposed leaflets, but its grains are much smaller: ten thousand would hardly be enough to make a pellet the size of a pin's head. And there are some still smaller. It would take sixty-four thousand grains of Indian corn starch to make a pin's head or, to be more exact, to fill the inside of a cube measuring one millimeter on a side; and in the case of the beet it would take ten millions. You see that in spite of their excessive smallness, a smallness that makes them invisible to the naked eye, the starch grains of the potato are giants in comparison.

"It is chiefly by the varying size of their microscopic grains that the starches of different kinds are distinguished from one another. In substance and structure they are all alike.

Placed in warm water, their grains swell, burst, expand their leaflets, and the starch, from whatever source, is changed into a glutinous jelly.

"Starch is the food supply of plant-life. Wherever we find buds that are intended to develop by themselves, wherever we find germs, there also we shall find a supply of starch serving as a sort of food reserve. Hence this peculiar provision is met with in tubers, bulbs, bulblets, seeds, and fleshy roots. Now when these buds and germs develop, the starch becomes, in the process of vegetation, a kind of sugar which, being soluble in water, can be sent to all parts of the young plant and serve it for food.

"By certain artificial devices this same change of starch into sugar can be brought about. The simplest of these devices is the application of heat, which always enters into the preparation of farinaceous food. Let us take a few examples. A raw potato is uneatable. Boiled in water or roasted in the ashes, it is excellent. What has happened, then? Heat has converted a part of the starch into sugar, and the tuber has become a sugary farinaceous paste. The same can be said of the chestnut. Raw, it is no great delicacy, although at a pinch it can be eaten; cooked, it is worthy of all the praise we can give it. I appeal to you to back me up in this assertion. Here, then, we have another transformation of starch into sugar by the action of heat. Beans, peas, both as hard as bullets in the dry state and of no agreeable flavor, are unmistakably sweetened by being boiled in water and having their starch acted on by heat. Our various farinaceous foods behave in the same way. Ingenuity brings into play a more powerful agent than heat alone to convert the starch into sugar. It is boiled in water and during the boiling a little sulphuric acid or oil of vitriol is added. Under the influence of this energetic fluid the starch is changed into a sugary syrup. It is of course to be understood that this syrup, as soon as it has been thus produced, is separated from the oil of vitriol which has served to make it.

"The sugar thus obtained is a soft, sticky substance, and almost as sweet as honey, but very different from ordinary sugar, which is solid and comes in beautiful white loaves.[3] It is called starch-sugar or glucose. Confectioners use it a great deal. When you crunch a sugar-plum—and I am persuaded that you do not underestimate the excellence of sugar-plums—do you know what you are eating? A composition of starch and starch-sugar. I pass over the almond in the center; that is beside the question."

"Do you mean to say," demanded Jules, "that a bag of sugar-plums comes from such stuff as potatoes and oil of vitriol?"

"Such is undoubtedly the origin of the delicious sugar-plum," was the reply; "and indeed many of the delicacies of the pastry-cook, of the confectioner, and of the manufacturer of refreshing beverages, which you believe to be sweetened with ordinary sugar, really owe their sweet taste to syrup made from starch—a much cheaper product than sugar. You see the potato furnishes something else besides the modest dishes with which it supplies our table.

"Nor is that the whole story. Starch-sugar, or glucose, is exactly the same as the sugar of ripe grapes. With potato-flour, water, and a few drops of oil of vitriol there is artificially produced, in enormous boilers, the same sugary substance that the vine produces in its bunches of grapes with the help of the sun's rays. Now grape sugar turns to alcohol by fermenting. Glucose must undergo a similar change. And, as a matter of fact, in northern countries too cold to admit of the cultivation

3   The old fashioned loaf-sugar is here meant.—*Translator.*

of the vine, alcoholic liquors are made from starch previously changed into sugar. On account of their origin these liquors go under the general name of potato-brandy. All seeds and roots rich in starch can be used in similar manufacture.

"Beer is a product of this sort. First barley is made to germinate by being kept moist and warm. In the process of germination the starch is changed into glucose for the nourishment of the young shoots. When the little plants begin to develop, the grain is dried and ground to flour. This mixed with water furnishes a sugary liquid which ferments, turning partly to alcohol and finally becoming beer."

CHAPTER XXI

HISTORY OF THE POTATO

"Next to wheat no plant in our part of the world is of so much importance for food as the potato. Its use was not introduced into this country until toward the end of the eighteenth century. The first appearance of the potato among our people is a curious piece of history. Why should I not relate it to you? It will show you what noble efforts and perseverance are sometimes necessary to bring about the adoption, on the part of those wedded to blind routine, of the simplest, most natural idea, and one so rich in future possibilities.

"The potato is native to South America; it came to us from the high plains of Colombia, Chile, and Peru. Its first appearance in Europe dates from 1565. A century and a half later the potato flourished in England. Its introduction into general use in France was slower. The first dish of potatoes, then a high-priced rarity, was served at the table of King Louis XIII in 1616.

"The royal dish is to-day at the command of the poorest; but this was not effected without a good deal of trouble, as you will see. For a long time the American tuber remained in our country a simple object of curiosity to which were attributed injurious properties, and which agriculture would have nothing to do with. Finally, toward the end of the eighteenth century a worthy man succeeded in overcoming these prejudices and popularized the culture of this valuable food plant. His name is

Parmentier. Remember this venerated name, my friends; he who bore it banished famine by making the potato supply the deficiency of wheat.

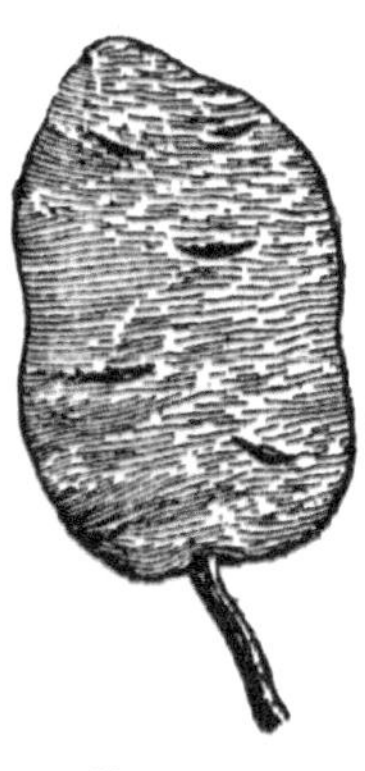

POTATO

"Parmentier communicated his ideas to Louis XVI. 'The potato,' said he, 'is bread already made and requiring neither miller nor baker. Take it just as it comes out of the ground and bake it in hot ashes or cook it in boiling water, and you will have a farinaceous food rivaling wheat. Poor land unfit for other crops will raise it, and it will henceforth relieve us of all fear of those terrible dearths that France has so often suffered in the past.'

"Louis XVI listened to this proposal with eager attention, but the difficulty was to make others listen also. In order to interest the world of fashion in the culture of the disdained tuber the king appeared at a public festival one day with a large bouquet of potato blossoms in his hand. Curiosity was aroused at the sight of these white flowers tinged with violet and set off by the dark green of the leaves. They were talked of at court and in town; florists made imitations of them for their artificial bouquets; in ornamental gardens they were used for the borders; and as the surest way to royal favor the nobles sent potatoes to their tenant farmers with orders to plant and cultivate them."

"Behold the potato fairly started on the right road!" interposed Jules. "It cannot fail to become popular now, under the protection of king and court."

"Not so fast, my little friend. Persuasion is a good deal better than command. The tubers patronized by royalty were thrown on the dunghill. At most, here and there a farmer, afraid of being reprimanded, allowed them to grow as best they could in some neglected corner."

"And then?"

"Then the only thing to do was to convince, not the nobleman who cared nothing for the potato except as a means for winning the king's favor, but the peasant himself directly interested in this affair. It was necessary to overcome his repugnance, a repugnance that made him reject the potato even as fodder for cattle; he must be taught by his own experience that the tuber of ill repute, far from being a poison, is excellent food. All this Parmentier thoroughly understood and he set to work without delay."

"This time he is sure to succeed."

"Not at first and not without great pains. In the suburbs of Paris he bought or rented for farming large tracts of land which he caused to be planted with potatoes. The first year the harvest was sold at a very low price. A few people bought some."

"Now we are nearing the goal."

"Not yet. Good is not accomplished so easily. The second year the potatoes were given away for nothing. Nobody wanted them."

"And Parmentier was left with the whole crop on his hands?"

"The excellent man could not find a welcome for a single basket of potatoes. In the country they laughed maliciously at his obstinacy in cultivating a vile root that no peasant would even feed to his pigs. But Parmentier did not despair. A singular idea came to him: to see whether the charm of forbidden fruit would not accomplish what he had failed to effect by his writings, his advice, his personal example, and his generous offers.

"A large field was planted with potatoes, and when the crop was ripe a fence was built about the field as if to protect a most valuable harvest. And more than this, Parmentier caused it to be trumpeted abroad throughout the neighboring villages that it was expressly forbidden to touch the potatoes under penalty of all the rigors of the law against marauders. During the day the guards kept strict watch over the field, and woe betide whoever should try to climb over the fence!"

"It seems to me," said Emile, "that with all those prohibitions and guards and fences Parmentier was more likely than ever to have all his potatoes to himself."

"Such was not his purpose; far from it. The guards kept good watch during the day, but they had orders to stay at home at night and leave unmolested any who might attempt to get into the field. 'What, then, is this plant that is guarded with such jealous care?' the peasants asked one another, attracted by the strictness of the prohibitory measures. 'It must be very precious. Let us try to get some when the night is dark.'

"Some bold marauders climbed the fence, hastily pulled up a dozen tubers, and scampered off again, looking back to make sure they were not pursued. Not a guard was to be seen. Word soon spread that the field was not guarded at night. Then the pillage began in earnest: the tubers hitherto so despised were carried off by sackfuls. In a few days there was not a potato left in the ground.

"People came and told Parmentier of the devastation of his field. The worthy man wept for joy; the one robbed blessed his robbers. By his ruse he had endowed his country with an inestimable food-supply; for, once placed in the hands of those who would consent to cultivate it, the potato was valued at its true worth and spread rapidly."

"Oh, what a curious story!" cried Louis, when Uncle Paul had finished; "what a curious story! Who would have thought it took all that trouble to make people accept a food that to-day is of such value to us? Is it, then, so very hard to spread a good idea when it is new?"

"Very hard indeed," replied Uncle Paul, "as those well know who make it their mission to fight against prejudice and ignorance."

CHAPTER XXII

ASCENDING SAP

"**N**OW LET us see how the plant is nourished by the various substances of which we have just studied the most important. Every form of plant-life is made up, not of a compact and uniform mass of matter with no occasional empty spaces, but, on the contrary, with the aid of a microscope it is seen that an infinite number of very minute cavities called cells are interspersed throughout the body of the plant. These cells may be regarded as extremely small closed sacs, sometimes round, sometimes oval, but more often with irregular and angular outlines by reason of the mutual pressure exerted by the cells. The cell-wall is composed of an excessively fine membrane. In the pith of the elder, all riddled like a sponge, you have an example of cells large enough to be seen without a microscope. Other cavities are long, pointed at both ends and swollen in the middle like a spindle. They are called fibers. Still others form canals of uniform size throughout, as fine as a hair and long enough to extend from the roots to the topmost leaves. These canals are called ducts. Look closely at the cross-section of a very dry vine-branch, and you will see a multitude of orifices into which it would be possible to thrust a hair. Those are the openings into so many broken ducts. Everything in the plant, absolutely everything—root, stalk, wood, bark, leaves, flowers, fruit, seeds, no matter what—is composed of a mass of cells, fibers, and ducts.

"That understood, let us consider the root of the plant. In its new parts, at the tip-ends of its finest ramifications, tip-ends that we have called spongioles, it is composed of cells just formed and consequently tender and fitted for absorbing easily the moisture in the soil. Spongioles, then, fill themselves much as sponges would do. That done, conduits offer their services for conveying the liquid to the top of the plant: they are the ducts just referred to, and comparable here to the water-pipes in our own fountains. But if in fountains water runs by its own weight, going from the highest to the lowest point, it is not so with the liquid absorbed by the roots, a liquid running from below upward. What then is the force that makes it ascend?

"This force is in the buds or, to speak more correctly, in the leaves. Each leaf is the seat of an active evaporation whose object is to rid the plant of the great quantity of water required for dissolving in the soil and then conveying to the leaves the nutritive substances present in the soil. This evaporation leaves a void in the cells that have given up the evaporated water. But this void is immediately filled from the neighboring cells, which give up their contents and receive in turn the contents of the next lower layers. From cell to cell, from fiber to fiber, from duct to duct, a similar transfer takes place at points farther and farther away from the evaporating surface, until the tip-ends of the rootlets are reached, where a continuous absorption makes good the loss of moisture by evaporation. The process reminds one somewhat of the working of our pumps, in which the piston leaves behind it a void that is immediately filled by the water in the pipe, which in its turn gets water from the bottom of the well. This liquid which ascends in every plant, absorbed by the spongioles of the rootlets and put in motion by the evaporation from the leaves, is called ascending sap, or crude sap. The sap is called ascending because it passes from below upward, from the roots to the branches; and it is called crude because it has not yet undergone the preparation that will turn it into the nutritive liquid of the plant. Thus we have learned our first lesson, namely: ascending sap is carried especially to those parts of the plant where buds are numerous, where leaves abound; it seeks by preference the ends of the branches, where evaporation is most active.

"We know that the surface wood is the newest; it is formed of cells, fibers, and ducts whose cavities are free and whose walls are permeable. The interior wood is older; its cells, fibers, and ducts are encrusted, stopped up, decrepit, out of use. The liquid accordingly makes its way where circulation is possible, and ceases to flow where the passage is obstructed. That is to say, the ascent of the sap takes place through the sap-wood and chiefly through the outermost layers, or those of most recent formation. Repeated experiment leaves no doubt on this point. When a tree is cut down at the time of the sap's greatest activity, we find the sap-wood moist and the older wood perfectly dry. Finally, in herbaceous plants the sap ascends through the whole body of the stem. Suspended during the winter on account of the absence of foliage, this ascent of the sap becomes remarkably brisk at the awakening of vegetation. Then it is that fruit-trees shed tears, so to speak, where the pruning-hook has left its mark; or, in other words, the ascending sap oozes from the openings of the severed ducts. These tears are especially noticeable in the grape-vine, where it has recently been trimmed.

"Now what would you expect to find in this liquid if you collected some of it as it trickles in the form of tears either from the vine or from a fruit-tree? Many things, doubtless, you will say, since this precious liquid is the prime source of all that the plant contains in itself. If such is your thought, undeceive yourselves:

ascending sap is little more than clear water, and often it is very difficult for science to prove beyond a doubt the presence in it of various substances in solution, so minute a fraction of the whole do they compose. Among these substances the most frequent are compounds of potash, of lime, of carbonic acid gas, traces of phosphates, and compounds of nitrogen or ammonia. In short, the liquid from which the plant is to derive its nourishment is the weakest sort of broth, composed of an enormous quantity of water and a very small proportion of dissolved substances. These inconsiderable substances are the only or almost the only things utilized by the plant; and the water that has collected them in filtering through the soil, and has then carried them from the roots to the leaves through the sap-wood, the water that forms almost the whole of the ascending sap, is destined, as soon as the journey is accomplished, to leave the plant and return as vapor to the atmosphere whence it descended in the form of rain."

CHAPTER XXIII

DESCENDING SAP

"ASCENDING SAP, a liquid composed of a large quantity of water and a very small proportion of dissolved nutritive substances, is absorbed in the ground by the roots and carried to the leaves through the sap-wood. It is not yet a nutritive fluid for the plant; it becomes so in the foliage by a double process. First, on being distributed to the leaves, which furnish a vast surface for evaporation, it exhales its superabundant water in the form of vapor and thus concentrates its usable ingredients. Then, under the influence of the sun's rays and through the medium of the green matter contained in the leaves, it undergoes modifications that work a fundamental change in its character. Among the processes here taking place, one of the best known is the decomposition of the carbonic acid gas taken from the air by the leaves and from the soil by the roots.

"We have seen that this gas, the plant's chief source of nourishment, is composed of carbon combined with the breathable part of the air, or oxygen. Under the action of the sun's light the leaves decompose this gas, liberating the oxygen in a condition henceforth fit for the respiration of animals and for combustion, while the carbon remains in the plant, mixes with the substances brought by the ascending sap, and with them becomes the nourishing liquid, the descending or elaborated sap, from which all future parts of the plant are to be formed. This liquid cannot be called wood, bark, leaf, flower, or fruit; it is not at all like any of these, and yet it is essentially a little of them all. An animal's blood is neither flesh, bone, nor fleece; but bone, flesh, and fleece are of its substance. Likewise the elaborated sap is a liquid designed for the sustenance of all parts of the plant; it contains matter for fruit and wood, leaves and flowers, bark and buds. It is the plant's blood; everything in the plant gets from it its nourishment, its wherewithal to develop. What a wonderful, what an incomprehensible process its production appears to us! In the crowded ranks of the leaf-cells, where one would suppose everything to be at rest, what activity, what transformations beyond the reach of human science! Liquids swell the cells, ooze from one to another, transpire, infiltrate, circulate, exchange their dissolved substances; vapors are exhaled, gases come, others go; the sun's light separates what was united, unites what was separated, and the raw materials of the ascending sap combine henceforth with the materials of life.

"The elaborated sap descends from the leaves to the twigs, from the twigs to the branches, from the branches to the stalk or trunk, and from the latter to the root, distributing itself here and there on its way. It circulates between the wood and the bark. It is this sap that, in the spring, when it is in great abundance, forms between the wood and the bark a thin layer of slightly viscous moisture and makes the bark easy to peel from its branch. Which of you in the month of May has not taken advantage of this peculiarity to peel off all in one piece a tube of bark from a very smooth twig of willow or lilac in order to make a whistle, trumpet, or other noisy plaything, the delight of boys of your age?

"Nothing is easier than to prove the passage of sap from above downward. If you remove from a tree-trunk an annular band of bark, the nourishing liquid oozes and accumulates at the upper edge of the wound, but nothing of the sort takes place at the lower edge. Arrested thus by a break in its path, the sap accumulates above the uncovered ring and causes there an abundant growth of wood and bark, which piles up in the form of a thick circular swelling, while below the ring the trunk preserves its former size.

"A tight ligature, by compressing and obstructing the passages through which the nutritive fluid has to pass, causes the formation of a similar swelling above the line of stoppage. You may have seen a sapling, bound too tightly to the stake intended for its support, strangled by its own growth if the gardener has forgotten to loose the band in time. Little by little the trunk swells above this band, which is finally overgrown by the bark and even hidden within its substance. Indeed, it is not rare to find a tree with its trunk caught fast in a narrow passage, as for example in the crevice of a rock, and swollen above the obstacle into an unsightly excrescence. The stoppage of the sap in its downward course explains this phenomenon.

"If the tree-trunk is not completely encircled by the stricture, if somewhere there is a strip of bark left free to serve as a passage, the nourishing juice takes this way to get around the obstacle, and so pursues its course to the roots. Then the tree continues to live. But if the barrier is absolutely insuperable, as in the case of an unyielding ligature or when the tree has been girdled, the sap cannot descend to the roots to nourish them; and with the death of these the end of the tree is not far distant.

"An important lesson remains to be drawn from these details concerning the circulation of this nutritive liquid in plants. Henceforth, when we fasten a plant to its prop or supporting stake, we shall be careful not to tie the string too tight or else to loosen it at the proper time, since otherwise we should run the risk of strangling the plant and so causing its death."

CHAPTER XXIV

TREE-PRUNING

"SELF-PRESERVATION IS the first law of a tree's life, and next to that the preservation of its species, which is to be perpetuated by means of seeds. All this is perfectly natural, for no posterity would be possible to the tree unless its own existence were maintained in the first place. Accordingly the tree lives first for itself, accomplishing this object by covering itself with buds that develop into branches covered with leaves. It is indeed on the leaves that the fundamental principles of the plant's life are based; it is in their substance that, with the sun's help, the descending sap is elaborated, this sap being the nutritive fluid, the life-blood as it were, of the vegetable organism. The propagation of the species comes next in importance. This duty devolves on the flower-buds or those that blossom and produce fruit, in the center of which are the seeds.

"Thus, left to its own impulses, a tree, if vigorous and enjoying favorable conditions, at first uses all its sap in making buds for the increase of its own woody structure; it covers itself with stout branches and abundant foliage before making up its mind to blossom. Later, when its limbs are strong and the ardor of growth begins to abate, the flower-buds appear, but usually in small numbers because a prodigal production of fruit causes rapid decline. Copious blossoming comes only toward the latter part of life; a tree never blossoms better than when it is about to die, as if, foreseeing its end, it strove before succumbing to leave behind it a numerous progeny. A thriving tree blossoms little or not at all; a sickly tree makes haste to blossom. But it is to man's interest that a tree should blossom and bear fruit as early and as abundantly as possible; we demand from it not the branches it would give us without our intervention, but baskets of fruit induced by our care. From this struggle between the natural tendencies of the tree and our own needs has sprung the practice of pruning, or the art of manipulating fruit-trees so as to obtain from them an abundant harvest.

"Here let us examine the general principles that are to guide us in the practice of this art. The shape to be given the tree's superstructure of branches and foliage is the first question we must consider. This shape is far from being unimportant; it is, on the contrary, very important, since the circulation of the sap and the distribution of the sun's rays, essential conditions to plant-life, are strictly dependent on it. If the tree is left free to develop by itself and to take its natural form, the sap from the roots will, under the impetus of its ascent, always seek by preference the highest points, where growth will in consequence proceed with vigor, while the lower parts will languish and die out for want of sufficient nourishment. If the branches are not properly thinned the central ones, deprived of the sun's vivifying rays, will remain poor, puny, more or less blanched. On the other hand, the tree ought to fill, as far as possible, the place assigned it, in order that there may be no unproductive space.

"These conditions prescribe the tree's shape. First of all, it should be symmetrical, in order that the distribution of nourishment may be even and no part of the tree be gorged with sap while another part is deprived of it. Secondly, the sun's rays should be allowed to penetrate everywhere so as to ripen the fruit and facilitate in the foliage the important work of sap-elaboration. To attain these different objects custom has fixed upon three principal shapes: the trellis, the pyramid, and the goblet. In trellis pruning the tree spreads its branches symmetrically, right and left, against a wall. The wall serves it as support and as shelter from the wind; it also gives the foliage and fruit additional heat and light by reflecting the sun's rays upon them. When pruned to take the pyramid form, the tree has its branches so trimmed as to decrease in length regularly from the base to the summit and to remain far enough apart to admit the light to the center. The whole forms a sugar-loaf, a cone, into the midst of which sun and air enter freely. It is the shape most in accord with nature. Finally, the goblet-shaped tree has a certain number of branches of equal vigor disposed in a circle around a central space that remains empty and thus receives its share of sunlight without hindrance."

CHAPTER XXV

PINCHING—BUD-NIPPING

"WHEN THE desired shape has been obtained the next thing is to keep it, despite all opposition on the part of the tree, which revolts in its own peculiar fashion; that is, it strives to restore the natural conformation of its branches. Suppose, for example, that a pear-tree, pruned after the manner of wall-fruit, has grown all out of symmetry and developed one side more than the other. How shall the two halves be restored to correct proportions? How shall the too vigorous part be weakened and the too feeble part strengthened? Several methods offer themselves.

"On the vigorous side let us cut back the branches with the pruning shears, leaving only the base of each with a small number of buds; in other words, let us cut them very short. On the weak side, on the contrary, let us leave the branches intact or cut them very long, thus leaving them the greater part of their buds. What will come of this treatment? Since abundant foliage, the active laboratory of the descending sap and also a kind of pump that sucks up the sap and causes it to ascend from the roots, is the prime cause of vigorous vegetation, the weak part, with its numerous buds developed into leafy shoots, will grow stronger, while the strong part, with its small number of buds, will become weaker. Both effects will tend to the same result: the restoration of the desired symmetry.

"With the ends of the fingers and the help of the thumb-nail, it is customary to pinch off from the too vigorous side the tips of the young branches while they are still tender. This operation we may call pinching. The sap that would have been used for the development of these branches is diverted from its course and carried toward the weak shoots, which it renews and stimulates. If the weak side itself needs pinching to arrest shoots that impair the desired symmetry, the operation is postponed as long as possible, while on the strong side it is carried out very early. The sap thus turned away from the vigorous side toward the ailing one has a whole season in which to restore the lost equilibrium.

"Instead of limiting ourselves to pinching off the tips of the young shoots with our thumb-nail, we can suppress them altogether while they are still tender. This is done as early as possible on the strong side, only the indispensable shoots being left. If it is necessary on the weak side, it is not done until the latest possible moment. This operation we may style bud-nipping, since the word 'bud,' by which we designate the germ of the future branch when it is still enveloped in scales, applies also for the sake of convenience to the branch already developed but still young and tender. It is evident that nipping off the buds from the strong part tends, even more than pinching, to promote the desired growth of the weak part. The more branches we suppress entirely, the fewer will be left to share the sap needed by the branches we wish to strengthen.

"What turns aside the sap from the part pruned, pinched, or nipped, toward the part left intact, is evidently the more or less complete suppression of foliage. It is primarily the leaves that by the continual evaporation of which their surface is the seat determine the ascent of the liquid drawn from the soil by the roots. The more numerous these leaves are at any one point, the more abundant the flow of sap to that point; the scarcer they are, the less the flow of sap. To diminish at any point the number of leaves by pinching, bud-nipping, or any other means, is therefore to diminish at the same point the flow of sap, which will go in some other direction, to the parts that have more leaves and hence a more rapid rate of evaporation to summon the sap. It is plain, then, that a middle course may be followed between the pinching that partly suppresses the foliage of a young branch and the bud-nipping that suppresses it entirely. This middle course consists in cutting a certain number of leaves from the too vigorous shoots; and they should be cut clean without tearing, by severing the stem and leaving its base undisturbed.

"The easiest way for the sap to run from the roots to the foliage is from bottom to top in a vertical line. Anything that interferes with this course hinders also the upward impetus. Thus in branches with sharp elbows and abrupt bends the rush of sap is slackened just as the rate of flow of a water-current is diminished by the windings occurring in its bed. Thus, again, in a branch having a decided incline downward the sap moves with difficulty, because its movement toward the extremity of this branch is in a direction contrary to that which is natural to it. The application of this principle is evident. If we wish to moderate a too vigorous growth of branches, we bend them toward the ground; if we wish to stimulate a too feeble growth, we straighten up the branches until they assume a vertical posture.

"We can also turn to account the exhausting effect of fruit-bearing. The more fruitful a branch is, the weaker it becomes, since the use of sap in fruit means so much the less for foliage, and it is foliage that invigorates the branch. Accordingly we will leave the greatest possible quantity of fruit on the strong part of our tree, and suppress it on the weak part."

CHAPTER XXVI

MAKING FRUIT TREES BEAR

"IF ONE side of a tree is pruned very short and the other very long, the natural course of the sap is to some extent diverted from the first side toward the second, which is richer in buds and consequently in foliage. We have just seen how this principle is utilized to check the growth of too vigorous a part in order to stimulate that of one that is too feeble and thus redress the balance between the two. But what would be the result if the whole tree were pruned at once?

"Let us first see what takes place in a single branch. Pruned long, it preserves the greater part of its buds, all of which call for nourishment from the sap flowing in that direction; pruned short, it keeps only a few buds, which having the sap of the entire branch at their disposal, will receive each a supply that is superabundant in proportion to the fewness of the buds. For example, what twelve would ordinarily have had for consumption, two or three will now have to themselves; and because of this superabundance of nourishment each bud will develop much more vigorously than it would otherwise have done. Hence if the whole tree is pruned with an unsparing hand, all the sap drawn from the soil by the roots, having no longer a tendency to go to one side rather than the other, will be distributed evenly; and the few buds left intact by the pruning-shears will show a luxuriance of growth in proportion to the supply of nourishment placed at their disposal. Thus thorough pruning applied to the whole tree has the effect of giving it new vigor, of rejuvenating it in some measure, or, in other words, of replacing its worn-out branches with vigorous ones. Accordingly when a tree has become exhausted by abundant fruit-bearing, it is pruned without stint one year in order to restore its vigor of growth.

"Let us now see what we should do if we had quite the opposite end in view; that is, if we wished to make a tree blossom and bear fruit. Here two principles will serve us as guides. First, in the fulness of its vigor a tree puts forth long branches and thick foliage, but does not cover itself with blossoms, bearing in fact only a few. It is not until it has become somewhat enfeebled that it begins to flower in profusion. Secondly, what would in the tree's youthful strength have been a branch-producing bud becomes in its enfeeblement a flower-bud; so that a flower may be regarded as a branch which, instead of developing freely and covering itself with leaves, has remained stunted, thrown back upon itself, for lack of vigor, and has exchanged its leaves for floral organs,—sepals, petals, stamens, pistils. Weaken a tree and you weaken the buds; such, in a word, is the prevailing principle.

"To weaken the buds individually, the pruning-shears will be plied but sparingly, leaving the buds almost intact; then these, being many in number, will have so much the less for each one separately, and some of them, especially toward the lower part of the branch, will find themselves too feeble to contend with the others and therefore will take the form of flower-buds, whereas they would have produced branches and not flowers if a more thorough pruning had rid them of their rivals.

"To weaken the tree as a whole, all that we have to do is to pinch off or cut off with the thumb-nail the tender tips of the young branches; then we bend these branches back so as to give them a number of crooks and turns that will impede the circulation of the sap. Finally, the woody branches of the preceding year are broken by the hand, sometimes wholly, sometimes half, so that the tip is left hanging down. If the tree is not too vigorous these three methods, pinching, bending, and breaking, are generally sufficient to make it bear.

"But when we have to do with very exuberant vegetation, more energetic methods are necessary. One of these we may call arching. The branches are all bent down so that each forms an arch; that is, the tip-end of each is pulled down to the ground and fastened there in any way that may be easiest. This abnormal position of the branch, with its top downward, is contrary to the ascending movement of the sap, which consequently flows less freely to the buds. The resulting dearth is conducive to fruit-bearing, and as soon as this effect is assured the branches are allowed to return to their natural position; otherwise the tree would become exhausted.

"Another method is as follows. Pruning is done very late, when the young shoots are already some centimeters long. The sap used up in the growth of the shoots cut off by the pruning shears is a great loss to the tree, which, being no longer able to supply ample nourishment to the lower buds of the branches, turns them into flower-buds.

"If these means do not suffice to make the tree bear fruit, there are more violent ones which are employed only in the last extremity. Toward the end of winter, before the sap has started, an incision some millimeters wide and deep enough to penetrate the outer layers of wood is made all around the base of the trunk. Sap, as we know, ascends through these exterior layers, the newest, the most permeable by liquids; so if we partially intercept its passage it will flow less abundantly to the buds and the weakened tree will soon begin to bear.

"Still another expedient is to strike at the very source of the sap, the roots. The foot of the tree is laid bare in the springtime, its main roots being denuded of their covering and left thus exposed all summer to the open air and the hot sun. No longer enjoying the coolness and darkness necessary to their office, they furnish less nourishment to the tree, and this scarcity causes the formation of flower-buds. A still more drastic method, but one that would kill the tree if employed imprudently, is to strip the roots of the refractory subject without mercy, cutting and mutilating a certain number of them and then putting back the earth that has been removed. A diminution in the flow of sap must necessarily result from this surgical operation. Finally, if the tree is small enough for the purpose, it is dug up at the end of autumn, with care to preserve the roots as far as possible, and planted again somewhere else. The disturbance caused by this change of place suffices to make the tree blossom the next year."

CHAPTER XXVII

THE SEED

"THE OVARY of the flower, after being fertilized by the pollen, becomes the fruit, the apple on the apple-tree, the cherry on the cherry-tree, the walnut on the walnut-tree, the grain of wheat in the wheat-ear, and so on for all plants. The fruit contains seeds in greater or less number, and sometimes only one, as in the peach, plum, and almond; often several, as in the apple and pear; while in other instances they can be counted by hundreds and thousands, as in the melon, the pumpkin, and the poppy-head. The natural function of the fruit is first to supply nourishment and then to protect its seeds by means of coverings, these being sometimes fleshy, sometimes thin and dry, sometimes hard and in the form of strong shells. In their turn the seeds have as their task the propagating of the species. Every form of plant-life, from the giants of the forest, the oak, beech, fir, and others, to the tiniest moss, has its beginning in the seed. Every plant has its flowers, its fruit, and its seeds. It is in the seed that vegetation is preserved in a thriving condition through the ages; it is by the seed that every tree, every shrub, every blade of grass propagate their kind and leave a numerous progeny.

"Who would not like to know," continued Uncle Paul, "something about the formation of the seed that is sown in the ground to become either a little plant or an enormous tree? What is inside it? How can an oak come from an acorn and a pear-tree from the pip of a pear? I will try, my friends, to satisfy the very natural curiosity such a mystery cannot fail to arouse in you.

"Let us look at the fruit of an almond-tree. First it has an outside skin, green and tender, which at maturity opens of its own accord, dries up, folds back, and lets its contents out. Examining the latter, we find a shell, sometimes fragile enough to be broken with the teeth, but at other times very hard and yielding only to the hammer. Breaking the shell, we come to the seed. Of what use are the two parts we have just removed? We must be very stupid if we cannot recognize in them the coverings intended to protect the seed, the wrappings that shelter the delicate germ from cold, heat, rain, and the teeth of animals. The outer envelope, covered with a short, velvety down, serves as a protection against the weather; the inner one is a veritable strong-box which we have to break between two stones before we can get at its contents. Similar means of defense are found in all fruit, but with wide differences in the different kinds of plants. The cherry, plum, peach, and apricot have the hard shell, the strong-box, of the almond, and also an outer envelope of juicy flesh. The apple and pear have their seeds or pips, as they are called, snugly ensconced in five little cavities grouped in the shape of a five-pointed star, as may be seen in a cross-section of the fruit. These little cavities have walls of a tough, scaly material somewhat resembling horn, while all about them is a thick rampart of flesh. Beans and peas are arranged in a sort of long sheath that opens in two pieces. Chestnuts are packed in a bag covered with long prickles. All these protecting coverings, whatever their shape and character and degree of toughness, form part of the fruit.

"Let us go back to the almond. The shell being broken, we come

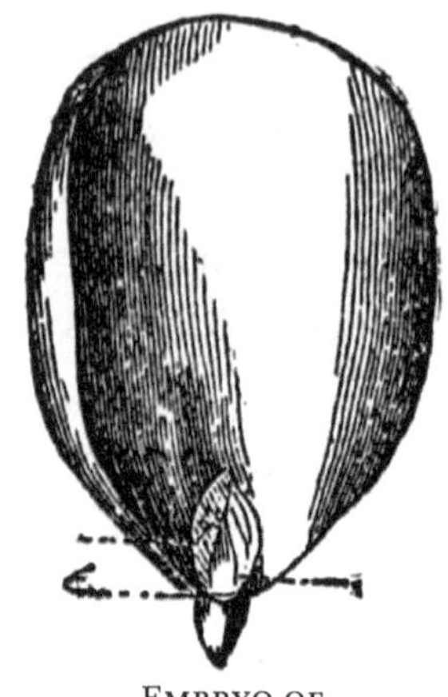

Embryo of
Almond Tree

to the seed, which is all in one piece. This seed, as we have just seen, is protected by two coverings, the inner one of which is a very firm, hard casing called the stone. As a protection is it enough? Not quite. Beneath the exterior defensive armor comes the fine inner covering that wraps the seed closely and shields it from contact with the hard shell. This covering is double and is composed on the outside of a reddish skin and inside of an extremely thin and flexible white cuticle. Similar double clothing is found on all seeds. The inner one is always very fine, as indeed it should be, since it comes next to the most essential and delicate part of the seed. Do we put coarse cloth, rough woolen stuff next to the tender flesh of a new-born babe? Certainly not; but rather the finest of linen, and over that the woolen fabric. The plant does the same with its tender young seeds. The outer envelope, much firmer and tougher than the inner, looks very differently in different plants. In the almond and walnut it is a reddish skin, and so it is also in the stones of the peach, apricot, and plum. In the pips of the pear and apple it is a tough brown casing. In beans it is smooth and shiny, sometimes quite white, sometimes black and white, sometimes speckled with red spots. In addition, peas and beans of all kinds have at one point on their surface a sort of little oval eye. To this eye was once attached a small short cord that fastened the seed to the wall of the pod and served as a pipe for supplying it with nourishment. All seeds have this attachment, or nursing-cord, as we may call it, but not all have so clearly marked as in the bean the eye where the cord is fastened.

"After the two coverings of the seed have been removed, which is very easily done when the almond is new, there remains a white object, firm and savory, the eatable part of the fruit of the almond-tree. That object is the seed proper; that is to say, the part that would have become a tree if planted in the ground. It is round at one end and rather pointed at the other. From the pointed end projects a little nipple, and all around the edge runs a slight furrow indicating that here the seed may be split in two. Let us insert the point of a knife into this furrow and exert a little pressure. One half will come away and the other half will show us what you see in this picture.

"The little pointed nipple (r) is called a radicle. It is the part that, if allowed to grow, would push down into the earth, send out branches there, and become the root. At the point marked g is a compact bunch of tiny leaves, all white, forming a kind of bud, but one that is much feebler and more delicate than buds that grow on branches. It is called a gemmule. This bud will unfold and send forth the first leaves. Finally, the narrow line of demarcation between the radicle and the gemmule is called the tigella, and from it the trunk of the tree will take its start. Such is the almond-tree in its seed. The large tree that will send out a mass of branches and foliage into the air and thrust powerful roots into the ground is now contained in an insignificant corpuscle just large enough to be seen."

CHAPTER XXVIII

THE SEED'S FOOD-SUPPLY

"WHEN IT has leaves and roots that are sufficiently developed, the little almond-tree will nourish itself by drawing what it needs from the earth and air. But until then it must live, it must grow stronger, and it must increase a little in size. As nothing can come from nothing, the germinating seed must find somewhere the material for its first growth. This cannot be in the soil so long as the radicle is nothing but a point, incapable of any work; neither can it be in the air so long as the little leaf-bud has not unfolded and developed into foliage. The seed, then, must have a certain supply of nutriment stored up within itself. Let us turn our attention to this prepared stock of food.

"In the almond we have studied the gemmule or leaf-bud, the radicle, and the tigella; but there still remain two large pieces, easily separable from each other, and constituting by themselves alone almost the entire bulk of the seed. These two pieces are the plant's first pair of leaves, but leaves of a peculiar structure, being very thick, fleshy, and relatively enormous in size. They are the alimentary reservoirs, the storehouses of food from which in its beginning the young plant must draw its sustenance. When germination begins, these two large leaves, swollen with nutritive matter, yield little by little a part of their substance to the tiny plant and suckle it, as it were. They might therefore be called vegetable udders, nursing-leaves, but science calls them cotyledons. The unhatched chick in its shell has the yolk of the egg to furnish substance for its growth, the young lamb has its mother's milk, the germ of the plant has the juice of the cotyledons.

"The same structure, with two cotyledons of great size and easy to observe, may be found in the broad bean, pea, kidney bean, and acorn, and in the stones of the peach, apricot, and plum. It would also be found in the pips of pears and apples as well as in the seeds of most of our cultivated plants, but more difficult to distinguish in proportion to the smallness of the seed. In every instance the seed would be found to have two cotyledons as food-storehouses, and also a gemmule and a radicle united by the tigella. Other plants, on the contrary, like maize, wheat, and the other cereals, as also the lily, tulip, and iris, have but one cotyledon, one nursing-leaf for the new vegetable organism.

"It is not always easy, especially when the seed is very small, to ascertain whether it has two cotyledons or only one; but as soon as germination has begun, this difficulty disappears. Then the seed with two cotyledons is seen to push up two leaves, the very first to appear, situated opposite each other, and very often differing in shape from those that come later. In the radish, for example, they are heart-shaped; in the carrot, long and narrow like little tongues. These two leaves that precede the others are known as seminal leaves. They come from the two cotyledons, which generally open in the air and grow green while nourishing the young plant with a part of their substance; but sometimes, as in the acorn, they remain hidden underground. On the other hand, seeds having but one cotyledon come up with only one seminal leaf, generally narrow and long. This is what we observe if we watch the germination of a grain of wheat.

"A simpler and quicker method may be used for ascertaining how many cotyledons a seed has. Hold a leaf up to the light and you will see its texture traversed by a multitude of little cords which serve it as a kind of framework. These cords are called veins or nerves. Now then, if you compare the leaf of a pear-tree with a blade of wheat, or reed, you will see that in the former the veins are more and more subdivided and ramified, joining one another and thus forming a network with irregular meshes, while in the latter the veins do not branch, but run in parallel lines without forming meshes. We should find the same difference of framework between the leaves of the elm, poplar, and plane-tree, on the one hand, and those of the iris, narcissus, and tulip, on the other. This difference being established, I will add that with few exceptions, of no interest to us here, every plant with netted-veined leaves has two cotyledons in its seed, and that every plant with parallel-veined leaves has but one. Consequently it is only necessary to glance at the foliage in order to know whether the seed has two cotyledons or only one. I will say further that pines, firs, and the other resinous trees have as many as ten cotyledons, which show themselves as a delicate tuft of leaves when the little plant comes out of the ground."

Uncle Paul then led the children into the garden to fix in their minds by observation the lesson they had just learned. "Gather haphazard," said he, "the first leaves you come to; then examine them and tell me how many cotyledons the seed must contain. First, here is the iris, with large blue flowers and sword-shaped leaves."

"I see," said Jules, "veins running in regular lines side by side, without ever joining one another. Since these veins are parallel the iris seed has only one cotyledon."

"And this blade of grass, this also that I pick from a corn-stalk?" asked his uncle.

"They, too, have parallel veins, both of them; and so their seeds must have only one cotyledon."

"And this grape-leaf, this leaf of the cherry tree?"

"It's my turn now," Emile hastened to interpose. "The veins form a sort of lace with very fine meshes. The grape and the cherry have two cotyledons."

"It is as easy as that, my friends. The leaf with its arrangement of veins shows us the fundamental characteristics of the plant. It tells us whether the germ is fed by one nursing-leaf or two, whether the young plant comes up with one seminal leaf or two."

CHAPTER XXIX

GERMINATION

"THE GERM in the heart of the seed is in a state that may be likened to deep sleep: its life is, as it were, arrested, suspended. But under the stimulus of certain conditions it awakens, throws off its coverings, gathers strength from its stored-up food, unfolds its first leaves, and appears above ground. This opening of the seed is called germination. Moisture, warmth, and air are the determining causes; without their coöperation the seed would remain a certain length of time in good condition for sowing, after which it would wither and lose its germinating power.

"No seed germinates without the help of moisture. Water plays a multiple part. First it soaks into the germ and the parts surrounding it, causing these to swell more than the envelope, so that the latter, however hard a shell it may be, is burst open. Through the cracks of this broken envelope the gemmule pushes out on one side and the radicle on the other, and henceforth the little plant enjoys the benefit of sun and air. Germination is more or less slow according to the degree of resistance offered by the walls of the seed. If these are hard and stony it is only with extreme slowness that the germ absorbs moisture and manages to burst its cell. Therefore, to shorten the period of germination care is taken to thin the shells of excessively hard seeds by rubbing them with a stone.

"Besides the mechanical part played by water in opening the seed, it has still another relating to nutrition. The various changes undergone by the alimentary contents of the perisperm and the cotyledons in becoming liquefied and capable of absorption cannot take place without the aid of water. Furthermore, this liquid is indispensable for dissolving the nutritive ingredients, introducing them into the young plant, and distributing them evenly throughout. It is plain, then, that if the seed remains dry it is absolutely impossible for it to germinate, and that in order to preserve seeds the first condition is to protect them from moisture.

"With moisture there must also be warmth. As a general rule, germination proceeds most satisfactorily when the thermometer registers between ten and twenty degrees centigrade, our spring and autumn temperature. Outside these limits, be it above or below, germination is retarded, ceasing altogether in extreme temperatures.

"The coöperation of air is not less necessary. Seeds might have the proper temperature and sufficient moisture, but if air were lacking germination would not follow. This capital condition explains to us why seeds planted too deep fail to come up; why germination is much easier in soil that is mellow and can be permeated by the air than in soil that is compact; why delicate seeds should be covered with very little earth or even simply sown on the surface of the moist ground; and, finally, why ground on being broken often becomes covered with fresh vegetation from the sprouting of seeds that have for years lain dormant in the soil, needing only to be stirred up and brought into contact with the air in order to germinate.

"Under like conditions of temperature, moisture, and air, by no means all seeds require the same length of time for germinating. Common garden cress germinates in about two days. Spinach, turnips, and beans take three days to come up; lettuce, four; melons and pumpkins, five; cereals, about a week. Two years and sometimes more are needed by the rose-bush, the hawthorn, and various stone-fruit trees. Generally seeds with thick and hard shells are slow in germinating on account of the obstacle they oppose to the penetration of moisture. Finally, when sown fresh, immediately after coming to maturity, seeds germinate quicker than when old, because old seeds have to recover by a prolonged sojourn in the ground the moisture lost through prolonged drying.

"According to their kind, seeds retain for a longer or shorter period their power of germinating; but why this vitality is more enduring in one instance and less so in another, we cannot tell. Neither the bulk of the seed nor the character of its outside coverings, nor the presence or absence of a perisperm, appears to decide its longevity. Such and such a seed lives for whole years, even centuries, while another loses its germinating power in a few months, from no cause that we can discover. Thus the seeds of the angelica will not come up unless they are sown immediately after maturing; but beans have been known to germinate after being kept more than a hundred years, and rye after a hundred and forty. Excluded from the air, certain seeds may be kept for centuries, always ready to germinate whenever favorable conditions shall present themselves. This explains why strawberry, bluet, and camomile seeds from ancient tombs have germinated just as new seeds would have done. Finally, rush seeds have been made to germinate that were dug up from great depths in the Island of the Seine, the original site of Paris. Doubtless those seeds dated from the time when Paris, under the name of Lutetia, consisted of a few mud and reed huts on the marshy borders of the stream. But despite these remarkable exceptions let us never forget that recent seed is preferable to old for sowing; it comes up better and in greater abundance.

"We have just seen that certain seeds are very slow in coming up, as for example the peach, apricot, and plum, whose thick shells resist the moisture required for germination. Put directly into the ground in the very places that the young plants are to occupy later, these seeds would be exposed to not a few dangers during their leisurely germination. Prolonged rains might make them rot; various marauders that are partial to them, such as rats, field-mice, jays, magpies, and crows, might dig them up and devour them. Besides, they would occupy for a long time, with no profit to any one, the ground in which they had been planted. All these objections are avoided by making a preliminary planting after a method known as stratification, from the Latin word *stratum*, meaning bed or layer. In a large, deep earthen pan, with holes in its bottom, or in any other suitable receptacle, such as a box, a pot, or a tub, likewise pierced with holes, it is the practice to place first a layer of small pebbles. The holes at the bottom and this layer of pebbles are to give easy access to the air and drain off the excess of water after each irrigation. Next comes a bed of fine sandy soil, then a layer or stratum of seeds arranged side by side, and on top of that a second bed of earth. On this is placed another stratum of seeds, which in its turn is covered with earth; and so the process goes on with alternating layers of seeds and earth until the receptacle is full. Then it is watered and placed in a cellar or a dark shed. All that is necessary after this is to keep the contents of pan or tub sufficiently moist by an occasional sprinkling. Enclosed thus in a small space easy to watch over, with no danger from marauding animals, and without needlessly occupying ground that might be used for other purposes, the seeds can now take their own time to break their hard shells and can germinate with all the slowness natural to them.

"When the shells at last crack open and the radicle appears, it is time to proceed to the final planting. The half-germinated seeds are then put into the ground one by one in an open field, each at the exact spot the young plant is to occupy.

"Stratification offers still another advantage. Fruit trees as well as other trees have a stout tap-root which bores vertically into the ground to a considerable depth and gives a good deal of trouble if transplanting is undertaken. To alter this tap-root into a root not growing so deep, but branching horizontally, would be decidedly advantageous. In speaking of the root we saw what the nursery-man does to obtain this result. He passes the sharp edge of his spade under the base of each tree-trunk so as to sever the tap-roots of his young plantations. In stratification the method is much simpler and success surer. With his thumb-nail the gardener nips off the tip of the tender radicle before the final planting is done. That is all. Deprived of its growing end the young root henceforth branches out horizontally instead of descending vertically."

CHAPTER XXX

THE BLOSSOM

"HERE IS the fennel-flower, which, with the corn-flower and the poppy, is so common in our fields of grain. It is purplish red, while the poppy is scarlet and the corn-flower, or bluet, is of an azure like that of the sky, as its alternative name indicates. On the outside of the fennel-flower are five green, firm pieces joined together at the bottom but terminating in long points at the top. Each of these pieces is called a sepal, and the five together form the calyx. Inside are five other pieces, thin, fine, broad, purplish red in color. Each one bears the name of petal, and collectively they form the corolla.

"Most flowers have two envelopes like these, one within the other. The outer one, or calyx, is nearly always green in color and firm in structure; the inner one, or corolla, much more delicate in texture, is tinged with those magnificent hues that please the eye so much in flowers.

"The sepals of the calyx and the petals of the corolla are sometimes separated from one another and sometimes joined together. In the fennel-flower the sepals are united below in a common sheath bristling with coarse hairs; but in their upper part they are separated into five narrow and pointed strips. The corolla we find to be composed of five pieces, five petals distinct from one another. On the contrary, in the blossom of the campanula the five petals of the corolla are joined at the edges

FENNEL FLOWER

and form a beautiful blue bell which looks as if made of one piece. The five large teeth that border the opening of the bell nevertheless show that the corolla is really composed of five petals, of which these teeth are the termination.

"The calyx and the corolla are the flower's clothing, a double clothing having both the substantial material that protects from cold and storm, and the fine fabric that charms the eye. The calyx, the outer garment, is of simple form, green in color, and of firm texture suitable for withstanding bad weather. It has to protect the still unopened flower, to shield it from the sun, from cold and wet. Examine a rose-bud and note with what delicate precision the five sepals of the calyx are united so as to cover the rest. Not the slightest drop of water could penetrate the interior, so carefully are their edges joined together. There are flowers that close their calyx every evening and snuggle down inside to keep from getting chilled.

"The corolla or inner garment unites elegance of form and richness of tint with fineness of texture. It is the flower's finery and is what especially captivates our eye, so that we commonly consider it the most important part of the blossom, whereas it is really nothing but an ornament.

"Of the two garments, the calyx is the more necessary. Many flowers have no corolla, but they always have at least a calyx, which in its simplest form is reduced to a tiny leaflet shaped like a scale. Flowers with no corolla remain unnoticed, and the plants that bear them seem to us to have no blossoms. It is a mistake: all trees and plants bloom, even the oak, willow, poplar, pine, beech, wheat, and multitudes of others whose blossoming is unheeded by the inattentive eye. Their flowers are extremely numerous, but as they are very small and have no bright-colored corolla they escape any but the closest scrutiny.

"It would be knowing a person very little only to be able to say that he wears such and such a coat; nor does one know a flower any better when one can merely say that it is clothed with a calyx and a corolla. What is there under this clothing?

"Let us examine together a lily, which by its size lends itself readily to study. It has no calyx,[4] but it does have a superb corolla formed of six petals gracefully curved inward at the edges, and whiter than ivory. I take away these six petals. What is left now is the essential part; that is to say, the thing without which the flower could not perform its function, could not, in short, bear fruit or seed. Let us carefully consider this remaining part. You will find it well worth the trouble.

"First there are six filaments or little white rods, each one surmounted by a tiny bag full of yellow powder. These six pieces are called stamens. They are found in all flowers in greater or less number, and in the lily there are six of them. The little bag that tops the stamen is called an anther. The yellow dust contained in the anther is called pollen; that is what daubs our nose when we smell the lily too closely.

---

4   This is inconsistent with what Uncle Paul stated two paragraphs above. He should have said here that the lily has but one floral envelope.—*Translator.*

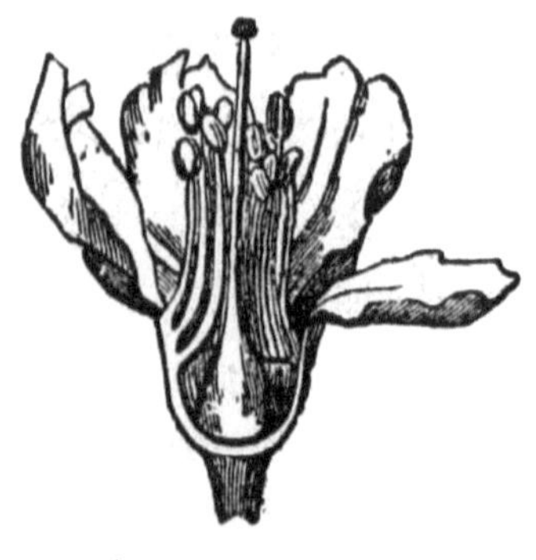

APRICOT BLOSSOM
CUT OPEN

"I take away the six stamens. There remains a central body swollen at the bottom, narrowed at the top to a long filament, and surmounted by a kind of head wet with a sticky moisture. In its entirety this central body bears the name of pistil; the swelling at the bottom is called the ovary, the filament growing out of it is the style, and the sticky head terminating this filament is known as the stigma.

"'What big names for such little things!' you will say. Little, yes; but of unrivaled importance. These little things, my friends, give us our daily bread; without the miraculous work of these little things the world would come to an end.

"With a penknife I cut the ovary in two horizontally. In three compartments grouped in a circle we see some tiny grains arranged so that each compartment has two rows of them. They are the future seeds of the plant. The ovary, then, is the part of the plant where the seeds are formed. After a certain time the flower withers, the petals wilt and fall, the calyx does the same, or sometimes it remains to play the part of protector a while longer, the dried stamens break off, and only the ovary remains, growing larger, ripening, and finally becoming the fruit that contains the seeds.

"Every sort of fruit—the pear, apple, apricot, peach, walnut, cherry, melon, grape, almond, chestnut—began by being a little swelling of the pistil; all those excellent things that the tree and plant give us for food were first ovaries."

"Then a big juicy pear began by being the ovary of a pear blossom?" queried Emile.

"Yes, my friend," was the reply; "pears, apples, cherries, apricots, even big melons and enormous pumpkins begin by being the little ovaries of their respective flowers. I will show you an apricot in its blossom."

Uncle Paul took an apricot blossom, opened it with his penknife, and showed his listeners what is here reproduced in the picture.

"In the heart of the flower," he explained, "you see the pistil surrounded by numerous stamens. The head at the top of it is the stigma; the swelling at the bottom is the ovary or future apricot."

"That little green thing," Emile exclaimed incredulously, "would have turned into a plump, juicy apricot such as I am so fond of?"

"Yes," affirmed his uncle, "that little green thing would have turned into an apricot such as Emile is so fond of. A similar little green thing would have turned into a big juicy pear, into a fragrant apple, or into a huge pumpkin, so heavy that it rests lazily on its stomach. To conclude, I will show you the ovary from which come wheat and consequently bread."

Uncle Paul took a needle; then with the skill and patience necessary for this operation he isolated one of the numerous flowers that collectively make up the ear of wheat. The delicate little flower displayed clearly, on the point of the needle, the different parts composing it.

"The blessed plant that gives us bread," continued Uncle Paul, "has very modest flowers. Two poor scales serve it for calyx and corolla. You can easily recognize three hanging stamens with their double-sacheted anthers full of pollen. The main body of the flower is the plump ovary which, when ripe, will be a grain of wheat. It is surmounted by the stigma, which has the shape of an elegant double plume. Such is the modest little flower that furnishes us all with the staff of life."

CHAPTER XXXI

POLLEN

66 IN A few days, even in a few hours, a flower withers. Petals, calyx, stamens fade and die. Only one part survives: the ovary, which is to become fruit. Now, in order to outlive the rest of the flower and remain on its stem when all else dries up and falls, the ovary at the moment of blossoming, receives an access of vigor, I might almost say a new life. The magnificence of the corolla, its sumptuous coloring, its perfume, all serve to celebrate the solemn moment when this new vitality is awakened in the ovary. This great act accomplished, the flower has had its day.

"Well, it is the dust of the stamens, the pollen, that gives this increase of energy without which the nascent seeds would perish in the ovary, itself withered. It falls from the stamens on to the stigma, which constantly wears a sticky coating designed to hold it; and from the stigma it makes its mysterious influence felt in the very depths of the ovary. Animated then with new life, the nascent seeds develop rapidly, while the ovary swells so as to give them the nourishment and the space they require. The final result of this incomprehensible travail is the fruit, with its contained seeds all ready to germinate.

"Let us cite a few of the numerous experiments that prove the absolute indispensability of pollen.

"Most flowers have both stamens and pistils; but there are plants that have their stamens and pistils in separate flowers. Sometimes the flowers with stamens only and those with pistils only are found on the same plant; sometimes they are found on sepa-rate plants. Plants having flowers with stamens only and flowers with pistils only on the same stock are called monœcious

plants. This expression means 'living in one house.' The flowers with stamens and those with pistils do indeed live together in the same house, since they are found on the same plant. The pumpkin, cucumber, melon, hazel-nut tree are monœcious plants.

"Where flowers with stamens and those with pistils are found on different stocks, the plants are termed diœcious; that is to say, they are double-house plants. Hemp, the locust tree, and the date-tree are diœcious.

"It is especially in monœcious and diœcious plants that the pollen's indispensability is plainly manifest on account of the natural separation of the stamens and pistils. Let us take for example the locust, a tree of extreme southern France, bearing seeds in pods similar to those of the pea, but brown, very long, and very wide, and containing in addition to the seeds a sugary pulp. Supposing we took a notion, if the climate permitted, to grow locust seeds in our garden, what locust tree must we plant? Evidently the one with pistils, because it alone produces the ovaries that become fruit. But that is not enough. Planted by itself, the locust tree with pistils will indeed blossom profusely every year, but will never in all eternity bear any seeds, for its flowers will fall without leaving a single ovary on the branches. What is wanting? The action of the pollen. Near the locust with pistils let us plant one with stamens. Now fructification proceeds as we wish. Puffs of wind, insects that pilfer from one flower and carry to another—these convey the pollen from the stamens to the stigmas, the torpid ovaries spring to life, and the locust pods grow and ripen perfectly. With pollen, seeds; without pollen, no seeds.

"Another example. In spots of fertile land in Northern Africa, spots of land called oases, the Arabs cultivate numerous date-trees which provide them with dates, their principal food. Date-trees, too, like the locust, are diœcious. Now, in the country of the date-tree, a sandy plain parched by the sun, spots of watered and fertile land are rare and have to be turned to the utmost possible account. Accordingly the Arabs plant only date-trees with pistils, the only ones that will produce dates. But when they are in flower, the Arabs go long distances to fetch bunches of blossoms with stamens from wild date trees in order to shake the pollen on the trees they have planted. Without this precaution there is no harvest.

"But I am coming to an example that will be more familiar to us. The pumpkin is monœcious: flowers with stamens and flowers with pistils inhabit the same house, the same vine. Before they are full-blown they can easily be distinguished from each other. The flowers with pistils have under the corolla a large swelling which is the ovary, the future pumpkin. The blossoms with stamens have not this swelling. Well, from one pumpkin vine standing apart in the garden let us cut off all the buds with stamens before they open, and leave those with pistils. For greater surety we will wrap each one of these latter in a piece of gauze large enough to let the flower develop without hindrance. This operation must be carried out before the buds open, in order to make sure that the stigmas have not already received any pollen. Under these conditions, not being able to receive the vivifying dust, since the flowers with stamens are cut off, and since also the gauze wrappings keep out the insects that might bring the pollen they had pilfered from some neighboring pumpkin vine, the pistillate flowers will wither after languishing awhile, and their ovaries will dry up without growing into pumpkins. If, however, we wish any selected blossoms to fructify in spite of their gauze prison and the suppression of the staminate blossoms, we take a small camel's hair brush and gather a little pollen which we put on the stigma. That is enough, the pumpkin will come.

"The absolute necessity of pollen for the formation of fruit explains to us the harmful effect of violent winds and prolonged rains in blossoming time. Swept away by blasts of wind, or washed away by rains, or simply spoiled by long-continued moisture, the dust of the stamens no longer acts on the ovaries, and the flowers fall without fructifying. This ruin of the harvest from lack of pollen is known as blight."

CHAPTER XXXII

THE GRAIN OF WHEAT

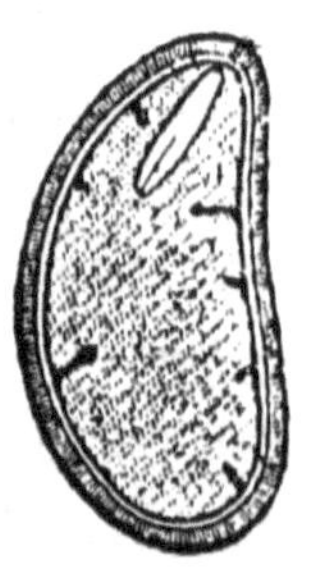

LONGITUDINAL SECTION OF IVY SEED

"NOW TURN your attention to this picture of an ivy seed cut through lengthwise. Where is the germ or little plant in its egg? It is that little white thing, rather long and narrow, embedded in the substance of the seed at one end. A fine line marks the division of the two cotyledons, which are now pressed close together. Next to them comes the tigella, or little stalk, ending in the radicle, or rootlet. Notice, my friends, how small these cotyledons are, how different from the enormous nursing-leaves of the almond, acorn, broad bean, kidney bean, and pea. These poor little plant-udders must soon get dried up, and if there were no other resources available at the time of germination the ivy would speedily starve to death.

"But look: under the skin of the seed we find a goodly store of farinaceous matter, in which the germ is embedded. Almost the whole of the seed consists of this accumulation of flour. So here we have the food-supply that will supplement that contained in the cotyledons, a very insufficient provision in itself. This granary of plenty within which the germ is lodged, this storehouse of food is called the perisperm. The almond, acorn, pea, bean, with a host of others, are quite lacking in anything of the sort, having under the skin only the germ and nothing more, absolutely nothing. The reason for this difference is plain enough. The almond, bean, pea, acorn, with their big cotyledons bursting with nutritive matter, do not need a supplementary ration; the germ will be sufficiently suckled by the udders nature has provided in the form of these cotyledons. But the ivy, with its poor little cotyledons, calls for help, and finds it in the farinaceous storehouse of the perisperm.

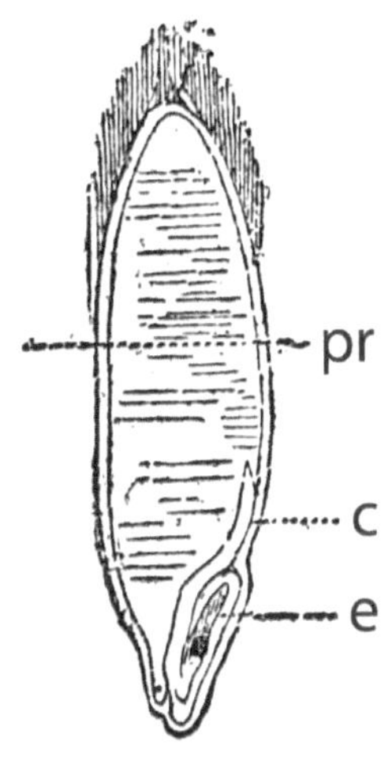

LONGITUDINAL SECTION OF A GRAIN OF WHEAT

"Thus a seed may have a double supply of nourishment to meet the needs of the young plant: that contained in the cotyledons and that stored up in the perisperm. Cotyledons are never lacking, but the perisperm is not found in all seeds. There is none in the almond, acorn, chestnut, apricot, bean, or pea; but to make up for this lack their cotyledons are of considerable size. On the other hand, buckwheat, chickweed, and ivy, whose cotyledons are small, are provided with a perisperm. All this may be reduced to one general rule. Cotyledons and perisperm play similar parts: they both help to nourish the little plant in its infancy. So, generally speaking, the seed with large cotyledons has no perisperm, while the seed with small cotyledons has one.

"I have just told you that many plants have only one cotyledon. I will add that this cotyledon is usually very small. It is especially in these plants that the perisperm is present. The grain of wheat offers a notable illustration of this truth. Cut lengthwise and looked at through a magnifying-glass, this seed would reveal to us what is represented in the picture I now show you. At the bottom and toward one side is the germ, forming but a very small part of the seed. At *c* is the single cotyledon, whence will come the first leaf, the seminal leaf. At *e* is the gemmule, which will furnish the next leaves. At the opposite end is a short nipple, the radicle, whence the root will spring. Now compare the tiny cotyledon of the wheat with the two voluminous ones of the almond. The latter, with their rich store of nourishment, will easily be able to feed the young plant until it has vigorous roots; but the cotyledon of the wheat, so poor and slender—can it nourish the young plant? Certainly not. Then the wheat germ must without fail have a storehouse of provisions. This storehouse is the perisperm (*pr*), a farinaceous mass constituting nearly the whole of the seed. This same perisperm, the first food of the wheat's first shoot, is also the chief food of man; it is what, under the millstone, becomes flour, of which bread is made. But how can the farinaceous substance of the perisperm nourish the plant? A very simple experiment will show us. Put some wheat in a saucer and keep it slightly moist. In a short time the seed will germinate. As soon as the young sprouts show their green points take one of the grains: you will find it softened all through. You can crush it between your fingers and squeeze out a white fluid, very sweet to the taste and much resembling some sort of milk. What has taken place ought not to be beyond your power to surmise from the account I gave you of the wonderful change starch may undergo. The perisperm of the wheat-grain consists chiefly of starch. During germination this accumulation of starch is converted into a sugary substance, into glucose in fact. Thence comes the sort of plant-milk with which the seed is now swollen. The germ is immersed in this sweet liquid; it imbibes it, soaks it up almost as a fine sponge would; and with the matter thus absorbed it augments its own substance, which lengthens into root, stem, and leaves. With what furnishes us bread the grain of wheat suckles the starting wheat-stalk."

CHAPTER XXXIII

CULTIVATED PLANTS

"THREE MODES of plant-propagation are in use among horticulturists, namely: layering, slipping, and grafting. To get an adequate notion of the great usefulness of these operations let us dwell for a moment on the origin of our cultivated plants.

"You perhaps imagine that from the beginning of time, in view of our need of food, the pear-tree was eager to bear large fruit, plump and juicy; that the potato, just to accommodate us, stuffed its big tubers with farinaceous matter; that the cabbage, in its desire to gratify us, conceived the idea of gathering those beautiful white leaves into a compact head. You imagine that wheat, pumpkins, carrots, grapes, beets, and no one knows what besides, possessed with a great interest in man, have always worked for him of their own accord. You think that our grapes of to-day are like those from which Noah extracted the juice that made him drunk; that wheat, ever since it appeared on the earth, has never failed to yield its annual harvest of grain; that the beet and the pumpkin had at the beginning of the world the plumpness that makes them prized by us now. You imagine, in short, that our food-plants came to us originally just as we have them now. Undeceive yourselves: the wild plant is usually of very little nutritive value to man. His is still the task of so cultivating it as to derive advantage from its natural aptitudes by improving them.

"In its native country, on the mountains of Chile and Peru, the potato in its wild state is a poor diminutive tuber about as large as a hazel-nut. Man takes the worthless wild stock into his garden, plants it in rich soil, tends it, waters it; and behold, from year to year the potato thrives more and more, gaining in size and in nutritive properties, and finally becoming a farinaceous tuber as large as your two fists.

"On the sea-coasts, exposed to all the winds that blow, there grows a wild cabbage with a tall stalk and a few green leaves of bitter taste and rank odor. But beneath its rude exterior it may perhaps hide invaluable aptitudes. Apparently this suspicion occurred to him who first, so long ago that the record of it is lost, took the sea-coast cabbage under cultivation. The suspicion was well-founded. The wild cabbage has been improved by man's incessant care: its stalk has become firmer and its leaves have multiplied, whitened, acquired tenderness, and massed themselves in a compact head, so that we have the crisp and succulent cabbage of to-day as the admirable result of this notable metamorphosis. There on the sea-coast rock was the first beginning of the excellent plant; here in our gardens is its present attainment. But what about its intermediate forms which, through the centuries, marked the gradual development of the species to its present high state of perfection? Each of these forms was a step forward, and each had to be preserved, kept from degenerating, and made the subject of still further improvement. Who could tell the story of all the labor and pains it has taken to produce the cabbage-head as we now have it?

"And the wild pear-tree—are you acquainted with it? It is a frightful bramble-bush, all bristling with sharp thorns; and the pears themselves—a most repellent fruit, sure to choke you and set your teeth on edge—are very small, sour, hard, and full of grit that reminds one of gravel-stones. Surely he must have had an extraordinary inspiration who first pinned his faith on this crabbed specimen of underbrush and foresaw in the remote future the butter-pear on which we regale ourselves to-day.

"In the same way, by the painstaking culture of the primitive vine, whose grapes were no larger than our elderberries, man has, in the sweat of his brow, developed the luscious fruit of the modern vineyard. From some poor species of grass now forgotten he has also produced the wheat that to-day supplies us with bread. A few wretched herbs and shrubs, far from promising in appearance, he has cultivated and improved until they became the vegetables and fruit trees so prized by us at present. This old earth of ours, in order to make us work and thus fulfill the law of our existence, has behaved to us like a harsh stepmother. To the birds of the air she gives food in abundance, but to us she offers of her own free will nothing but wild blackberries and sour sloes. But let us not complain, for the stern struggle with necessity is precisely what constitutes our grandeur.

"It is for us, by our intelligence and labor, to work our way out of the difficulty; upon us it is enjoined to put into practice the noble creed, God helps those who help themselves.

"Thus from the earliest times it has been man's study to select from the countless forms of vegetation at his disposal those that best lend themselves to improvement. The greater number of species have remained useless to us, but others, predestined no doubt, and created especially with a view to man's needs, have responded to our efforts and acquired through cultivation qualities of prime importance, since our sustenance depends on them. Nevertheless the improvement attained is not so radical that we can count on its permanence if our vigilance relaxes. The plant always tends to revert to its primitive state. For example, let the gardener leave the headed cabbage to itself without fertilizing, watering, or cultivating it; let him leave the seeds to germinate by chance wherever the wind blows them, and the cabbage will quickly part with its compact head of white leaves and resume the loose green leaves of its wild ancestors. In like manner the vine, set free from man's constant attention, will degenerate into the little-esteemed wild species that haunts our hedge-rows and yields a scant harvest that will not, all together, be worth a single bunch of cultivated grapes. The pear-tree, if neglected, will again be found on the outskirts of our woods, once more bristling with long sharp thorns and bearing under-sized and extremely unpalatable fruit. Under like conditions the plum-tree and the cherry-tree will bear nothing but stones covered with a sour skin. In short, all the riches of our orchards will in similar circumstances undergo such deterioration as to be worthless to us.

"This reversion to the wild state occurs even under cultivation and in spite of efforts to prevent it when seed is used for propagating the plant. Suppose the seeds from an excellent pear are put into the ground. Well, the trees that spring from those seeds will bear for the most part only mediocre or poor, even very poor, pears. Another planting is made with the pits of the second generation, and the result shows still further decline. Thus if the experiment is continued with seeds taken each time from the immediately preceding generation, the fruit, becoming smaller and smaller, bitterer and harder, will at last return to the sorry wild pear of the thicket.

"One more example. What flower equals the rose in noble-ness of carriage, in perfume and brilliant coloring? Suppose we plant the seeds of this superb flower; its descendants will turn out to be miserable bushes, nothing but wild roses like those of our hedges. But we need not be surprised at this. The noble plant had the wild rose for ancestor, and in trying to propagate it by its seed we have simply caused it to resume its native characteristics.

"With some plants, let us note in conclusion, the improvement attained by cultivation is more stable and persists even when the seed is used for purposes of propagation; but this persistence is only on the express condition that our vigilance shall not relax. All plants, if left to themselves and propagated by seed, revert to the primitive state after a certain number of generations in which the characteristics imposed by human skill and care gradually disappear."

CHAPTER XXXIV

DIFFERENT WAYS OF PROPAGATING

"SINCE OUR fruit-trees and ornamental plants, if propagated by seed, revert sooner or later to the wild type, how can they be propagated without risk of degeneration? This must be done by means of the buds instead of the seeds. Buds or branches of a plant or tree must be transplanted from one stock to another; this is called grafting; or they may be planted directly in the soil by processes known as layering and slipping. These are invaluable methods, since they enable us to stabilize in the plant the improvements attained after long years of labor, and thus to profit by these improvements, which we owe to our predecessors, instead of beginning all over again a course of training that would demand far more than a single life-time.

"Layering, slipping, and grafting insure the faithful reproduction of all the qualities of the parent stock. As are the fruit, flowers, foliage of this parent stock which has furnished the buds or slips for transplanting, so will be the fruit, flowers, foliage of the resulting plant or tree. Nothing will be added to the qualities we wish to perpetuate, but on the other hand nothing will be subtracted. To the double flowers of the original from which came the layer, the slip, or the graft, will correspond the double flowers of the plant developing from this layer, slip, or graft: the same shade of coloring will be reproduced, and the fruit will have the same size, savor, and sweetness. The slightest peculiarity

which, for unknown reasons, appears in a plant grown from the seed, and which sometimes is found only on a single branch, as the indented outline of the leaves or the variegation of the blossoms, is reproduced with minute accuracy if the graft, slip, or layer is taken from the branch having this modification. By this means horticulture is daily enriching itself with double flowers or a new shade, or with fruit remarkable for its size, its early or late ripening, its juicy flesh, its more pronounced aroma. Without the help of graft and slip these fortunate accidents, occurring but once and no one knows how, would lead to no further profit after the death of the plant thus favored by chance; and horticulture would find itself compelled to repeat over and over again its attempts to bring about improvements which, almost as soon as effected, would invariably be lost for want of means to fix them and render them permanent.

"If history had preserved the record, what long and painful efforts to develop our various cultivated plants from worthless seedlings should we not read there! Just think of what a happy inspiration it must have taken to select exactly the kind of vegetable or other plant susceptible of improvement, what patient experimental attempts to subject it to cultivation, what wearisome labor to improve its quality from one year to another, what care to prevent its degenerating and to hand it down to posterity in perfect condition. Think of all this and you will see how the smallest fruit, the smallest vegetable, represents more than the toil of him who has raised it in his garden. It represents, perhaps, the accumulated effort of a hundred generations, an effort indispensable if we are to have a succulent pot-herb as the descendant of a worthless weed. We live on the fruit and vegetables created by our predecessors; we live on the labor, strength, ideas of the past. May the future in its turn live on our strength both of arm and thought! So shall we worthily fulfill our mission.

"It was not chance that gave man the idea of layering, slipping, and grafting, but rather the thoughtful observation of nature's methods all about him. He who was first, for example, to note how the strawberry grows and multiplies, received the first lesson in layering. Let us in our turn examine this curious process.

"From the parent stock of the strawberry vine a number of runners start out, long, slender, and creeping on the ground. These runners are also known as stolons or creeping suckers. After reaching a certain distance they expand at the end into a little tuft which takes root in the ground and is soon self-supporting. The new tuft of the strawberry vine, as soon as strong enough, in its turn sends out long runners which follow the example of the first ones; that is to say, they creep along the ground, end each in a rosette of leaves, and take root. The picture shows us a first tuft, more vigorous than the others. From the axil of one of its leaves starts a runner whose terminal bud has developed into a small plant already provided with roots of some vigor. A second runner sprung from this plant bears a third rosette whose leaves are beginning to unfold. After sending out an indefinite number of similar runners the mother plant finds herself surrounded with young suckers, established here and there, as many as the season and the nature of the soil permit. At first these suckers are attached to the mother plant by the runners, and sap flows from the old plant to the young ones; but sooner or later there is a severance of ties, the runners dry up and are henceforward useless, and each offshoot, properly rooted, becomes a separate strawberry vine. Here we find, without any of man's ingenuity or skill, all the details of layering; and it was undoubtedly the natural process that suggested the artificial method. A long branch bends down to the ground, takes root there, and then becomes detached from the parent stock by the death or destruction of the connecting part. The horticulturist lays a long shoot in the ground, waits until it sends down adventitious roots, and finally severs the connection with his pruning-shears. That is layering."

CHAPTER XXXV

LAYERING

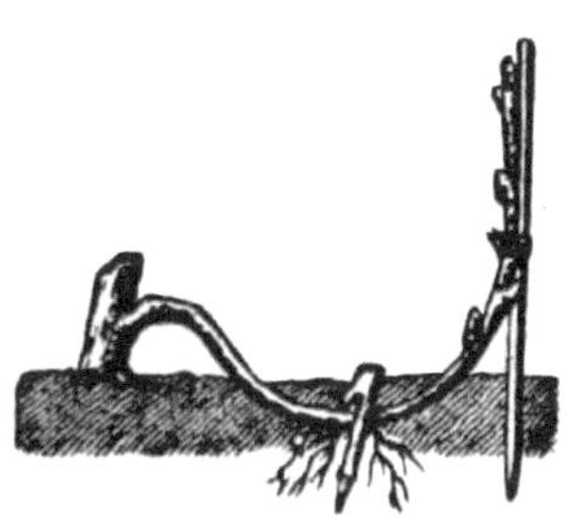

LAYERING

"SOME PLANTS, and among them the pink, send out from the base of the mother stalk straight, pliant shoots which can be used for obtaining so many new plants. These shoots are bedded by being bent elbow-wise and having the angle stuck into the ground and fastened there with a crotch; then the end is raised upright and held so by means of a stake. Sooner or later the buried elbow sends down adventitious roots, but until then nourishment is drawn from the parent stock. When the buried parts have sent down enough roots, the connections are cut between the old plant and the new ones, and each of these latter, set out by itself, is thenceforth a distinct plant. This operation is called layering, and the several shoots used in obtaining new plants are called layers.

"Let us now put into practice the method we have just been studying in theory. In a vineyard, we will suppose, a number of the vines have died from some cause or other, and it is necessary to replace them. Layering offers us the readiest means and will occasion least delay to the harvest. Near the place occupied by the dead vine we select a stock provided with a vigorous shoot of sufficient length and conveniently situated. Then we dig down where the old vine stands and pull up all of the lifeless stalk as well as the roots, since these are seats of decay that might infect the whole neighborhood. Finally, in the soil thus stirred we dig a ditch two or three decimeters deep, and in this we lay the shoot we have selected, taking care in bending it down not to break or splinter it. The part thus put into the ground is then covered with a tolerably thick layer of earth, and on this, to complete the filling of the ditch, is thrown a basketful of manure. The tip of the shoot is raised upright, tied to a stake, and trimmed in such a manner as to retain only two eyes or buds above ground. As to the eyes on the part extending from the mother stem to the point where the shoot plunges into the ground, they are nipped off because they would needlessly appropriate a part of the sap. This operation is called vine-layering, and the shoot bent down and placed in the ground we speak of as a vine-layer. The best time for this work is the beginning of winter, because the long rest enjoyed by the shoot in the ground throughout the season when vegetation slumbers disposes it to sprout with more vigor upon the renewal of sap-circulation in the spring.

"Let us now watch the behavior of the partly buried vine-shoot. If it had remained all in the open air, it would have borne fruit; it would have had its three or four bunches of grapes. Why should it not do so under the conditions imposed by the vine-dresser, conditions that have altered nothing in its relations to the mother stem? It still remains in uninterrupted communication with the vine that sustains it; it receives its share of ascending sap drawn from the soil by the roots of this vine; the buds remaining to it will develop leaves which, with the help of sunlight, will convert this crude sap into elaborated sap; in short, it lacks nothing to enable it to function almost as it would have done had it not been partly buried. And in fact the vine-layer does bear that same year; if well cared for, it bears several bunches of grapes. So the proverb says: The vine-layer pays its owner from the very first year. Meanwhile, acted on by the coolness and moisture of the soil and the stimulus of fertilization, it puts forth adventitious roots where it has been placed underground, and these roots grow in number and vigor until the time comes when they suffice to nourish the young vine without the help of the mother stem. It is in the third year that the rooting is far enough advanced for the young offshoot's independent existence. Weaning is then undertaken, and the nursling is deprived of its nurse; that is to say, a stroke of the pruning-knife close to the ground and on the side toward the parent stock separates the latter from the vine-layer, which becomes henceforth self-supporting.

"With its long shoots so near the ground the vine offers every convenience for carrying out the operation just described; but as a general rule shrubs and trees are far less favorably situated: their branches are not long enough or flexible enough or (a prime essential) near enough to the ground to be bent down and laid in the trench dug for receiving the layer. How is this difficulty to be overcome? The way is very simple. We have already observed the effect of cutting back; we know that a stem cut back, that is to say cut off close to the ground, develops around the border of its wound numerous adventitious buds which grow into so many shoots. They are precisely the sort of shoots we need, long, flexible, and starting from the level of the ground. Each of them, if treated as a layer, partly buried in a trench where it is fixed with a crotch, and held, above ground, in a vertical position by means of a prop, takes root sooner or later according to its species, and can then be transferred as an independent plant to any desired spot. Such is the simple method known both as layering and as arching, because it is essentially the same as ordinary layering and at the same time necessitates the bending of the young shoot so as to describe an arch.

"The following method dispenses with this bending, which is impracticable when the wood is too brittle. In the spring the stalk or trunk that is to furnish the layers is cut back. All around this cross-section young shoots soon make their appearance, after which it is only necessary to wait until they are long enough but have not yet lost their tenderness, a state most conducive to the growth of adventitious buds; then the parent trunk is earthed up, or in other words light soil is heaped all about the stump so as to cover the lower part of each shoot. The earth is piled up in the shape of a truncated cone with a cup-shaped hollow at the top to receive water from time to time and thus maintain the necessary degree of moisture and coolness. Kept damp and cool in this manner, the young shoots will before long send down adventitious roots, and the following year there will be a cluster of rooted plants that can easily be detached with a knife. That is what is called layering by earthing up or by sprouting.

"If it is found undesirable to cut back the parent stem in order to obtain shoots for layering, and if at the same time the shoot that we wish to root is too high to be bent down and inserted in the ground, the following expedient may be employed. A flower-pot broken in two lengthwise or a leaden cornucopia is hung on the tree, and the branch to be rooted is placed lengthwise in the pot or cornucopia. The pot is then filled with mold or moss kept damp by frequent watering, and the result, sooner or later, is the growth of adventitious roots. When these are suitably developed, gradual weaning is next in order; that is to say, underneath the pot a slight cut is made, and this is deepened day by day. The end here in view is to accustom the layer little by little to do without the mother stem and support itself. At last the separation is complete. This gradual weaning is no less advantageous when the layers are placed in the ground: it assures the success of the operation.

"If the wood is tender, adventitious roots spring without difficulty from the interred part, and the methods already described suffice for the success of the layering; but woods of dense structure are more or less obstinate about taking root, and might remain in the ground indefinitely without yielding. In such cases our art must intervene, based on the plant's manner of living. Let us recall the effect of a band drawn tightly about a stalk or trunk. Above this line of strangulation the descending sap accumulates more and more, since it can no longer continue on its course between the wood and the bark, this latter being compressed by the ligature. It accumulates and produces a ring-shaped swelling where the plant tries to discharge on the outside the superabundance of matter arrested in its passage. Let this protuberance be heaped about with fresh earth, and adventitious roots will speedily be developed to allow the sap to continue its descent. A tiny streamlet, running free, follows its channel without effort and without any undermining of obstacles. But if we obstruct its passage the accumulating body of water will gain power to open new vents for itself through the dam. Sap does likewise. Circulating freely in its natural channel, it is not diverted from its course by any allurements on its way; and unless the conditions present in wood and bark favor the growth of new roots, no sap will be expended for this purpose. But if its usual passage is barred, the sap devotes its energies to the formation of adventitious roots in order that it may, through them, resume its interrupted course. A like result follows if a ring of bark is removed from the buried part of the branch or shoot that we wish to take root. The arrested sap produces a ring-shaped swelling on the upper edge of the wound, and from this swelling spring roots.

"Now let us apply these theoretical principles. If the wood is compact and for that reason rebels against the laws of simple layering, we will take a piece of wire and strangle (that is the word) the branch we are operating upon; that is to say, we will bind it tight, but without breaking the bark. The compression should be made just below a bud or eye, and about midway of the part that is to be underground. This process is called layering by strangulation.

"Or again, still midway of the part to be bedded in the earth, and immediately under a bud, we cut the bark all around the branch without injuring the wood; a second incision is made a centimeter and a half lower down; then tearing off the strip of bark between the two circumcisions, we remove it all in one piece. This method is known as annular incision from the ring of bark thus taken away.

"Or as a third expedient, still midway of the part to be bedded in the trench, we make with a sharp instrument an oblique incision from below upward, cutting into the wood as far as the marrow. In this way we are enabled to raise a tongue comprising half the thickness of the shoot, and this tongue is held in its lifted position by a small pebble inserted in the slit. This is what we call a Y-shaped incision, because the raised tongue forms with the rest of the stem an opening like that between the two branches of the letter Y. Through the half that remains intact communication with the mother stem is maintained and the needed share of crude sap is received, while from the cut and upraised half adventitious roots are put forth because the course of the descending sap is arrested there.

"In order to bring into contact with the damp soil a greater extent of wounded fiber fit for putting forth adventitious roots, it is customary to split the upraised tongue in two and keep the two parts gaping by interposing a small pebble. This method of double incision is used for trees that offer the greatest resistance to successful layering.

"To sum up, all these methods and others derived from them have for their object the fostering of adventitious roots by arresting the course of the descending sap at a certain point beneath the soil."

CHAPTER XXXVI

SLIPPING

"PROPAGATION BY means of a slip or scion cut from the parent tree and so placed that it will develop adventitious roots we may for convenience speak of as slipping. The cut end of the slip is set in the ground in some cool, moist, shady spot where evaporation is slow and the temperature mild. For delicate slips the shelter of a bell-glass is often necessary in order to insure the requisite moisture in the atmosphere and thus prevent the slip from drying up before it has sent down roots to make good its losses. For greater surety, if the slip has many leaves, most of the lower ones are removed in order to reduce the evaporating surface as much as possible without compromising the plant's vitality, which resides especially in the upper part. But in many cases these precautions are needless; thus, to propagate the grape-vine, willow, and poplar, it suffices merely to thrust the detached scion into the ground.

"Trees whose wood is soft and well filled with sap are the ones best fitted for slipping; to this class belongs the willow, with its notably tender fiber. On the other hand, wood that is dense and hard gives us sure warning that this mode of propagation will be found very difficult or even impossible. Thus it would invariably fail with the oak, the olive, the box-tree, and a great many more hard-wood trees. Furthermore, slipping offers far less certainty of success than layering, since the layer remains in communication with the parent stock and is thus supplied with nourishment until it has acquired roots of its own, whereas the slip, all such communication being abruptly cut off, is obliged from the outset to rely on its own resources and pass without help through the difficult period of rootlessness. Among fruit-bearers there are scarcely any except the grape-vine, the currant-bush, the quince-tree, and a few varieties of plum and apple trees, that lend themselves to this method of propagation. Among the larger trees the willow and the poplar take root with no difficulty whatever when started from the slip. Finally, a great many ornamental species, herbaceous plants or bushes like the rose, jasmine, and honeysuckle, multiply easily by this method, the usual one adopted with them by the flower-gardener.

"Let us go back now to the very simplest case, the one calling for the fewest precautions. A damp piece of ground on the water's edge is to be planted with poplars or willows. Toward the end of winter the forester in charge cuts a sufficient number of vigorous young branches as large around as a stout cane or even a man's fist, or perhaps larger, and from one to four meters long. He removes all the lower twigs, clips the intermediate ones to half their length, and leaves the upper ones intact if the tree is to be pyramid-shaped; otherwise he gives the top a truncate form. Finally the lower end is cut to a point with the hatchet, to make it easier to thrust into the ground. Now the slip is ready for planting, and all that is necessary is to push it well down into the earth by its pointed end and leave it to itself. Without any further attention, if the ground is sufficiently damp, adventitious roots will start, and each of the stakes thus rudely hacked will become a poplar or a willow.

"But other forms of vegetation are far from manifesting this facility in rooting which makes possible the growth of a tree from a stake driven into the ground, it may be with the blow of a club; therefore delicate precautions are necessary for success if these obdurate subjects are to be propagated by slips. Let us take the grape-vine as an example. Its slips for planting are shoots of the same year's growth. These are tied in a bundle and their cut ends placed in water to soak for a week or more. Why this long immersion of the part that later is to be planted in the ground? Because the outside bark is dry and tough, difficult for tender roots to pierce, especially if the soil is dry. Accordingly the bark is softened by soaking for some time in water; and also, when the slips are taken out of the water, they are lightly scraped where they are to be in the earth, but left untouched where they are to be in the air. In this way the outer layer of bark is removed after being softened in water; and there is so much the less resistance offered to the growing roots; but the inner layers, where the vine's vital activities go on, are scrupulously spared. The slight wounds inflicted by this scraping, let it be further noted, favor the starting of roots by arresting the sap. After being prepared in this manner the slips are set out. In soil that has been well worked so that the young roots may push downward without hindrance, vertical holes are made with a long iron or wooden dibble, and in each of these holes a slip is inserted to the depth of about half a meter. Fine earth is then sifted into the hole and well rammed down to insure perfect contact with the slip, and the operation is finished.

"Just as the process of layering is facilitated by the formation of a ring-shaped swelling where the descending sap is arrested in its course either by a ligature or by the removal of a ring of bark, so the same artifice can be advantageously employed in propagating by means of slips. Around the shoot selected as slip for the next year's planting an iron wire is tightly bound; or, instead of this, a ring of bark is cut away. By autumn a swelling will have formed all about the stem, whereupon the shoot is detached and placed in the ground for the winter in order that the swelling may become a little further enlarged and somewhat softened. In the spring the shoot is taken up again, trimmed so that it shall have only four or five buds left, and planted like an ordinary slip. From the ring-shaped swelling caused by the accumulation of sap roots will start.

"All the advantages offered by the ring-shaped swelling may be secured with no expenditure of ingenuity on our part. Take hold of a small branch and pull it down so as to split it off from the main stem. Thus torn away it will bring with it a sort of spur or splinter from the trunk directly under the severed branch. This spur, trimmed with a knife to give it a less ragged outline, will render the same service as the ring-shaped swelling: the descending sap will be stopped in its course at this point, will accumulate, and will foster the growth of adventitious roots.

"Instead of breaking off the branch by tearing it away at its base, one can, with a stroke of the pruning-knife above this base and another below it, cut the older limb bearing this branch so that the latter carries with it a piece of the former. With this piece as a sort of natural bourrelet or swelling, success is rendered more assured than in any other way.

"To conclude, let us say a few words about slipping by means of buds, a kind of planting that uses buds instead of seeds. This method, which requires the nicest care of any, is adopted only in exceptional cases. Let us suppose we have a very few shoots, or only one, from some extremely rare variety of grape-vine, and we wish to obtain from this single shoot the greatest possible number of slips. To this end the shoot is cut into small pieces about five centimeters long, each bearing a bud midway of its length. These pieces are then each split in two lengthwise, and the part with the bud is retained, the other thrown away. Thus prepared, the pieces are planted in fertile soil with the split surface underneath and the bud just peeping out of the earth. But to insure any likelihood of success with this method, certain special conditions not called for in ordinary planting must be observed, as will be readily understood. The delicate slips are arranged with care in an earthen pan or pot, and covered with a bell-glass to assure them a moist and warm atmosphere. After roots have started the slips are transplanted, each being placed in a separate pot where it gains strength and awaits the proper time for planting in the ground."

CHAPTER XXXVII

GRAFTING

"GRAFTING IS the process by which a twig or a bud[5] is transplanted from one branch to another, or from one tree to another. That which is to serve as support and sustenance to the transferred part is known as the stock, while the twig or bud received by it is called the graft.

"One absolutely necessary condition must be fulfilled if this operation is to be successful: the transferred part must find on its new nursing-branch nutriment to its taste, that is to say, a sap like its own. This requires that the two plants, the stock and the one that furnishes the graft, should be of the same species or at least belong to closely related species, since likeness of sap and its products can result only from likeness of organization. It would be a mere waste of time to try to engraft the lilac upon the rose, or the rose upon the willow, for there is nothing in common between these three species either in leaves, flowers, or fruit. This difference in structure is invariably accompanied by a marked difference in respect to nutrition. Hence the rose-bud would starve to death on a lilac-branch, and the lilac-bud would meet with the same sad fate on a rose-bush. But lilac can very well be grafted on lilac, rose-bush on rose-bush, vine on vine. And one can even go further than this: a peach-bud will flourish on an apricot-tree, a cherry-bud on a plum-tree, and

5   In English this transfer of a bud is commonly called "budding."—*Translator.*

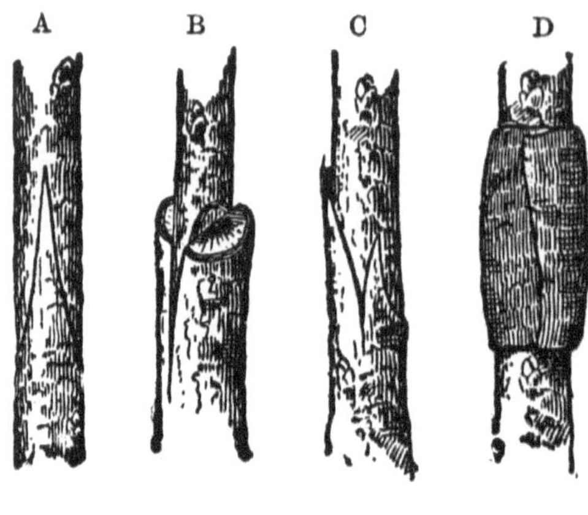

A—Saddle Grafting
B—Cleft Grafting
C–D—Whip Grafting

vice versa; for between the members of each of these pairs there is a close and easily discernible analogy. In short, there must be the closest possible resemblance between the two plants if grafting is to succeed.

"The ancients were far from having any clear idea on this absolute need of likeness in organization. They tell us of grafting the holly with the rose to obtain green roses, the walnut tree with the grape to produce enormous grapes as large as walnuts. In our own time has not the project been seriously considered of grafting a vine shoot on to a mulberry tree in order to restore vigor to the grape whose roots an underground grub has attacked? Such graftings and others between plants completely unlike have never been successfully undertaken except in the imagination of those who dreamt them.

"We have already seen that, grown from seed, our various fruit trees do not, as a rule, reproduce the quality of fruit of the parent stock; an invincible tendency to revert to the wild state causes the fruit to lose, little by little, from one generation to another, the improvement it had acquired through cultivation. Thus the pear, through repeated plantings of the seed, would become increasingly sour, small, and hard, until it had at last returned to the sorry state of the wild pear growing on the edge of the woods. But this defect attending growth from the seed is redeemed by one very desirable quality: the tree thus grown regains more or less the robustness of its wild type; it is incomparably more vigorous, healthier, longer-lived, than the artificially perfected tree whose strength is compromised by the very excess of its fructification. One has vigor, the other fine fruit. The two attributes cannot go together; if one increases, the other decreases. Well then, these robust specimens reared from the seed are just what we require for grafting. Used as stocks, they supply the quality inherent in them, namely, vigor; and the cutting engrafted upon them furnishes the other quality, excellence of fruit.

"Accordingly it is the practice to plant the pips of pears and apples, and the stones of apricots and peaches; and on the trees thus obtained to graft cuttings from pear, apple, apricot, and peach trees that bear fruit of recognized superiority. In this way there are united in the same tree the root and trunk of the robust and almost wild kind with the leaves and blossoms of the weak but artificially improved kind. Every variety of pear tree is by nature fitted to receive a pear graft, every variety of peach tree to receive a peach graft, and so on with all fruit-trees. There is no objection to selecting as stock any wild pear, cherry, or plum tree that may have sprung up of itself in hedge or thicket. It is thus for example that the cherry is grafted on two others of like sort, the wild cherry and the cherry of Saint Lucia, both frequenters of uncultivated hillsides. The first bears fruit hardly as large as a pea, black, round, and full of a very dark and rather bitter juice; the second has still smaller fruit with scarcely any pulp and uneatable. No matter: with grafts from a suitably chosen source they will cover themselves with the finest cherries. In like manner our superb garden roses can be grown on the wild rose stock, the common dog rose of the hedges, whose modest blossoms have only five petals of a pale carnation color and are well-nigh odorless. Sometimes, again, two species of similar characteristics are chosen for grafting purposes. Thus the pear grafts well on the quince-tree, the fruit of the latter being, after all, a sort of big pear; the apricot can be grafted on the plum; the peach on the plum and, still better, on the almond, so like the peach in its foliage, its early blossoming, and the structure of its fruit.

"As a curiosity let us mention the mixing of several kinds of fruit on the same stock. By means of grafting the same tree can bear, all at one time, almonds, apricots, peaches, plums, and cherries, because these five kinds admit of reciprocal grafting; another tree may be covered simultaneously with pears, quinces, berries of the mountain ash, medlars, and service-berries. These are very odd instances, certainly, but of no practical interest. It would be a waste of time to dwell longer on them did they not teach a useful lesson. They demonstrate that however many fresh grafts are added to a tree, the new-comers exert no influence outside their own sphere. Whether offshoots of the tree itself or aliens, the grafts develop, blossom, and fructify, each after its own kind, without contracting any of its neighbor's habits. Among the curious phenomena observed in this artificial juxtaposition of mutually independent grafts, we will mention a pear-tree on which were represented, by means of grafting, all the different varieties of cultivated pears. Sour or sweet, dry or juicy, large or small, green or bright-colored, round or long, hard or mellow, each and all ripened on the same tree and grew again year after year without change, faithful to the specific character, not of the supporting tree, but of the various grafts planted on this common stock.

"The mere bringing together of analogous plants does not

suffice for the success of the operation of grafting; there must be a considerable extent of contact between those parts of the graft and the stock that have the most vitality and are consequently best fitted to coalesce. This contact should be in the inner layers of the bark and in the seat of plant-growth situated between the wood and the bark. The vital activity of the plant, in fact, resides especially in this region. It is between the wood and the bark that the elaborated sap descends; there is where new cells and new fibers are organized, to form on one side a sheet of bark and on the other a layer of wood. Hence it is there and only there that coalescence is possible between the graft and the stock."

CHAPTER XXXVIII

GRAFTING

(Continued)

"There are three principal kinds of grafting, namely: grafting by approach (also called simply 'approaching' or 'inarching'), grafting by shoots or scions, and grafting by buds (commonly known as 'budding'). The form given to the two cut ends that are brought together and the disposition of the parts thus placed in contact give rise, in practice, to numerous subdivisions that need not be mentioned here. We will confine ourselves to the essentials.

"Grafting by approach is analogous to layering, with this difference, that the tree to be grafted takes the place of the soil that receives the layer. In layering we induce the growth of adventitious roots by partly burying in the ground a branch or shoot still adhering to the stock that nourishes it. When, acted upon by the soil, roots have started in sufficient number, the shoot is gradually cut loose until at last it is quite severed from the parent stock. In grafting by approach it is also proposed to make a branch, a shoot, a tree-top, while still united to its own stem or stock, take root, so to speak, not in the ground, but in the substance of a neighboring tree.

"Let us suppose that two shrubs are growing close together and that we wish to engraft on one of them a twig or shoot of the other. The parts to be placed in contact receive each a longitudinal gash that penetrates to the marrow, or even deeper, and the two gashes are made of equal length. These parts are then brought together, care being taken to make the young and growing portions in the one exactly meet those in the other; that is to say, the inner layer of bark in each, with the channel traversed by the elaborated sap, is carefully fitted to the corresponding part in its neighbor. The whole is thereupon made fast with a ligature, and the two wounds are left to the slow operation of vital forces. Fed by its own stem or trunk, from which it is not yet separated, the shoot to be transplanted mingles its sap with the sap of its neighbor; on both sides there are new growths to cicatrize the wounds, while the two parts gradually coalesce until, sooner or later, the graft becomes incorporated with its future support. And now the graft must be weaned; that is, it must, little by little, be deprived of the sustenance furnished by its own stock. This is accomplished as in simple layering, by gradually cutting through the shoot below the point of union. As soon as the graft is thought to be getting all its nourishment from the new stem, it is completely severed from the mother tree. This mode of grafting, the most elementary of all, sometimes takes place accidentally and unassisted. In a hedge or any dense growth of bushes, if two branches chance to come into close and prolonged contact, there will be at this point, first, a slight abrasion and then a complete wearing away of the bark until the two raw surfaces end, it may be, in growing together. It is not improbable that natural occurrences of this kind furnished man with his first notions of grafting.

"Grafting by approach is an excellent method to apply whenever in the arrangement of a fruit-tree's branches there is a vacant space that needs filling. Regular distribution, sym-

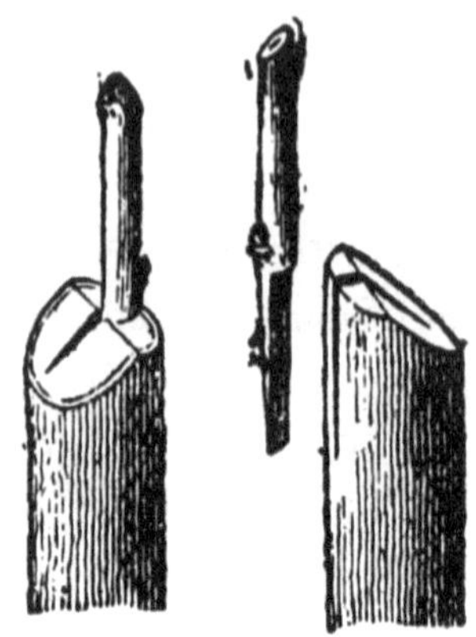

CLEFT-GRAFTING

metry of arrangement, is a condition demanded if only to satisfy the eye, which is always offended by disorder; but there is another and still more convincing reason for this regularity. The more evenly a tree's branches are distributed, so that each shall receive an equal share of sap, sunlight, and heat, so much the more fruit will it bear. Suppose, then, there is a lack of branches in some part. To fill this gap and thus restore the tree's symmetry, grafting by approach offers a ready means. From a branch near the vacant space and itself sufficiently supplied with twigs or shoots, one of these latter, of good length, is selected; then it is properly cut or gashed and the gash is brought into contact with a similar gash at the point where it is desired to start a new growth; and, finally, a ligature is applied to hold the two parts together. As soon as coalescence is complete the graft is severed below the point of union, and the lower section, after being straightened up again, is ready to serve once more as branch to the limb that bears it. In this way, with no loss to themselves, the more abundant branches furnish offshoots to the poorer ones.

"Grafting by means of shoots or scions cut from the parent stock at the outset is analogous to slipping. It consists in transplanting on to a new stock a shoot detached from its mother branch. The most common method is cleft-grafting. It is done in the spring when the buds begin to open. Shoots of the preceding year are chosen for grafts, care being taken to select those that are vigorous and that have attained no later than August the hard and woody condition necessary for resistance to the severities of winter. One precaution at the very outset must be taken. When the graft is put in place it will be of the utmost importance that it shall find in its new position nourishment proportionate to its needs. It would infallibly perish if it should prove to be in a more advanced state of vegetation than the stock selected to nourish it. The latter, therefore, ought to be rather ahead of than behind the former in this respect. To secure this result, between one and two months before the operation is to be carried out it is well to cut the grafts and place them in the ground on the north side of a wall, where they will remain quiescent while the branches to which they are to be transferred will make progress and their sap will start.

"We will suppose there is a worthless pear-tree in our garden, grown from a pip or transplanted from its native wood, and we propose to make it bear good pears. The course to pursue is as follows. We cut off entirely the upper part of the wild pear tree, trimming the cut with our pruning-knife so that there are no ragged edges, since these would not scar over readily and might become the seat of a far-reaching decay. If the trunk is of moderate size and is to receive but one graft, it is cut a little obliquely with a small level surface on the upper edge, as shown in the picture. In the middle of this horizontal facet a split is made to the depth of about six centimeters. That done, we take one of the grafts set aside as already indicated, and we cut it so as to leave only two or three buds, of which the topmost one should be at the tip of the branch. Then, just under the lowest bud we whittle the end of the graft into the shape of a knife-blade, letting the bud stand just above the back or dull edge of the blade. For greater stability when the graft is put in place, a narrow inverted ledge is cut at the top of the blade on both sides. A glance at the picture will show you all these little details. Finally, the graft is slipped into the cleft of the stock, bark exactly meeting bark, wood meeting wood. The whole is brought tightly together by binding, and the wounds are covered with grafting mastic, which may be bought already prepared. If this mastic is lacking we can use what is known in the country as Saint Fiacre's ointment, a sort of paste made of clay, or rather a mixture of clay and cows' dung, the fibrous nature of the latter preventing the former from cracking. A winding of rags holds the ointment in place. Thus wound, the stump does not suffer from exposure to the air, which would dry it up. In course of time the wounds cicatrize, and the bark and wood of the graft coalesce with the bark and wood of the severed trunk. Finally the buds of the graft, nourished by the stock, develop into branches and at the end of a few years the top of the wild pear tree is replaced by that of a cultivated pear tree bearing pears equal to those of the tree that furnished the graft.

"The operation of cutting back a branch or trunk to receive the graft always promotes the growth of numerous buds. What is to be done with the shoots that spring from these? Evidently they must be suppressed, for they would appropriate, to no good end, the sap intended for the graft. Nevertheless the suppression must be done cautiously. Let us not forget that what primarily causes the sap to ascend is the evaporation of moisture from the leaves. As long as the graft has not opened its buds and spread its leaves, it is well to let the young shoots of the stock remain untouched. They act as helpers, in that their foliage draws upward the juices extracted from the soil by the roots; so that, far from having an injurious effect at this time, their presence is most useful. But the day will come when the graft alone will suffice for this work of pumping up the sap, and then it is best to get rid of these messmates which, of heartier appetite than the graft, would soon starve it out. First the lower shoots of the stock are suppressed, then gradually those higher up, care being taken not to destroy the top ones until the graft has developed shoots two or three decimeters long."

CHAPTER XXXIX

GRAFTING

(Concluded)

"THE PART of a plant or tree above ground and the part under ground are mutually dependent, the development of one implying a corresponding development in the other. If there is a superabundance of foliage, the roots will be unable to furnish it sufficient nourishment; on the other hand, if the roots are unduly vigorous, there will be too much sap for the foliage—an excess of nourishment which, there being no use for it, will encumber the plant and be injurious to it. Hence if the trunk to be grafted is strong it must have several grafts, in order that the number of buds to be nourished may be in right proportion to the number of nourishing roots.

"To this end the trunk is cut, not obliquely as for a single graft, but horizontally. Then it is split all the way across, following a line that passes through the central pith, and two grafts are implanted in the cleft, one at each end. It is evident that not more than two can be placed in the same cleft, because the bark of the graft must of necessity come in contact with the bark of the stock to insure inter-communication and coalescence between the sap-canals of the two. If the size of the stock requires more than two grafts, instead of splitting the trunk diametrically several times, it is preferable to make lateral clefts which, leaving the center untouched, cause less danger to the solidity of the stock.

BUDDING

"Recourse can also be had to the following method, in which no clefts whatever are called for, clefts being difficult to cicatrize when the wood is old. The grafts are cut like the mouthpiece of a flute; that is to say, at the base half is taken off lengthwise while the other half is left, but is whittled down, thinner and thinner toward the end, much like a flute's mouthpiece. Thus shaped, the grafts are inserted between the wood and the bark of the stock, an operation facilitated by the flow of sap in the spring, when the bark separates easily from the wood. If there is danger of tearing the bark under the strain of the graft acting as a wedge, a slight incision is made in the bark to give it the play it needs. In this way the circumference of the stock receives the number of grafts deemed necessary. It only remains now to bind the whole securely and cover the wounds with mastic.

This method is called crown-grafting, because the grafts are arranged in a crown on the circumference of the cross-section.

"Grafting by buds corresponds to that variety of slipping in which buds, each one by itself on a small fragment of the branch, are set into the ground. It consists in transplanting on the stock a simple bud with the bit of bark that bears it. It is the method most commonly employed. According to the time of year when the operation is undertaken, the graft is called an active bud or a dormant bud. In the first case the grafting is done in the spring, when nature is awaking from her winter's sleep, so that the eye or bud implanted in the stock coalesces with it and very soon develops into a young shoot. In the second instance the bud is set in place some time in July or August, at the period of the autumnal sap, so that it lies dormant or, in other words, remains stationary during the following autumn and winter, after uniting with the stock.

"The implement here required is the grafting-knife, furnished at one end with a very sharp blade, and at the other with a short spatula of bone or very hard wood. The first thing to do is to remove the bud to be transplanted. On a branch in which the sap is working we make with the grafting-knife a transverse cut above the bud and another below; then, holding the branch in one hand and the grafting-knife in the other, as the picture shows, we remove the strip of bark lying between these two cuts and delimited laterally by the line $g\ g'\ g$ and its opposite, in figure F. This strip, which we call the shield, is shown by itself in H. The leaf that sheltered the bud in its axil has been removed, but the base of the stem of this leaf has been left and will be useful later for taking hold of the shield and handling it more conveniently. The shield must be cut away without any tearing and in such a manner that no sap-wood is left clinging to the bark. The latter must be perfectly intact, especially in its inner layers, the seat of vital activities. Finally, the bud should have its proper complement of young, greenish wood, which constitutes the germ, the very heart of the bud. Should this germ be removed by unskilful manipulation, the bud would have to be thrown away, for the graft would surely fail.

"The next step is to make a double incision in the bark in the shape of a T, penetrating as far as the wood but without injuring it. With the spatula of the grafting-knife the two lips of the wound are raised a little while the bud with its shield is taken up by the piece of leaf-stem attached to it and inserted between the bark and the wood. All that now remains to be done is to draw the lips of the little wound together and bind the whole with some sort of material sufficiently pliant and elastic not to compress and finally strangle the bud as it develops. A rush, a slender thong made of a long and flexible grass-blade, or, better still, a piece of woolen yarn is well suited to the purpose. But if despite all precautions the ligature should after a while prove too tight on account of the swelling of the graft, it would be necessary to loosen it without delay. As soon as the graft has 'taken,' as we say, the young shoots starting out on the stock are gradually suppressed in the cautious manner prescribed for cleft-grafting.

"When the stock is too small to receive a bud in the usual manner, the following expedient is resorted to. From a shoot of about the same size as the stock a rectangular strip of bark with bud attached is cut with four incisions of the grafting-knife. This strip is immediately laid upon the stock to serve as a pattern while the point of the knife is passed all around it. In this way there is cut from the stock a strip of bark having exactly the same shape and size as the pattern, which latter is thereupon inserted in the vacant place and made fast there by a ligature. This process may not inappropriately be called veneering.

"In flute-grafting the bark both above and below the bud is cut transversely all around the stem, and then another cut is made lengthwise between these two slashes. A cylinder of bark may thus be peeled off in one piece. From the stock, which should match this cylinder in size, a similar cylinder is removed and its place taken by the other one bearing the bud we wish to transplant."

CHAPTER XL

ROTATION OF CROPS

THEY ARE eating dinner at the farm. A large platter of pork cutlets and beans is smoking in the center of the table. Every one has been served. It is a pleasure to see these good people eat, they have such hearty appetites. Jacques, the big ox-driver, is the first to finish. He throws his bone away. Azor is there to seize it. He lies flat on his stomach and takes the bone in his fore paws. Hear him bite on his hard pittance. How it cracks! Let any one beware of teasing Azor now. An angry growl and a baring of his four formidable canine teeth would warn the rash intruder to have done with his joking at once, for if not—well, I will not be responsible for the consequences. Azor is not a surly dog; far from it; but he is well within his rights when he brooks no nonsense at his meals. He has done his duty most valiantly as a dog. Night before last some wolves were prowling about the sheep-fold, and he drove them off. Let Azor gnaw his bone in peace.

Ha, there! The big tortoise-shell cat, Master Minet, is otherwise minded. He draws near, hair erect, tail as large around as your arm, to try to frighten Azor and rob him of his allowance. Azor, without dropping the bone, gives a low growl and lifts one paw. That is enough, the cat flees. So, my bold Minet, what were you after here? The bone is not for you; your teeth are not strong enough to bite it. Go away! Martha is calling you to give you some bread soaked in gravy. That will suit you better than a bone as hard as a stone.

Ah, here come some more guests. The door stands open and in come the hens from the poultry-yard. *Tap, tap, tap, tap*; they peck the crumbs fallen from the table. Azor has no use for such diet—tiny morsels much too small for him; nor does the cat want them either, they are too floury. But the hens feast on them.

And all, human beings, dog, cat, hens, dine at the same time; only each must make the best of what the others cannot use. Azor is content with the bone that big Jacques threw away; the cat is satisfied with a little bread soaked in gravy, a dish quite inadequate to Azor's needs; the hens pick up the crumbs disdained by Jacques, Azor, and the cat. Martha, it seems, had prepared dinner only for the farm people, and behold, by utilizing the scraps that are worthless to some, many others join in the midday meal. From the scraps disdained by man the dog will gain strength to defend the flock; from those rejected by the dog the cat will acquire keen eyesight and sharp claws to see and to seize the mouse; from what is of no value to the cat the hens will make eggs; and everything, absolutely everything, will go to the profit of the farm.

"Agriculture in its turn," remarked Uncle Paul, turning to account this homely illustration in domestic economy, "prepares dinner for the crops in its own peculiar manner. It spreads the ground with manure, that fertile dressing so relished by growing plants. The table is set, or in other words the field is ready, well plowed and harrowed, and well manured. Whom shall we call first to the table, for it is plain we cannot invite all at once. Whom shall we call first? It shall be wheat, let us say, a plant with tastes hard to please, but one that in return gives us bread. So wheat is sown. In this soil, full of all sorts of good things, it cannot fail to thrive, however unfavorable the season may be. It will select what suits it best and leave the rest.

"Now that is done. The harvest is in, and it handsomely comes up to our hopes. The wheat has converted into magnificent grain the fertilizer put into the ground. Out of decay it has created nourishment. Surely it has well acquitted itself of its charge. It has made a clean sweep: all that could be turned into wheat it has appropriated, and there remains nothing further to be done. What would happen, then, if wheat were sown again in the same field? Exactly the same thing that would happen to Simon if he had nothing to eat but the bone that Jacques threw away. He would die of hunger. Simon must have man's food, wheat must have wheat's food. So if the first crop has exhausted the supply of material for making wheat, how can you expect to raise a second crop? Evidently that is asking the impossible; it is running the risk of reaping only a very mediocre harvest or even none at all. Therefore it is the rule not to sow wheat twice in succession in the same field. And what is true of wheat is true also of all other crops. Where a plant has prospered one year, the same plant will not do well the second year, because the ingredients required by this plant are more or less exhausted. It is foolish to invite guests to a table that is stripped bare.

"If the table were spread again, if more fertilizer were added to the soil, that would be quite a different matter, and wheat would grow as well as it did the first time. But such a procedure would be bad management, for the very utmost should be made of one meal. Before further expenditure in the way of fertilizer let us exhaust the virtue of the fertilizer already applied. Azor dined well on what Jacques discarded; the hens were well fed with what Azor and the cat left. Let us take an example from this succession of eaters who utilize each in his own way the remnants worthless to the others. The wheat has exhausted, or nearly exhausted, all that is suitable for wheat; but just as Jacques the ox-driver left the bone, it has left in the soil a good many ingredients that make excellent food for other crops. In order, therefore, to utilize to the last ounce the first spreading of fertilizer, we must invite to the repast a guest of different tastes. This guest may be, for example, the potato. In soil that would have furnished but starvation diet for wheat the potato will find quite enough to live on, its tastes not being the same as the cereal's.

"Thus we have two successive crops for one coating of manure: we have sacks of potatoes with no additional outlay in fertilizer. Is that all? Not yet. After the wheat and the potatoes there is, to be sure, but meager nourishment left in the upper layer of the soil; but in the lower layers there remains the part of the fertilizer that the rain has washed down and dissolved and that the short roots of the preceding crops could not reach. To utilize this underlying matter and bring it up again to the surface in the form of forage let us now sow a plant with vigorous roots, such as clover, sainfoin, or, still better, lucerne, which will penetrate deeper. And so we get our third crop.

"After clover we can try a fourth crop, of a different kind; but it is evident that as the guests succeed one another at the same table the remnants become more and more scanty and difficult to utilize. Accordingly we must choose a hardy plant and one that is content with little. Finally a time will come, and at no very distant date, when the board will be bare: the coating of manure will have given up its last particle of nutritious matter. Then the table must be garnished afresh, the field fertilized anew before beginning again with the same crops or attempting others. Let us demand no more. You understand, my young friends, that in order to utilize to the utmost this precious substance that gives us every kind of food, such as bread, vegetables, forage, meat, fruit, dairy products—to make the very best use of this we must, instead of raising the same crop in the same field year after year, adopt the plan of varying our crops, changing from one of one kind to another of a different character, so that what earlier plantings have left in the soil may be turned to account by later ones. This succession of different sorts of farm produce is called rotation of crops."

CHAPTER XLI

ROTATION OF CROPS
(CONTINUED)

"WHEN SOIL is spoken of as worn out and needing rest, the speaker uses a figure of speech meaning that the soil has been exhausted by the crops it has borne. The crops do indeed take from the land a great quantity of substances necessary for plant-life; and when these substances are no longer present in sufficient amount, the soil refuses to produce; it is exhausted. To restore its original fertility would require a large outlay in fertilizer and hence it is often more advantageous to accomplish this object by one of the following methods.

"Sometimes the land is allowed to lie fallow; that is to say, it is left to itself without any care whatever for whole years. Weeds spring up freely, and at the same time water, air, and frost act on the soil, disintegrating and mellowing it and inducing the formation of certain substances necessary to vegetation. The weeds are converted into mold, and finally the land, rested and recuperated, is ready to bear a new crop. Restoration by this process is very slow, taking several years, and hence it is customary to shorten the period of waiting by working the soil and even manuring it, although it may not yet be the intention to sow any seed. In these circumstances the land is called fallow land.

"There is, however, one way to obtain an uninterrupted succession of crops from the same land unless the soil is very poor. All plants derive their nourishment from the soil and the atmosphere; but some take more from the atmosphere, others from the soil. The plants that get their sustenance chiefly from the air are those that have luxuriant foliage. The potato is one of these. You know that it is through their leaves that plants obtain the carbonic acid gas diffused in the air. The greater the spread of foliage, the more abundant will this absorption be. The plants that depend almost wholly on the soil are those with only a few small, slender leaves, thus taking but little carbonic acid gas from the air. Such is wheat.

"Moreover, from the potato plant we take only the tubers, which form but a small part of the whole, and we turn under the stalks and leaves, which are thereupon converted into humus. Thus the potato has the property of enriching the soil at the expense of the atmosphere, and it gives back more than it takes. It is, then, one of the enriching rather than impoverishing plants in respect to its action on the soil. Cereals, on the contrary, are utilized by the harvester both as to seed and haulm, nothing but the meager roots being left in the ground; and as, on account of their very scanty foliage, cereals derive almost their entire sustenance from the soil, they take from it much more than they give back to it. They accordingly belong to the class of plants that impoverish rather than enrich the soil in which they grow.

"It is impossible, thus, except by a ruinous expenditure of fertilizer, to raise a crop of grain every year on the same land. But if we should let potatoes succeed wheat, and wheat succeed potatoes, what would be the result? The latter crop, deriving a large part of its nourishment from the air, would flourish in soil comparatively exhausted by wheat; and on having its leaves and stalks turned under it would give back to the soil a part of its former fertility. Wheat could then be successfully raised again on the same land.

"This practice of raising successively on the same land different crops as little harmful to one another as possible and capable of utilizing to the utmost the dressing put on to the land, is nothing but that very rotation of crops that I have already told you something about. Its purpose is to economize fertilizer and at the same time to secure an uninterrupted succession of crops. The underlying principle consists in making an enriching plant succeed an impoverishing one; that is to say, a plant with luxuriant foliage is made to succeed one with scanty foliage. The chief enriching plants are clover, lucerne, sainfoin, potatoes, turnips, and beets. Cereals, on the contrary, are all impoverishing plants. It is a general custom to raise on the same land a more or less extended series of different crops, the series running four, five, or six years, or even longer, after which it begins over again in the same order. This rotation of crops is designated according to the number of years the series covers, as for instance a five-year or a six-year rotation. A six-year rotation might run, we will say, somewhat as follows:

> 1st year—potatoes—enriching crop.
> 2nd year—wheat—impoverishing crop.
> 3rd year—clover—enriching crop.
> 4th year—wheat—impoverishing crop.
> 5th year—sainfoin—enriching crop.
> 6th year—oats—impoverishing crop.

"Let us examine in detail this series that we have taken as an example. The first year the soil is thoroughly manured. One of the effects of manuring is to start a great crop of weeds that would infest the land and impoverish the crop were they not carefully removed. Hence the necessity of weeding. To weed a piece of ground is to destroy the weeds either by hand or with some implement. But it is not every crop that admits of weeding: the plants must be a certain distance apart, as otherwise they will be trampled under foot, cut off, or uprooted in the weeding process. Wheat cannot be weeded, its stalks are too close together; but potatoes are far enough apart for weeding without difficulty. Now, weeding destroys all useless, injurious grasses and other unwelcome intruders; their future reappearance is prevented by pulling them up before their seeds ripen, and thus at last the ground is cleaned and made ready for a choice crop. This will explain to you the great advantage of letting the potato or some other crop that can be weeded take precedence of the cereals.

"The second year comes wheat. Cleaned by the tillage that has gone before, the ground is no longer covered with grass and weeds. Nor does it need fresh manure, for if the potatoes have consumed certain elements in the soil, these are not exactly the same that wheat requires; and, furthermore, the dead plants, turned under and reduced to vegetable mold, compensate by what they have derived from the atmosphere for what the tubers may have taken from the soil. Wheat is therefore just the crop to raise now.

"But it would be much against one's interest to exact from the soil another crop of wheat the third year. Exhausted by the grain it has just produced, the soil would yield but a scanty harvest unless it were freshly manured, a process that would make of the whole operation, not a piece of farming, but an example of gardening, and would also entail too great expense. For that reason the third year is devoted to the raising of an enriching crop, such as clover. After furnishing a supply of fodder, what is left of the clover is turned under, and all its remnants of roots, stems, and leaves are reduced to mold, which renders the soil fit for another wheat harvest the fourth year. A third enriching crop to be turned under after the final mowing, is likewise needed for the fifth year; and this crop may be sainfoin. At the end of the series comes another cereal, oats, for example. The rotation is now complete, and the program begins all over again.

"Crop-rotation is capable of innumerable variations, and the series may be longer or shorter, but there should be the slightest possible departure from the rule that a cereal crop ought always to be preceded by some crop that enriches the soil."

CHAPTER XLII

LAND-DRAINAGE

"IN THE bottom of a flower-pot you will find a small round hole. Over this hole it is customary to lay a bit of broken tile, and on this, if the plant to occupy the pot is delicate, a few small pebbles. This done, the pot is filled with vegetable mold. Why this hole, this bit of tile, these pebbles? That is what we are now about to consider.

"Water is absolutely indispensable to plants, since it is the medium that dissolves the various nutritive ingredients of the soil and thus renders them capable of assimilation by the roots. Accordingly the soil penetrated by these roots must be constantly supplied with sufficient moisture either by rainfall or by artificial irrigation. But air is not less indispensable. It disinfects the soil and by causing slow combustion of the humus gives rise to a slight but uninterrupted liberation of carbonic acid gas, one of the nutritive substances required by vegetation. Should the roots be cut off from this life-giving agency, they would languish and finally decay. Thus it is that if vegetation is to thrive the soil in which it grows must have at the same time both air and water. But if the bottom of the flower-pot has no opening, or if its opening is stopped up, the water from the watering-can will not flow through, nor will there be any air admitted from below, and for lack of this the roots will decay. On the other hand, if the water, after saturating the earth, runs out freely by the hole in the bottom of the pot, the damp soil will become a sort of sponge to which the air will have access from all sides, and the plant will thrive.

"This reasoning applies to the most extensive agricultural operations as well as to the care of a potted plant. After water has soaked into the ground it should find some channel to carry it off; otherwise the roots will decay for want of air. That is why clayey soils, which retain water when they are once saturated, are unsuited to agriculture, while light soils, having sand mixed with the clay and thus readily allowing the water to drain off, are well adapted to it. For the same reason, again, a sandy subsoil accelerates vegetation, and a clayey subsoil retards it. A sandy subsoil offers the same advantage as a flower-pot open at the bottom, whereas a clayey subsoil is like a flower-pot closed at the bottom. In the first case the surplus of water drains off and the air has free access; in the second the superabundant moisture finds no outlet and the air cannot reach the roots.

"Now let us suppose we have a marshy soil to deal with. Because of the stagnant water either on the surface or a little below it nothing can grow on this piece of ground except rushes or other hardy plants designed by nature for this kind of soil. Accordingly we proceed to dig a number of small ditches, of a depth somewhat greater than that attained by plant-roots, and we fill the bottom of these ditches with small stones, on which we finally throw back the earth we have removed. These underground ditches are suitably inclined, and all empty at the lower end into a main canal. The water saturating the soil collects in these ditches, filters through the layer of pebbles, and empties into the main canal, which carries it off to some river or other stream. Our marshy soil is now like the potful of earth with a hole at the bottom, the bit of broken tile, and layer of little pebbles: the air has free access and brings fertility with it. This operation of ours is called drainage, a word formed from 'drain,' which is both a verb and a noun. In the latter sense we apply it to the narrow ditch dug for carrying off superfluous water.

"A drainage system like that just described is the simplest possible, but there is one serious objection to it: the layer of small stones soon becomes clogged with soil washed down by the water, and the latter can no longer run off. Hence it is customary to use fagots instead of stones, since they offer less obstruction. But still better results are obtained with earthenware conduits laid in the ditches. Sometimes these conduits take the form of drain-tiles such as are used on roofs, and they rest on sills or ground-pieces of the same material; or, again, they may be tubular in form, the successive sections loosely fitted together so that the water to be carried off may enter where the sections join.

"The effect of drainage is not merely to carry off the superfluous water and thus promote the aëration of the soil to the depth reached by the roots; it also keeps the soil cool and moist by the constant presence of water in the drainage ditches or pipes. When a heap of sand is watered at its base, the moisture is seen to mount higher and higher until it reaches the top. In like manner the water collected in our drainage ditches soaks into the upper soil in a dry time and thus reaches the roots of plants growing there, so that water which is superfluous or even harmful at certain periods is held in reserve and gradually distributed at the right moment.

"Another advantage of a drainage system is that it prevents that cooling of the soil which would result from prolonged evaporation. In taking the form of vapor water chills the objects that help to promote the evaporation. For this reason we feel a decided chill on emerging from a bath; the film of moisture that covered us is passing off in vaporous form. Similarly a constant evaporation at the surface of a water-soaked tract of land chills the ground and we have a cold soil. But if the water is carried off by proper drainage, evaporation ceases and there is no further chilling of the surface soil. Now, a high temperature is always favorable to vegetation.

"Draining is so beneficial that it is not confined to marshy ground, which without it would be quite unproductive, but is applied also to ordinary arable land. Wherever the soil is too clayey, or even where the surface soil is good but the subsoil clayey, rain-water cannot drain off readily and the ground remains soggy and cold. Eventually, however, it dries up, but there being no way for the air to permeate the soil, the latter is left hard and unyielding, so that the roots are by turns drowned in liquid mud and held fast in a tenacious paste that has been baked by the sun. Drainage overcomes these difficulties, and consequently all rich soils that hold rain-water for some time before infiltration are much improved by being properly drained."

CHAPTER XLIII

PARING AND BURNING

"YOU SEE that man over there on the hillside," said Uncle Paul, pointing to a laborer who, with a large hoe, was paring the ground, so to speak, by shaving off great squares of earth covered with grass and weeds and shrubs. "You see how he stands those pieces up, either in pairs, back to back, or one at a time, so bent or vaulted that they will stay upright by themselves. Thus the air is allowed to circulate and dry them rapidly. If we come back in a few days, after sun and air have done their work and the drying process is complete, we shall find our man there again at his work; and we shall see how he piles up the turf with the earthy side upward and outward. In the middle of the pile he leaves a cavity which he fills with brushwood and dry leaves. Then he sets fire to the whole. A second pile is constructed in the same manner and likewise set on fire. Soon the entire hillside is covered with a great number of these small furnaces, burning slowly and sending out long trails of smoke. In a few days, three or four at most, the fires burn themselves out, and then, as soon as all the piles are cold, the mixture of ashes and calcined earth is spread over the ground with a shovel. This agricultural operation is known as paring and burning, and is carried out for the purpose of rendering arable a tract of land not yet under cultivation and still covered with wild vegetation.

"The operation of paring and burning produces two effects,

one with reference to the clay in the soil, the other having to do with the ashes left from the burning of the weeds. Clay, as you know, is a tenacious, binding substance, impervious to both air and water. Consequently a soil that is too clayey is unfavorable for vegetation, furnishing the roots with insufficient air and moisture. Now, when clay is heated to a high temperature, it acquires very different properties: it no longer makes paste by the addition of water, but is porous, permeable, and readily admits air and water. The paring-and-burning process, therefore, improves an argillaceous soil by calcining the clay and rendering it permeable. That is as much as to say that if paring and burning are beneficial to heavy or clayey soils, they are, on the other hand, harmful to those that are light or sandy.

"Finally, the operation just described affects the soil through the ashes of the burnt weeds. After the combustion of all vegetable matter there remains an earthy powder or ash comprising the mineral substances contained in that vegetable matter, substances unchanged by combustion because of their great resistance to heat. The most important of these is potash. All the ingredients that once belonged to the burnt plants are evidently adapted to the formation of new plants. The ashes, then, of the weeds consumed in the process of paring and burning will be very useful to the plants about to be raised on the land that has been burnt over. By the burning, however, it is impossible to turn to account all that the weeds contained: what escapes in the form of smoke is so much lost. Hence care should be taken not to carry combustion too far. In this connection the calcined clay renders still another service. By becoming porous through calcination its nature is altered so that it can absorb and retain the gaseous products of combustion and thus save just so much waste. But if a soil lacks clay, paring and burning are harmful, and it is better simply to turn the weeds under, whereupon they will be converted into mold instead of being dissipated in the atmosphere as smoke.

"Ashes other than those resulting from paring and burning are also used as an agricultural fertilizer, though they are rarely put to this use just as they are, because the contained potash, a highly valuable substance, is first extracted by leaching. After this process the ashes are called buck-ashes. They contain silica and also carbonate and phosphate of lime, all in a condition most favorable for assimilation by plants. Of less strength than ordinary ashes, leached ashes nevertheless produce good results, especially on clayey soil. Coal ashes, too, it should be added, serve to lighten a heavy soil since they contain a large proportion of calcined clay.

"The subject of ashes leads us naturally to that of soot, a substance composed of vegetable matter incompletely decomposed by heat and containing ammonia, which renders it highly efficacious as a fertilizer. It is applied to young plants, giving them an increased vigor of growth. By its acrid quality, moreover, it is excellent as a protection against insects that attack vegetation."

CHAPTER XLIV

WINE-MAKING

"WHEN WINE is heated, there is first an escape of an inflammable vapor that burns with a bluish flame. A person needs only to have seen once this preparation of hot wine to recall that curious flame flickering over the boiling liquid and darting up little blue tongues. Now, this inflammable vapor comes from alcohol, a fluid substance that gives to wine its peculiar properties and is hence sometimes called spirits of wine. There are, then, in wine two distinct liquids, one easily reducible to vapor and called alcohol, the other slower to vaporize and recognizable as water. This does not mean that the wine has been watered: the water in question is not there as the result of fraud; it belongs naturally to the wine and comes from grapes just as alcohol does. Wine is therefore a natural mixture of a small proportion of alcohol with a great quantity of water. In our ordinary wines the proportion of alcohol for each hundred quarts of liquid varies from nine to fourteen quarts.

"Wine is made from the juice of grapes. This juice, as it is pressed out of the sweet grapes, has none of the taste or smell peculiar to wine, for it does not yet contain any alcohol; but it does have an agreeably sweet taste, the same taste that makes grapes so desirable a fruit for the table. This pleasant flavor is due to a sort of sugar present in the grapes. Examine carefully a handful of raisins such as you buy at the grocer's: you will detect on their surface, certain tiny white grains that crunch under the teeth and have a sweet savor. Those grains are little particles of sugar that have collected on the outside of the grapes during the process of drying. Grapes, then, must contain sugar.

"Well now, this sugar is exactly what causes the formation of alcohol. What is sugar in the fresh juice of grapes is alcohol in the same juice after it has fermented and turned to wine. Let us consider briefly how this change comes about.

"The vintage is first of all subjected to a process of treading by men who trample on the grapes in large vats, after which the resulting mixture of juice and skins is left to 'work,' as we say. Before long this liquid mush begins to heat of its own accord, and presently there sets in a sort of boiling which liberates big bubbles of gas as if there were a fire underneath. This working process is called fermentation, and its seat is in the sugar of the grape-juice. Little by little the sugar decomposes, splits apart as we might say, into two substances very different from each other and also very different from the sugar whence they came. Of these two substances one is alcohol; the other is a gas already known to us—carbonic acid, the same gas that plants feed on and that animals give forth in breathing; the same, finally, as that produced by burning coal. The alcohol remains in the liquid, which thus gradually loses its original sweet taste and acquires instead a vinous flavor. The gas, on the contrary, works its way to the surface, agitating the mass with a sort of tumultuous movement like that of boiling water, and is dissipated in the atmosphere.

"Let us bear in mind that carbonic acid gas is as invisible as the air itself, that it has no odor, no color, and finally that it kills quickly if inhaled in any considerable quantity. That explains the danger lurking in a wine-vat during fermentation, or even in a wine-cellar that lacks sufficient ventilation to carry off the perilous gas. No one should enter such places without holding before one a lighted taper at the end of a long stick. While the taper continues to burn in the usual manner, one can proceed without fear: there is no carbonic acid gas present. But if the flame becomes dim, gets smaller and smaller, and finally goes out altogether, one must beat a hasty retreat, for the extinction of the taper is a sure sign of the presence of carbonic acid gas, and further advance would mean exposing oneself to imminent death.

"But to return to the subject of wine-making, we were saying that the sugar which imparts its sweet taste to the must (that is, the unfermented grape-juice) changes its nature and divides into two parts: alcohol, which remains in the liquid and turns it to wine, and carbonic acid gas, which is dissipated in the atmosphere. When this process is finished the wine is drawn off, leaving behind the residuum of skins and pips. The final product is thus composed of a large quantity of water from the grapes themselves, a small quantity of alcohol from the sugar which has undergone the chemical change just described, and, finally, a coloring substance furnished by the dark grape-skins.

"White wine is made from white grapes, which have skins with no coloring matter; but it can very well be made from dark grapes, colored though they are. The secret consists simply in this: the crushed grapes are pressed before fermentation begins. In this way the juice is separated from the skins, and, these latter being removed, the wine will be white even with dark grapes. In short, the coloring matter in grapes which gives its hue to red wine is contained solely in the skins; and furthermore it is insoluble in water, but easily soluble in alcohol. Hence it is only after fermentation has made some progress that the liquid becomes colored by the dissolving of the coloring matter through the agency of the alcohol that has been generated. Accordingly, if the skins are removed before the juice ferments and generates alcohol, the wine remains white, since it no longer contains any coloring matter to dissolve.

"Some wines force out the corks from their bottles and are covered with foam on being poured into glasses. These are foamy wines, and to produce them the bottling must be done before fermentation is finished. The carbonic acid gas then continues to form, but as it finds no way of escape since the bottle is tightly corked, it dissolves in the liquid and accumulates there, though all the while endeavoring to free itself; and that is what makes the cork pop with a sharp report when the string that holds it down is cut; that is what causes the wine to rush foaming out of the bottle; and, finally, that is what gives the bead to a glass of wine and makes a slight crackling sound as the bubbles burst on the surface.

"Foamy wine has a pungent but agreeable taste owing to the carbonic acid it contains. We drink, dispersed through the liquid, the same gas as would kill us if freely inhaled; but it has no terrors except when thus inhaled. Mixed with our drinks, it imparts to them a slightly tart flavor, harmless and even salubrious, since it aids digestion. There is carbonic acid gas in nearly all water that we drink, and it is in fact by reason of this gas that water is able to hold in solution the small proportion of stony matter that contributes toward the formation of our bones. It is to this gas, finally, that effervescent lemonade, cider, beer, and Seltzer water owe their pungency and their foam."

CHAPTER XLV

THE STAG-BEETLE

"ONE OF the joys of your time of life, I am sure," resumed Uncle Paul, as he and his hearers seated themselves in the shade of an old oak tree amid the humming and whirring of insect life all about them, "is the study of the little creatures of field and farm and forest, so interesting in their mode of life, so varied in their forms and colors. You chase the splendid butterfly from flower to flower, you take up the cockchafer and put it on a bed of fresh leaves, with a straw you drive the cricket from its hole. The insect that amuses you can also instruct you. In our modest studies let us now have a little talk on this subject.

"What is this tiny creature with the stout coat-of-mail of chestnut color? Its large head, showing parallel folds that might have been carved by a sculptor's hand, is armed with two branching nippers which open like a pair of tongs and then close, mangling between their teeth the finger they have seized. Woe to the giddy-pate that lets himself be caught by them! The trap closes tighter and tighter and never lets go.

"But, vigorous as are its mandibles, the insect is not one to be afraid of, provided only you look out for those nippers. For all its threatening aspect, it is at bottom a peaceful creature. Catch it by one leg and it will fly round and round like the June-bug. It is called the stag-beetle, a name that explains itself, for it has branching mandibles resembling a stag's horns, and it belongs to

STAG-BEETLE

the family of beetles. Put the two words together and you have 'stag-beetle.'

"The singular creature has not always been as we see it to-day. In its youth, not later than last year, it had neither its present mandibles nor its six legs nor its chestnut-colored coat-of-mail. In fact, its form had nothing in common with what we now behold. Then it was a big, fat worm, with fine white skin, crawling on legs so small and feeble as hardly to deserve mention.

"The whole animal consisted of little more than a crawling stomach unprovided with any protection. The head alone was fortified with a substantial skull of horn, and it also bore, one on the right side of the mouth, the other on the left, two short but strong teeth adapted to cutting in pieces the wood of the oak, its sole nourishment.

"Such a worm, entirely naked, evidently cannot live in the open air, where the thousand little roughnesses of the ground would be continually wounding its delicate skin. It must have a safe shelter that it need not leave until it has become the well-armored insect we now see. The grub of the stag-beetle does in fact live inside the oak, which affords it at once food and lodging. There, in the depths of the tree-trunk, is its inviolable retreat.

"With its two teeth, as hard and sharp as a carpenter's tool, it cuts away, patiently, bit by bit, the fresh wood imbued with sap. Each fragment thus detached is a mouthful for the worm's nourishment; but as it is by no means a rich diet there must be a good deal of it to furnish enough nutriment. Therefore the gnawing goes on without cessation, in all directions, with a corresponding enlargement of the domicile, which soon becomes a labyrinth of galleries that go up and down and cross one another, penetrate farther into the trunk or approach the surface, at the pleasure of the occupant, whose choice is determined by its taste for morsels lying in this or that direction.

"For three or four years this is the worm's mode of life. To make itself big and fat is its sole business, and to this it devotes itself with vigor. I leave you to imagine what must become of an oak tree worked by a dozen of these gnawing creatures. Under the bark, which is almost intact, the trunk is one vast wound, perforated with galleries that are themselves littered with wormhole dust, and oozing with a brown juice that smells like a tannery. Unless the forester applies a remedy, and that speedily, the enormous oak will be ruined. Leaving this care to his charge, let us go on with our story.

"When it has become big enough and fat enough, after at least three years of continual feasting, the worm prepares to change its form. Near the surface, that its future exit may be the easier, the little creature hollows out a sufficiently large oval chamber and lines it with a sort of wadding made of the finest fibers of the wood. Thus the tender flesh of the rejuvenated insect will be protected from all rude outer contact.

"These precautions taken, the worm undergoes its transfiguration: it splits open all down the back, strips off its skin, throws it away like a discarded garment, and is born a second time, as one might say, but under a totally different form. It is no longer a worm—far from it—but it is not yet a stag-beetle, although the outlines of the latter are already discernible.

"The creature is quite motionless, as if dead. The legs, neatly folded over the stomach, are as transparent as crystals; the nippers are pressed close to the breast; the wings, not yet expanded, have the appearance of a short scarf encircling the flanks; and the whole is swathed in swaddling-clothes finer in texture than an onion skin. The entire organism is wrapped in a repose so profound that one might think all life extinct. It is white or crystalline in appearance, and so tender that a mere nothing will wound it. The coarse worm of the beginning has been succeeded by this most delicate of creatures.

"Out of the material amassed by the wood-gnawer's voracious appetite there is created an entirely new being. The flesh, at first nearly fluid, slowly acquires consistency; the skin hardens, assumes a chestnut hue, takes on the firmness of horn; in fact, when the warm season returns again the insect wakes up from that deep sleep, not of death, but nevertheless very much like it. The creature moves, tears apart the swathing bands under which its rebirth has taken place, strips off these wrappings, and here at last we have the insect in its full perfection. Behold the stag-beetle!

"It comes out from its native oak, spreads its wings in flight under cover of the foliage, and settles down, now on this tree, now on that, in the rays of the sun. The freedom of the open air and the enjoyment of the light of day constitute its supreme felicity for which it has been preparing during the three or four years of constant toil in the dark galleries of an old oak.

"Thenceforth it grows no larger. Just as it was on emerging from its cell, so it will remain to the end, without the least increase either in weight or in bulk. Thus it leads a very staid existence. In its grub state the famished creature gnawed wood night and day; its life was a perpetual digestion. Now, on the contrary, all that it needs in the way of sustenance is an occasional sip of the sweetened sap oozing from the bark of the tree.

"But its days of idle delight are numbered; it has scarcely

a couple of months to spend joyously among the oak trees. Then it lays its eggs, one by one, in the crevices of tree-trunks, to propagate its kind; and, that done, it very soon dies. It has played its part. From those eggs will come forth worms which will patiently work their way into the wood, hollow out galleries there in their turn, and begin all over again the very sort of existence led by their fore-fathers.

"The greater number of insects have the same life-history as the stag-beetle: they pass through different stages before taking on their final form. All without exception, the smallest as well as the largest, come from eggs deposited by the mother in chosen places where the needed nourishment, so variable in different species, is easy to find.

"From the egg emerges, not the finished insect with all its distinctive traits, but a provisional creature bearing, very often, no resemblance to the parent or to the matured offspring of that parent. This initial form we called a worm in speaking of the stag-beetle, and the name is in that instance appropriate; but in a multitude of cases it would be incorrect, having no agreement with the creature's appearance. We then call it a larva.

"The larva is therefore the insect under the form it presents on emerging from the egg. Its continuance in this form is longer than in that of the finally perfected creature. The larva of the stag-beetle remains a larva for three or four years, whereas the beetle itself lives but a couple of months. The sole occupation of this grub is eating, continual eating, that it may grow fat and store up supplies enough to carry it through its subsequent transformations.

"Having attained sufficient size, the larva constructs a retreat for itself, hollows out a little cell, and spins a cocoon where in perfect quiet the delicate task of transformation will be undertaken. It strips off its skin and becomes an inert, formative body known as a nymph.

"Finally, the nymph, having arrived at the right degree of maturity, casts off its wrappings and reveals itself as transformed into a perfect insect. It lays its eggs, and the same succession of changes is again repeated. The egg, the larva, the nymph, the perfect insect—there you have the four stages of the insect's life. These changes of form are called metamorphoses."

CHAPTER XLVI

SHEATH-WINGED INSECTS

"I SHOW you here the scarab, clothed all in black. Passionate lover of the sun, it rarely strays beyond the regions bordering on the Mediterranean. It belongs to the band of scavengers, a group of handsome insects which, feeding on ordure, are charged with the sanitation of the greensward defiled by grazing herds.

"Its favorite dish is the dung of horses and mules. With the toothed edges of its head it rummages in the dung; with its wide, serrate fore legs it cuts up this material, kneads it, and molds it into a ball about as large as an apricot. This done, the next thing is to seek out some quiet retreat far from the hubbub of its fellows who have been drawn to the spot for as much as a kilometer round about by the odor; and of course the booty must be trundled away to this secure retreat, there to be eaten at ease, without fear of predatory assaults from the envious.

"This task is performed in couples. One hooks on to the globule in front and pulls with head up; the other pushes from behind with head down. Heave ho! It starts, it rolls, under the combined efforts of the two partners. On the down grade the load again and again runs away with the team, which falls headlong, gets up again, and catches hold of the cargo once more with an ardor that nothing can discourage. Under the rays of a scorching sun this store of provision is thus dragged a long distance over the sand, across the greensward, and over ruts. Perhaps the scarabs find their bread at first not sufficiently compact, and seek to give it consistency by rolling it on the ground. Every one according to his fancy.

"At last a favorable spot is selected in a sandy tract. One of the two proprietors hollows out in all haste a dining-room, while the other stands guard without over the globular treasure, ready to defend it stoutly against any chance marauder. As soon as the dining-room is ready the provisions are stored away there, after which the two colleagues shut themselves up in their domicile, safe from unwelcome visitors, closing their door with sand. So there they are at table, with their heap of victuals in front of them; and now for a good feast! When the board is bare again, the two banqueters leave their dugout to gather together a new globule and resume their feasting.

"The scarab is not found everywhere, the more's the pity, for its manner of life is very curious to watch. Wanting this manufacturer of globules, we nevertheless do have everywhere other scavengers which work in somewhat similar fashion. Out of ordure they put together little balls of the size of a cherry, and sometimes they roll away their plunder, as does the scarab, bury it in the ground, and there regale themselves on it. Their trade of making these little balls or pills has given them the expressive name of pill-mixers.

"Let us pass on to other kinds. This one, for example, is called the calosoma. By reason of the elegance of its form and the richness of its coloring it is one of the most beautiful insects of our region. Its back has the brilliance of a gem such as no jeweler ever possessed. One would really take it to be made of gold, but gold of a peculiar sort and much richer than ours, flashing as it does with red, green, and purple glints. There is nothing to compare with this dazzling costume. It should be added that if the insect is taken between the fingers it emits, as a means of defense, a strong odor reminding one of a chemist's disagreeable drugs.

"The calosoma does not share the scarab's peaceful habits: it is an ardent hunter and leads a life of carnage. Its prey is the caterpillar, the bigger the better, whether smooth-skinned or hairy. If you happen to find a calosoma, put it into a good-sized bottle and give it for dinner a lusty young caterpillar as large as your finger. You will see with what ferocious satisfaction this drinker of blood will disembowel the poor worm, despite all its writhing and squirming, and will feast on its green entrails.

"The carabid, which is also a passionate lover of game, has the calosoma's activity and brilliance, but is of smaller size. Some are bronze in color, others golden, still others of a copper tint, or black edged with a superb violet. All explore with keen scrutiny the thick tufts of grass, and give chase to small prey such as larvæ, caterpillars, and worms. The most common example of this class wears a golden green coat and is a frequenter of gardens, where it makes war on all kinds of vermin. It is the little guardian of our beds of peas and beans, and of our flower borders. In honor of its services to the garden we call it the gardener.

"The calosoma and the carabid do not fly; they are made for running, as is evident from their long legs, their agile movements, and their lithe form. They chase the game in hot pursuit, or else lie in wait for it behind a leaf, but never pursue it on the wing. On the other hand, the scarab, the common June-bug, and a host of other insects fly very well."

"But why don't they all fly?" asked Emile.

"I will tell you," replied his uncle. "Look carefully at the June-bug a moment. It has two kinds of wings: on the outside two large and substantial scales of horn, and beneath these two fine membranous wings, expanded during flight, but carefully folded together and concealed when not in use. The outside scales are called elytra, or sheaths. They serve as a case for enclosing and protecting the delicate membranous wings, which alone are fitted for flying. The carabid and the calosoma have sheaths of splendid brilliance, it is true, but beneath these sheaths there are no membranous wings to spread themselves in flight and fold up again in repose. Hence these two insects are unable to fly.

"The dytiscus and the hydrophile, whose names signify 'diver' and 'water-lover' respectively, both frequent the waters of deep ponds, of ditches, and of pools. With their legs flattened out like oars, their very smooth bodies, arched above and keel-shaped below, they are first-rate swimmers and divers. It is a feast for the eye to follow the graceful agility of their oars when they row calmly on the surface or plunge beneath it.

"At the least alarm they dart quickly to the bed of the pond and take refuge amid the water plants. On the instant of diving their belly is seen to flash like a plate of polished silver. The reason of this borrowed sheen is found in a thin layer of air that they carry with them adherent to the belly. With this supply they will have air to breathe until, all danger past, they ascend again to the surface.

"In the matter of costume these two master-swimmers are of modest appearance. Both are of a very somber olive green, but in addition the dytiscus wears faded gold lace on its sheaths. If the pond dries up or ceases to please them, they can quickly betake themselves to another—not on foot, for their flattened legs, excellent as oars, are worthless in walking, but by flight, with the help of their membranous wings, ordinarily hidden under the sheaths, where the water cannot reach them.

"In old oak trees the larva of the capricorn-beetle, another ravager of forests, leads much the same kind of life as does the grub of the stag-beetle. Large in size, all black with gleams of chestnut, this insect is remarkable for its jointed horns, which are longer than its body. What can it do with these cumbersome ornaments? Does it wear them on its forehead to intimidate the foe? I would not venture to dispute the matter, but what I do know very well is that with its extravagantly long horns it frightens the inexperienced young pupil so that he dares not touch it, and he calls it the devil. All the same, the capricorn-beetle does not deserve the evil reputation it has got from the timid. It is perfectly harmless.

"Insects' horns are called antennæ. All have them, some longer and some shorter, now of one shape, now of another. In some instances they are flexible filaments, jointed chaplets; in others, short stems ending in either a cluster of little buds or a bunch of leaves pressed one against the other. See for example the burly and magnificent insect that browses the foliage of our pine-trees on warm summer days. It is called the pine-beetle. On a chestnut background it wears a sprinkling of white spots. The antennæ carry at the end a set of little plates or scales which open and shut like the leaves of a book.

"It is in place here to mention the common June-bug, furnished like the pine-beetle with antennæ bearing leaf-clusters at the end. I propose to tell you its story in detail; for, if this little creature is the joy of young people of your age, it is also the terror of the farmer.

"But first one word more to conclude our short story of sheath-winged insects. Their number is immense. Nearly all have membranous wings under the protecting case formed by the sheaths; and these can fly. Others, relatively few, are unprovided with membranous wings, and hence are unfitted for flight. This entire group bears the general name of *coleoptera*, meaning sheath-winged. A coleopter is any insect furnished with sheaths, whether it flies or not."

CHAPTER XLVII

THE JUNE-BUG

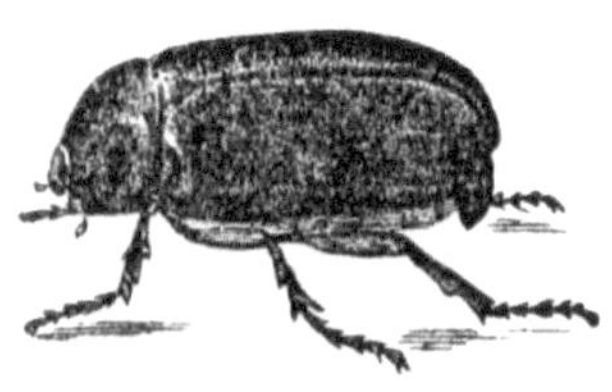

"IT IS a discovery of no small importance in your eyes, my young friends, when you find the first June-bug of the season on the young foliage. In the evening you get together in a corner and talk about it, you make plans for the morrow, and all your conversation is about the June-bug that has just arrived. You arrange to get up early the next day and shake the trees in order to bring down the sleeping insects; you get ready a box, pierced with holes, to receive the captives, and put in a handful of fresh leaves for them to feed on.

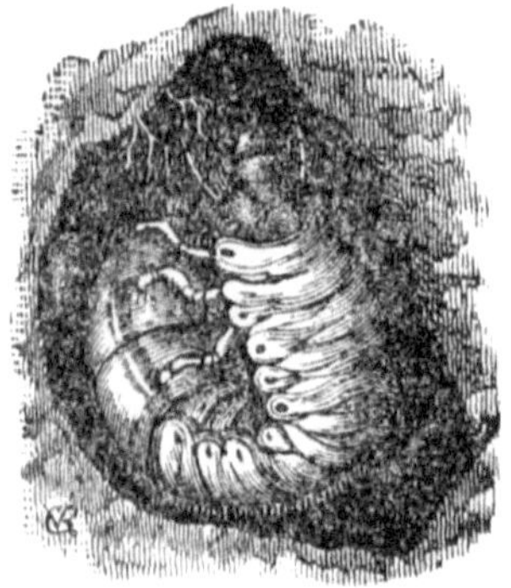

JUNE-BUG

"At the first streak of dawn you are up; you visit the willows, the poplars, the hawthorn hedges wet with dew. It is a fruitful hunt: the June-bugs, benumbed by the chill of night, fall like hail when you shake the branches. Soon you have a half a score of them, then a dozen, then twenty. It is enough. You go back to the house with your prisoners fluttering and struggling in the foot of an old stocking, in your handkerchief, or in your cap. You bring a supply of green leaves.

"And now for your experiments! You tie a long string to the leg of one of the beetles and put the insect in the sun. It inflates and deflates its belly, raises its wing-sheaths, and expands its wings. There it goes, into the air. Your experiment has succeeded. These delights of the June-bug season, my children—enjoy them as long as you can. Other pleasures pale beside them. In view of the amusement it affords you I gladly welcome the June-bug. But turn now to a less pleasing aspect of the matter.

"Like every other insect, the June-bug is at first a grub. In that form it lives three years in the ground, whereas in its final state, when it is found on trees and bushes, it lives but two or three weeks. This grub or larva is commonly called the white grub, also the fish-worm, and sometimes the ground-hog. Look at it carefully for a moment and tell me what you see."

"I see," answered Louis, "a fat, big-bellied worm, slow in its movements, and fond of lying curled up on its side. It is of a whitish color with a yellowish head."

"Yes, and what else?"

"It has six legs, not made for running on the surface of the ground, but for crawling underneath; and it has strong jaws for biting the roots of plants. Its head is capped with horn to help it in boring through the soil."

"Very good," was Uncle Paul's approving comment; "and you see how the stomach is distended with food, which shows in a darker tint through the white skin of the paunch. So gorged is the worm, in fact, that it cannot stand on its legs, but lies lazily on its side.

"For three years this fat grub lives under ground, always under ground, tunneling like a mole in all directions, and living on roots. Then it makes for itself a little chamber out of earth, very smooth inside, and shuts itself up there; after which it proceeds to transform itself into a nymph, and then into a June-bug. Everything serves it for food: the roots of grass and of trees, of cereals and of fodder, of vegetables and of flowers. In winter it buries itself deep in the ground and becomes torpid; at the approach of spring it returns to the upper layers of the soil, installs itself among the roots, and goes from plant to plant, leaving devastation in its path. You have, let us suppose, a fine bed of lettuce in your garden. From no apparent cause, some morning, you find it all withered. You pull up one of the plants, and it proves to have no root; the white grub has cut it away. Or you have a nursery of young fruit trees for your orchard. The terrible worm passes that way, and your nursery is good for nothing but fire-wood. Or you have sown several acres with wheat or rape, you have made a considerable outlay for fertilizer and labor; but there is promise of a handsome harvest with large profit to you. The larva of the June-bug works its way up from the depths, and then good-bye to your harvest; the stalks dry up as they stand, having no roots left to sustain them. When this formidable worm invades a country, famine would surely follow were it not that traffic facilities make possible the speedy importation of provisions from other lands. We live in a progressive age and, thanks to the means of transport and to the briskness of trade, people do not die of hunger in a province whose fields have been devastated by the white grub. They do not die of hunger, but what woe follows in the wake of the devouring larva! Year in and year out, it destroys millions of francs' worth of crops in France alone.

"The multitude of these little insects is truly terrifying. When they invade a field, the earth, undermined in all directions, loses its firmness and yields under the pressure of the foot. One year, in the department of the Sarthe, the ravages became so serious that it was necessary to undertake a systematic destruction of the pest. The June-bug was hunted on a large scale, and sixty thousand decaliters were gathered in, each decaliter containing about five thousand insects. Thus the total number taken amounted to three hundred millions. To give you some idea of the immensity of this number I will add that if you should try to count those three hundred million insects, one by one, it would take you more than twenty years, working ten hours a day.

"In the department of the Lower Seine there was at one time found to be an average of twenty-three larvæ of the June-bug to the square meter, or two hundred and thirty thousand devourers to each hectare. A hectare will raise a crop of one hundred thousand beets. Thus each beet was gnawed by at least two worms. Allowing eighty thousand rape-stalks to the hectare, we find each stalk feeding three worms, or very nearly. It is clear that under these desperate conditions no rape-seed oil or beet-root sugar can be produced. Every plant perishes. In the single year 1866 the Lower Seine lost from this cause about twenty-five million francs.

"In 1868, in different parts of France, notably in Normandy, the multiplication of June-bugs was so great as to spread alarm throughout the rural districts. Trees were completely stripped of their foliage, and in the evening, when the insects fly abroad, such clouds of them encumbered the atmosphere as to make it difficult to walk about. Almost everywhere there were June-bug hunts organized, and those who gathered the insects received from the public treasury from four to six francs per hundred liters. In one place alone, Fontaine-Mallet, near Havre, there were gathered four thousand and fifty-nine kilograms of the insects in four days. The school-master sent his pupils out after June-bugs, and four hundred and forty kilograms was the result of one day's collecting. All these insects were carted to Havre by the wagon-load and drowned in the sea. In certain communes they were brought to the town hall in such quantities that there was no way of disposing of them. The air reeked with the stench they made.

"It is said that in 1668 the June-bugs destroyed all the vegetation in one county of Ireland, so that the country presented the dead appearance of winter. The sound made by the insects' mandibles in browsing the foliage of the trees was like that of a carpenter's saw, and the hum of wings resembled the distant beating of drums. Enveloped in clouds of insects and blinded by the living hail, the inhabitants could hardly see to go about. The famine was horrible: the poor Irish people were even obliged to eat the June-bugs to keep from starving."

"Oh, how awful that must have been!" exclaimed the group of listeners.

"Yes, awful, indeed," assented Uncle Paul, "and I have a few more instances to relate, less lamentable than the Irish famine, it is true, but still of a nature to show us how prodigious were the legions of June-bugs in certain years. In 1832, in the neighborhood of Gisors, a stage-coach became enveloped at nightfall in a cloud of these insects. Blinded and terrified, the horses obstinately refused to go on. Finally there was nothing to do but turn about and go back, so completely did the humming swarm bar the way. Forty years ago the June-bugs descended upon Mâcon after ravaging the vineyards in its vicinity. They were scooped up in the streets by the shovelful, and to make one's way through the cloud of beetles one had to clear a passage by the energetic brandishing of a stick.

"Since the June-bug is so redoubtable a scourge to agriculture, since it is a foe with which one must reckon most seriously, how, you will ask, is it to be got rid of? There is one way, and only one: collecting and destroying both grubs and beetles. We can count to a certain extent on the help of moles, hedgehogs, ravens, crows, and magpies, all of which hunt the larvæ, especially in newly ploughed fields; and we can also count on the aid of a host of birds such as shrikes, sparrows, and others, which devour the beetles; but the number of the enemy is so great that this destruction by natural means does not always suffice. We must then lend an energetic hand ourselves. Which of the two is to enjoy the fruits of the earth, man or June-bug? Man, if he will but bestir himself and wage unceasing war on both the insect and its larva.

"The white grub, as I told you, bores into the earth more or less deeply according to the season. In winter it goes down half a meter, a depth at which it is protected from the frost. Upon the return of milder weather it comes up again, to be within reach of the roots; and from the first of April it can be found by digging down twenty centimeters. A favorable time, therefore, is chosen for turning up the earth and bringing the larvæ to the surface, whereupon women and children, following after the plough, gather up the white grubs in the furrows. A single hectare has been known to yield in this way from two hundred to three hundred kilograms of worms. The vermin are pressed down into the earth with lime, the whole making an excellent manure, and the enemy of harvests thus serves to accelerate their growth."

CHAPTER XLVIII

CATERPILLARS AND BUTTERFLIES

"O F ALL insects butterflies are the most graceful, the most worthy of childhood's eager desire. Oh, how beautiful they are! Poised on a flower, they seem to form a part of it and to animate it with the gentle beating of their wings. You cautiously draw near, you crouch down and make a quick clutch with the hand, but the beautiful creature is no longer there. It is waiting for you on another flower, quite unconcerned at your designs on its freedom. Let us leave it, then, to flit from one cluster of lilacs to another, and occupy ourselves a while with an account of its structure and habits.

"All butterflies have four wings suitable for flying, two upper and larger ones, and two lower ones half hidden under the others. Here we find no horny sheaths such as are worn by the scarab and the June-bug, no protecting case under which the membranous wings are folded to guard against laceration. The scarab is a clod-hopper, well acquainted with the harsh irregularities of the ground. He pursues his plodding course on foot, and it is only rarely that he spreads his wings in flight. The butterfly is a delicate creature of the air, very seldom using its legs for walking, but finding them of service when it alights upon a flower. It has, therefore, four broad wings, wide-spread and always ready for flight.

"And what wings! Words are lacking to describe them fitly.

Some are white as if coated with flour, others sky-blue, and still others sulphur-yellow. Again you find them of a flame-like red or dark crimson. Some have round spots like eyes, which look at you with their large pupils encircled by azure, mother-of-pearl, or gold; and you will see others speckled with black, adorned with silver lace, or fringed with carmine. If you touch them they leave on your fingers a brilliant powder beside which the filings of the precious metals would look dull.

"This dust might be called the butterfly's plumage. It consists of scales of extreme delicacy, placed regularly side by side like the tiles on a roof, and attached by one end to the membrane of the wing just as a bird's feathers have their quills implanted in its skin. Grasped roughly between the fingers, the wing parts with its delicate covering; it loses its ornamental scales and shows naked to the view. It is then a fine, translucent membrane traversed by a network of tiny ribs, or nervures, as they are called, which hold it expanded and give it firmness.

"At rest, butterflies do not all carry their wings in the same manner. Those that fly by day and go from flower to flower in

CATERPILLAR

full sunlight, hold their wings erect on the back and folded against each other. These butterflies are also recognized by their brilliant coloring, their lightness on the wing, their grace of form.

Those,[6] on the other hand, that fly either by night or at evening twilight bear their wings, in repose, either outspread or else lightly folded in a sort of roof-shape. They are of bulkier form and heavier than the first-mentioned, and sombre hues predominate in their costume.

"Whether friends of light or fond of darkness, whether courting the sunshine or lovers of the night, butterflies are invariably very abstemious, finding all the nourishment they require in the tiny drop of honey exuding at the bottom of a flower. Many flowers have long and narrow mouths; no insect muzzle is slender enough to reach into flasks like these and lap up the syrup, and therefore butterflies must have a special instrument adapted to the purpose.

"This instrument is the proboscis, as fine as a hair and long enough to reach to the exquisite drop, however deeply it may be hidden. When not in use, this proboscis is kept tightly coiled at the entrance to the insect's mouth. When it finds a flower to its taste, it uncoils this spiral and extends the proboscis in a long thread which plunges into the narrow-necked bottle and proceeds to suck up the coveted drop. If we wished to drink from a flask of similar shape, we should use a straw or reed. Its

6   The author does not, either here or later, distinguish by name, as might have been done, between butterflies and moths. The latter fly mostly in the evening or at night.—*Translator.*

proboscis is the butterfly's straw with which it takes its refreshment from the flowers.

"As with other insects, the butterfly is at first a larva or worm, very different, you understand, from what the creature will afterward become. The larvæ of butterflies are nothing in the world but caterpillars."

"Oh, how disgusting!" cried Emile, making a wry face.

"But nevertheless so it is," proceeded his uncle. "Caterpillars, repugnant creatures to us, change into those magnificent butterflies that we are never tired of admiring. What was ugly becomes beautiful, what was frightful finds itself the proud possessor of grace and charm.

"There are some caterpillars that have the skin quite naked and mottled with various colors in a manner not unpleasing to the eye. To touch these worms, even to handle them, inspires little or no fear, so harmless do they look. But there are others, of a larger size, which carry on the back, toward the rear, a menacing horn, a sort of hook, of which it seems prudent to beware. This apprehension, however, is groundless: the horn is inoffensive, being not a weapon but a mere ornament. Caterpillars thus equipped become large butterflies flying in the late evening twilight.

"Still others have an even more repulsive look, bristling as they do with clusters of prickles and with tufts of long hair. From these ugly creatures, whose very touch would be so disagreeable to us and would make us utter cries of fear, come some of the most beautiful butterflies of our part of the world. Such is the caterpillar that browses the leaves of the nettle and becomes the Vanessa Io or peacock-butterfly. It is black with white spots, and wears a rough armor of toothed prickles. The butterfly, the Vanessa, has wings of a bright brick-red adorned with a large eye of mingled black, violet, and blue. Who would ever imagine, unless he had seen the transformation or heard about it, that so ravishing a creature has such an origin?

"But for all their hairs and prickles caterpillars need cause us no alarm. Nothing about them justifies the fear they too often inspire. No caterpillar is poisonous, no caterpillar seriously injures the hands that touch it. Yet it is well not to repose full confidence in hairy caterpillars: sometimes the hairs become detached and cling to the fingers, causing rather lively itching sensations. But a little scratching ordinarily ends the trouble. Accordingly any one who should hereafter be afraid of caterpillars would not deserve the privilege of chasing butterflies.

"Every larva is a gluttonous eater, because it must grow big and accumulate the wherewithal for its subsequent changes of form. Nor are caterpillars lacking in response to this serious duty. The future butterfly's welfare is at stake. Made solely for eating, the larvæ gnaw and browse unceasingly. Each one has its own particular kind of sustenance, its chosen plant, and nothing else meets the requirements. The larva of the Vanessa selects the nettle and turns with aversion from all substitutes; that of the Pieris, a white butterfly with black spots, will have only the cabbage; that of the Machaon, a butterfly with large wings that end in a sort of tail, feasts on fennel; and so of others.

"After attaining the full size assigned to them by nature, caterpillars, like other larvæ, prepare for their transformation. Some shut themselves up in a cocoon made from a silken thread that they spin from their mouth, while others content themselves with binding together, by means of the small supply of thread at their disposal, particles of earth, bits of wood, and hairs plucked from their own body. Thus is obtained, at small expense, a sufficiently substantial temporary abode. Finally, still others, especially among the butterflies that fly in the daytime, merely seek a retreat on the side of some wall or against a tree-trunk, and there suspend themselves in a girdle of silk.

"These precautions taken, the caterpillar strips off its skin and becomes a nymph, but very different from that which the stag-beetle showed us. The coleopter, in its nymph stage, was already recognizable, with its branching mandibles, its legs folded on its stomach, and its wings enclosed in their sheaths. The butterfly, on the contrary, is not at all discernible under the casing of the nymph. This nymph, with skin as tough as parchment, is an object little indicative of its true nature and much more suggestive of the kernel of some strange fruit than of any animal form. Because of its shape, so different from that shown to us by ordinary nymphs, it has received a special name, that of *chrysalis*.

"This word means golden sheath. Sometimes, notably in the case of the Vanessa, the chrysalis is adorned with gilding; but in the great majority of instances the suggestive name is not deserved, a uniform chestnut hue, darker or lighter, being the usual color of the chrysalis. Ripened by long repose, this species of animal shell splits down the back and releases the perfect insect, complete in all its attributes. The butterfly passes a few festive days amid the flowers, and before dying lays eggs whence will spring caterpillars to continue the race."

CHAPTER XLIX

ANTS

"A NTS LIVE in communities, each containing many members, in underground abodes, where the young are reared. These communities are composed of three kinds of insects: males and females, recognizable by their large transparent wings, four to each ant; and the neuters, or workers, which have no wings. These last, the workers, build the house, take care of the community, rear the larvæ and bring them their food, distributing it to each one. The others do not work. To add to the population by furnishing an abundant supply of eggs is all that they are expected to do.

"As soon as the rays of the morning sun strike the ant-hill, the workers standing watch at the entrance hasten within, nudge their comrades with their antennæ to wake them up, run from one to another, urge them on, hustle them into activity, and put all the subterranean galleries into lively commotion. First of all, attention must be given to the larvæ, feeble transparent worms, without feet and unable to feed themselves and to grow unless they receive assiduous care from their nurses.

"Accordingly, aroused by the tumult caused by the workers rushing in from outside, the ants proceed to busy themselves with the larvæ and also with the nymphs, carrying them with all possible expedition into the open air and placing them where they will best be exposed for some time to the benign influence of the sun's heat. After this sun-bath they are returned to the darkness and stowed away in chambers expressly prepared for them. And now is the time for feeding the nurslings.

"Just as little birds receive the beakful of food, so do the larvæ take their nourishment. When they are hungry they raise themselves a little and seek the mouth of some one of the workers engaged in ministering to them. The nursing ant opens its mandibles and lets a tiny drop of sweetened liquid be taken from its mouth. Thus, one suck at a time, the nutritive juice is distributed until the entire brood is fed.

"But carrying the larvæ into the sun and feeding them will not suffice: they must also be kept in a state of extreme cleanliness. The workers bestow upon their charges the same tender care that the mother cat exercises toward her kittens. Over and over again they lick the nursling's body to give it perfect whiteness, and they tug cautiously at the wrinkled skin when the transformation draws near.

"Before casting this skin the larva spins itself a cocoon of silk, elongated and cylindrical in shape, pale yellow in color, very smooth, and compact in texture. Under cover of this protecting sac, the worm becomes a nymph. In this form the ant assumes its final shape, lacking only strength and a little firmness. All its members are distinct, but enveloped in a fine membrane which it must strip off to become a perfect insect.

"If you disturb an ant-hill you will see the workers hastening to carry away and put in a safe place certain cylindrical bodies having somewhat the appearance of grains of wheat and very inappropriately called ant-eggs. They are not the eggs of the insect, which are in reality much smaller; they are cocoons with their contents, larvæ at first, nymphs later.

"When the time comes for leaving its cocoon, the enclosed

ant is unable of itself to gain its freedom by piercing with its mandibles the silken envelope; it possesses nothing resembling the solvent liquid which the silk-worm holds in reserve in its stomach; nor has it at the forward end of its prison-cell a door for exit analogous to the curious paling provided for the great peacock-butterfly. It would perish in its silk sack if the working ants did not bestir themselves for its deliverance.

"Three or four of these mount the cocoon and strive to open it at the end corresponding to the prisoner's head. They begin by weakening the texture of the sac by tearing away a few threads of silk at the point where the opening is to be made; then, nipping and twisting the tissue so difficult to break through, they at last succeed in puncturing it with a number of holes near one another, whereupon the mandibles are applied at one of these holes just as one would apply a pair of scissors, and a narrow strip is cut away. At this hard labor the ants work in relays, toiling and resting by turn. One holds the narrow strip that has been cut, while a second enlarges the opening, and a third gently extricates the young ant from its natal sac.

"At last the insect comes forth, but unable to walk or even to stand on its legs, for it is still enswathed in a final membrane which it cannot strip off unaided. The workers do not forsake it in this new predicament; they free it from the satin envelope enwrapping all its members; with delicate care they extricate the antennæ from their sheaths; they disengage the feet and set the body at liberty. Then the young ant is in a condition to walk about and, above all, to take nourishment, which it greatly needs after all this fatiguing exertion. Its liberators vie with one another in offering the mouth and disgorging a little sweetened liquid. For some days longer the workers keep a watchful eye on their new companions and follow them about, acquainting them with the labyrinthine passages of their abode. Thus instructed, the young ants mingle with the others and share their labors.

"The nurses remaining at home to perform the household duties depend for their rations on the workers that go out to collect supplies. These latter bring them little insects, or pieces of those that they have dismembered on the spot when the entire prey is too large for conveyance. Whatever they may be, these provisions are passed around and are speedily disposed of by the assembled company. If the working ants chance to find ripe fruit or large pieces of game that cannot be divided into small parts, they adopt another mode of procedure. Placed in possession of so great riches, they content themselves with the juice alone, of which they imbibe copiously, then return home with stomachs full of liquid food which they disgorge, drop by drop, as fast as their hungry comrades present themselves.

"The ant in need of nourishment strikes rapidly with its antennæ those of the ant expected to render the desired assistance. Presently they are seen to approach each other with open mouths and tongues out in readiness for the transfer of the nutritive liquor from one to the other. During this operation the ant receiving the mouthful of sustenance keeps up an uninterrupted caressing, with fore legs and antennæ, of the ant ministering to its needs.

"Who is not familiar with the lice that infest plants, assembled in dense groups that contain each more members than one could easily count? There are black lice on the beanstalks, green ones on the rosebushes, their stomachs carrying, behind, two little tubes whence oozes from time to time a tiny drop of liquid. This liquid is the ant's main dependence for food. Let us follow an ant on its rounds among the plant-lice.

"It goes hither and thither among the motionless herd, which

Texas Red Ant

is nowise disturbed by its presence. Having found what it is after, the ant stations itself close to one of the lice, which it proceeds to caress with gentle taps of its antennæ on the little creature's stomach, first on one side, then on the other. The milch-louse allows itself to be seduced by these friendly overtures, and a drop of liquid oozes out at the end of the tubes, the ant sucking it up at once. A second louse is visited, and it too is solicited in the same caressing fashion. It yields its drop of liquid and lets itself be milked, after which the ant passes without delay to a third louse, which it coaxes in like manner. A fourth, probably already drained, withstands the wheedling, whereupon the ant, perceiving that nothing is to be hoped for there, proceeds to a fifth member of the herd and obtains what it desires. A few of these mouthfuls are enough to satisfy an ant, and then it returns to its home.

"Certain ants are great stay-at-homes: for them it would be a painful infliction to have to go out into the world. In order to spare themselves this necessity they raise plant-lice and pasture them in enclosures very near the ant-hill so that the milking may be done at leisure. These herded plant-lice are their precious possession, and the community is more or less rich as it owns more or less of this property. It constitutes the ants' flocks and herds, their cows and goats. They build underground stables among the grass-roots, and there keep the plant-lice which they obtain from a distance, just as we gather our domestic animals under the roof of barn or fold.

"Others display an even more curious ingenuity: they take possession of the lice living on some branch or twig of a growing bush, and, jealously watchful of their cattle, suffer no stranger to come and lay claim to the food-supply they themselves are preparing to appropriate. With their mandibles they drive off all intruders; they patrol the twig in vigilant defense and stand careful guard over their herds. If the danger becomes too menacing, they hasten to carry away their livestock and pasture it elsewhere, in a safe place.

"Or, as still another device, they take little pellets of earth and build around the twig a sort of pavilion, a structure with a very narrow opening, a sheep-fold, in a word, with a few leaves growing inside it and furnishing sustenance to the enclosed flock. In this quiet retreat the proprietors milk their ewes, safely sheltered from rain and sun and, most important of all, from alien ants.

"We have in this region a rather large reddish ant known as the red ant or Amazon ant, which cannot without help build its house, raise its larvæ, procure food, or even eat food; but with its hooked mandibles it is admirably equipped for fighting and pillage. Slaves are the object of its predatory raids, slaves to feed it, to go out after provisions, to build the ant-hill, and to rear the young. A small black or drab ant is the object of its slave-hunting excursions.

"In battalions of some thousands each the reds go forth in quest of a nest of drabs. They break into the ant-hill notwithstanding its occupants' resistance, and sack the underground city. Presently they take their departure, each with his plunder between his mandibles. They carry away, not the full-grown ants, since these could not be trained to serve in the strange ant-hill and would speedily make their way back to their former home, but the young ones, and the nymphs shut up in their cocoons.

"Hatched in the domicile of the reds, the ants issuing from the stolen cocoons look upon the natal ant-hill as their own and there fulfill their customary duties with diligence. They go out after provender, undertake all building operations, care for the larvæ of the Amazon ants, and feed their big and stupid conquerors who, once in possession of enough slaves, never leave home again."

CHAPTER L

THE ANT-LION

"ON THE margin of ponds and streams we may see, flying from one bulrush to another, certain insects with large transparent wings and abdomen long and slender like a piece of string. Some are of a bronze green color, others of a splendid indigo blue, while still others, somewhat larger, are clothed in mingled black and yellow. They are called libellulids or, more commonly, dragon-flies, and also devil's darning-needles.

"Do you recognize the insect? Haven't you ever run after it? Perched on a reed that trembles in the current, it seems to be

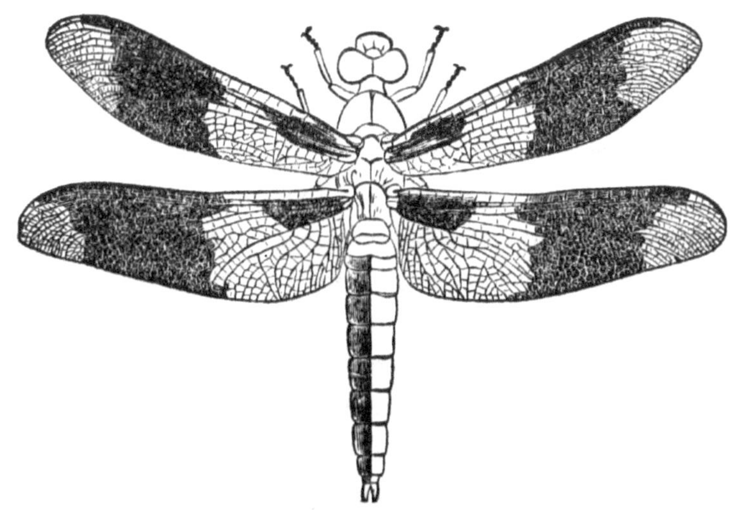

A COMMON DRAGON-FLY, NATURAL SIZE

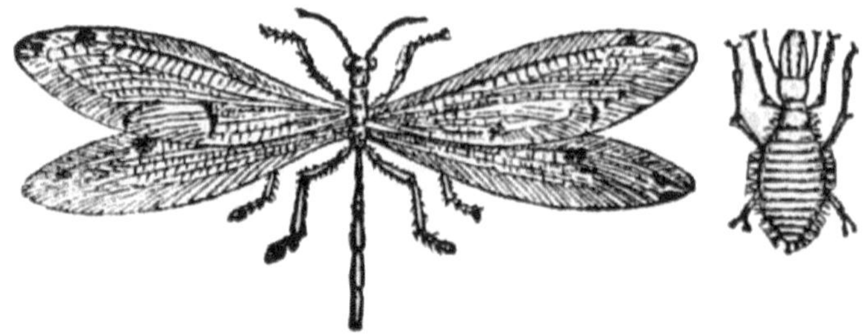

Ant-lion

dozing and waiting for you, its wings extended to the utmost. Your hand darts out to seize it. Good-bye, darning-needle! It is ten paces away from you."

"Yes, indeed," replied Louis, "every one has chased darning-needles, but I never knew of any one's catching them. And we don't have to go so far as the brook or the mill-pond to find them, either."

"No; not all of them are lovers of water. Some, in fact, avoid it and prefer sandy places parched by the burning sun. A modest gray is their uniform, but they make up for their lack of brilliancy by their curious mode of life while they are still in the larva form. The picture that I show you here illustrates what these gray dragon-flies look like at an earlier stage.

"A singular creature and not exactly ingratiating in appearance. It would not be very pleasant to encounter one in a lonely nook in the woods, little adapted though its size is for attacking us. Look at its ferocious pointed nippers, opening and closing like a pair of tweezers. Do they not betoken a thirst for blood? As a matter of fact, the little creature lives by carnage exclusively; it is a hunter whose game is the ant. Hence its name of ant-lion, or, as it might be put, the lion of the ants.

"Prey of that sort is incapable of serious resistance when once it has been seized by those terrible hooks; but it must first be seized, and there is the difficulty. The nimble ant scampers off at the first approach of danger, and if it should chance to be hard pressed it has only to run up a blade of grass and there be out of reach. The ant-lion, on its part, heavy of paunch and short of leg, drags itself along very awkwardly; and, moreover, if it ever undertakes to get over the ground—a rare occurrence—it always moves backward, which is not what might be called a speedy gait and does not adapt itself to keeping the object of one's pursuit always in sight.

"The chase being thus rendered impracticable, there remain the snare and the ambuscade. The creature must capture by cunning what its sluggishness of movement makes it impossible to get possession of otherwise. Let us see what form this cunning takes.

"Hunt at the base of sun-exposed walls and rocks, and if you find there some little nook with very fine and dry sandy soil, the ant-lion will seldom fail to be there too. Its abode is easily recognized by the regular funnel-shaped hollow scooped in the ground. The insect itself is invisible, being hidden under the sand at the bottom of the excavation.

"With the blade of a knife thrust obliquely into the ground lift up the bottom of the funnel, and you will have the little creature, rather abashed at first by the sudden destruction of its retreat, but soon recovered and striving to hide itself in the soil by a backward movement. Make haste to take it and put it into a glass under a layer of fine sand like that beneath which you found it. There at your leisure you can watch it as it hollows out its funnel, a pitfall for catching ants. You will see it put into practice the cunning wiles of an ambushed hunter.

"Let us for a moment stand as onlookers, mentally at least, while this work goes forward. Placed on a bed of sand and restored from its former dismay, the ant-lion proceeds to plunge its belly halfway into the soil; then, with this substitute for a plowshare, and always moving backward, it draws a circular furrow. Returning to its starting-point it draws a second furrow close to the first, then a third next to the second, and so on with a great many more, each one of smaller circumference than the preceding, so that they all together form a spiral which constantly approaches the center; and as this living plow is driven deeper and deeper at each circuit, and throws outward the soil that it turns up, the final result is a funnel of about two inches in diameter and somewhat less in depth. There you have the ant-lion's trap, the treacherous pitfall in which the ants are caught.

"Of course the huntsman employing such a device as this must himself keep well out of sight. The ant-lion is too well versed in its art to violate this elementary principle. It crouches down under the sand at the lowest point of the upturned funnel, with only its nippers showing, and these are pressed close to the ground, but wide open and ready to seize any luckless ant that may chance to tumble down the incline. Although the horrible pincers are exposed, they are not likely to excite suspicion, being easily mistakable from the edge of the excavation for some stray bits of dead leaves.

"These preparations completed, the insect lies in wait, perfectly motionless. Its patience and its hunger are subjected to prolonged trial. Hours and even days pass with no sign of game. Alas, how difficult it is in this world even for an ant-lion to win its mouthful of bread!

"But at last there comes an ant, on business bent that takes it into these parts. Preoccupied with its own concerns, it takes no heed of the pitfall. Hardly has it approached the edge of the chasm when the sand, which is extremely unstable, gives way under the little creature's feet. There is a land-slide, and with it down tumbles the incautious ant. In mid-course it succeeds by desperate efforts in arresting its descent. It struggles to regain the upper level; its tiny claws, trembling with fear, catch as best they may at the roughness of the slope; but as soon as touched these supports yield, and the down-rush begins anew with irresistible impetus.

"One grain of sand, more firmly planted than the rest, offers some resistance. Perhaps safety will be found in this point of support if it continues to withstand the strain. It holds firm, surely enough. The ant climbs up a little, heedful of its steps for fear of precipitating another slide. It has almost gained the edge of the excavation and seems about to find its feet once more on firm ground. Will it indeed escape scot-free?

"Oh, no. The hungry watcher at the bottom of the funnel will have something to say on that subject. He intends to make a good dinner on the ant. If things had followed their customary course and the imprudent victim, caught in the trap, had continued to slide down until within reach of the nippers, these would have seized their prey without further formality; but since the game seems about to escape, it is the huntsman's part to employ the manœuvres reserved for difficult cases.

"The ant-lion's head is flat and somewhat shovel-shaped. The insect plunges it into the sand and then, with a sudden movement of the neck, throws the shovelful up into the air so that it will come down again on the ant. Other shovelfuls follow in quick succession, better and better directed, and fall back in a hail-storm on the now nearly exhausted ant.

"Against this shower of sand resistance is impossible when one stands on a treacherous footing that gives way at each attempt to escape. The poor victim is swept away and rolls to the bottom of the funnel. Instantly the nippers seize their prey, and all is over. The huntsman goes to his dinner, not gnawing the fruit of his patient skill, since it is too tough for that, but sucking the juice like the refined epicure he is.

"When there is nothing left of the ant but a dry husk, the ant-lion loads it on to his head and with an upward toss throws it out of the funnel, in order not to defile his place of ambush with a useless corpse which might arouse the distrust of passers-by. Then a little careful mending restores the pitfall to its former mobility, and the huntsman waits patiently for another ant to take a false step and slide down into his lair."

CHAPTER LI

VENOMOUS ANIMALS

"AMONG VENOMOUS animals there are some whose poisoned weapon has no other purpose than to serve as a means of defense. Such is the bee, the worker in honey of our hives; such also is the burly, hairy bumblebee, which also gathers a store of honey, but keeps it underground in rude little pots of wax. Let us not molest them at their task, either intentionally or otherwise, and they will not molest us. If we irritate them, they straightway draw on the aggressor and stab him with their venomous dagger. This weapon they carry for defense, not for attack.

"But there are other and more redoubtable creatures that use their venom for killing quickly, and without any dangerous struggle on the victim's part, the prey on which they feed. Of course the offensive weapon is capable of becoming also a defensive one in moments of peril: that which serves to kill the prey serves likewise to repel the enemy. Among animals making this double use of their venomous weapon, first for attack and then for defense, let us note the scorpion and the viper.

"The scorpion is a hideous creature and of interest to us solely on account of its sting. It has a flattened stomach, dragging on the ground, and no distinct head. In reality it has a head, but so little differentiated from the rest of its body as to give a truncated appearance to the whole. On each side are four

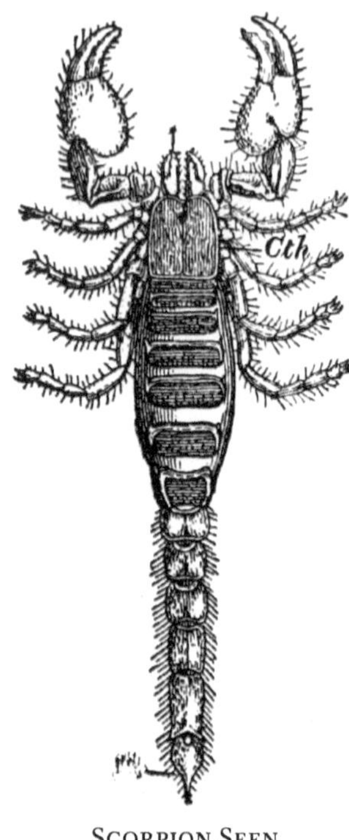

SCORPION SEEN
FROM ABOVE

feeble legs, and in front a big pair of nippers like those of the crab. Behind is a sort of jointed tail, the terminal joint of which, more swollen than the others, serves as reservoir for the venom. It ends in a hook, very sharp and with a microscopic perforation at the point, from which the venomous fluid escapes at the instant of attack.

"In this jointed tail with its terminal sting you behold the scorpion's implement of the chase, a terrible weapon which kills immediately, at one stroke, any small game the animal may have seized. It is carried bent over on the back, ready to inflict its deadly wound in front or behind with the suddenness of a released spring. The two-jawed nippers, of which only one jaw moves, are harmless despite their menacing appearance. They are a sort of tongs used by the animal to hold within reach and prevent from escaping the prey it is about to sting.

"The scorpion is carnivorous, feeding on all game adapted to its size, such as wood-lice, insects, spiders. Endowed with but little agility, it leaves its lair by night and under cover of the darkness hunts its sleeping prey. Let us suppose it to chance upon a big spider. That is indeed a succulent morsel, but its capture involves danger, for the spider on its side is armed with two venomous fangs in its mouth. Being both thus equipped with deadly weapons, which of the two will succumb? It will be the spider.

PLUMED VIPER, OR PUFF-ADDER, ONE OF THE VIPERIDAE

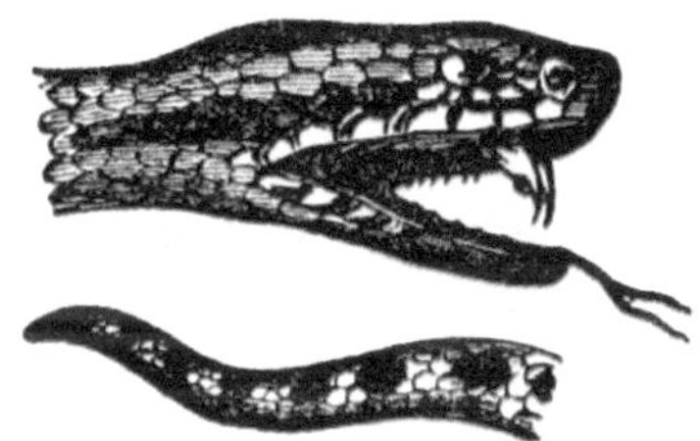

HEAD AND TAIL OF COMMON VIPER WITH ERECT FANGS

"The scorpion seizes it with its two nippers and holds the victim far enough away to avoid the risk of a bite. Then the coiled tail quickly straightens out over the scorpion and proceeds to inflict a sting on the helpless captive. It is all over. The stricken prey gives a momentary shudder in its death agony and then collapses, lifeless. The huntsman can now feast on his victim at leisure and in perfect security.

"We have in France, in the southern departments, two species of scorpions, of which the smaller and more common is of a greenish black. Its customary haunt is under the stones at the base of old walls, the favorite lurking-place of the wood-louse and the spider; but it also very often finds its way into human habitations, where it hides in dark corners. In rainy weather it snuggles under the linen laid away in cupboards, and even creeps under the bedclothes. Not a pleasant experience is it to find this baneful intruder, some fine morning, in the foot of one's stocking. One shakes out the frightful creature and treads it under foot. If it has stung you, the pain is no joke, though not seriously dangerous.

"The other species, much larger and far more to be dreaded, is found almost exclusively in Languedoc and Provence. It is straw-color in hue and inhabits sandy hillocks where the sun beats down with the fiercest heat. There, under some large stone, it digs itself a den, a spacious retreat, whence it issues only by night in quest of something to eat. It is never known to intrude into houses, nor does it ever leave the warmth of its desert solitudes. Unless you disturb it by lifting up the flat stone that roofs its abode, you run no risk of encountering the sting; but woe to the reckless one who should rashly venture to rummage in that retreat. The creature's sting is sometimes deadly, they say.

"The viper makes its home, by preference, on some warm and stony hillside, where it lurks under the stones and in the tangled underbrush. Its color is brown or reddish, with a darker zigzag stripe on the back and a row of spots on each side. Its belly is of a gray slate-color, and its head, larger than the neck, is blunted as if cut off in front.

"It is an extremely timid creature and never attacks man except in self-defense. Its movements are brusque, irregular, and heavy. Like all serpents it feeds on live prey, especially insects and small field-rats. To capture these quickly and to deprive them of the power to defend themselves, the viper first inflicts a venomous wound, as does the scorpion.

"All serpents dart out and in between their lips, with extreme velocity, a black, thread-like member, forked at the end and of great flexibility. Many persons take this to be the reptile's sting, though in reality it is nothing but its tongue, a tongue void of offense and used by its possessor to snap up insects and also to express, in the snake's peculiar manner, by quickly passing out and in between the lips, the passions that agitate the creature. All serpents have this sort of tongue, but in these regions it is only the viper that possesses the terrible weapon for inflicting venomous wounds.

"This consists, first, of two fangs, or long, sharp teeth, situated in the upper jaw. These curved teeth are movable, starting up for attack, at the reptile's will, or lying down in a groove of the gum and remaining there as inoffensive as a stiletto in its sheath. Thus the risk of a self-inflicted wound is avoided. These fangs are each pierced from end to end with a narrow channel having at the tooth's point a minute opening through which the venom is discharged into the wound. Finally, at the base of each fang is a tiny sac filled with venomous liquid. As with the bee and the scorpion, this liquid is harmless in appearance, free from odor, and without taste—little else than water, one would say. When the viper attacks with its fangs, the venom-sac presses a drop of its contents into the dental canal and the terrible liquid passes into the wound. In short, the whole operation exactly corresponds to the similar procedure I have described in speaking of the bee's sting.

"Let us suppose you are so imprudent as to disturb the reptile as it lies asleep in the sun. Immediately the creature uncoils itself and, with jaws wide open, smites your hand. It is all over in a twinkling. Then, with the same rapidity, the viper recoils itself and settles back again, continuing to threaten you, with its head once more the center of the spiral coil.

"You do not wait for a second attack; you beat a hasty retreat; but, alas, the harm is done. On your wounded hand you discover two tiny red spots, apparently of little more significance than the sting of a bee. No cause for alarm, you say to yourself if you are unacquainted with the effects of such a wound. But it is a false reassurance.

"Presently the red spots are encircled with a zone of livid hue. With a dull sensation of pain the hand becomes swollen, and gradually the swelling extends to the entire arm. Before long there follow cold sweats and a feeling of nausea, breathing is rendered difficult, vision is clouded, the intellect is torpid, and unless timely aid is rendered death may be the sequel.

"What is to be done in the face of such danger? One must press tightly or even bind fast the finger, the hand, the arm, above the wound, in order to prevent the passage of the venom into the blood. The wound must be made to bleed by the exercise of pressure all around it; it must be energetically sucked to draw out the venomous liquid. I have explained to you in speaking of the bee, and I now repeat it, that venom is not a poison. It will not act, however powerful it be, unless it mixes with the blood. Sucking it, therefore, is without danger if the lining of the mouth is intact.

"It is plain that if, by energetic suction and by pressing until the blood flows, we succeed in extracting all the venom from the wound, the latter will henceforth be of no serious importance. For greater security, as soon as possible the wound should be cauterized with a corrosive fluid, such as ammonia or nitric acid, or even with a red-hot iron. Cauterization acts in such a manner as to destroy the venomous matter. It is painful, I admit, but one must submit to that in order to escape something worse.

"Cauterization falls within the physician's province; but

the preliminary precautions—ligature to stop the spread of the venom, pressure to make the envenomed blood flow, and suction to extract the venomous liquid—are matters for our personal attention; and all this should be taken in hand immediately, since the longer the delay the more serious the case becomes. When these precautions are taken it is very seldom that the viper's bite has fatal consequences."

CHAPTER LII

THE PHYLLOXERA

"IN OUR talks on ants a few words were said concerning their milch-cows, plant-lice. You haven't forgotten those curious herds with udders in the form of two little tubes that emit, from time to time, a sweetened liquid. The ant comes and milks these cows, caressing them as it does so with its two antennæ. It fills itself with their milk, making its stomach serve the purpose of a milk-pail, and then runs back, all bursting with the delicious fluid, to disgorge it into the nurslings' mouths.

"These ant-cows are watched over with jealous vigilance; in case of need they are pastured within enclosures, for fear of marauders. So far all is for the best: the ants' cattle afford us some passing amusement, and apparently they are open to no serious reproach. But if we pursue our inquiries further the plant-lice will reveal themselves to us under a far more serious aspect.

"Let us speak first of rosebush lice. You wish to pluck a rose. Its perfume fills the air, its form and color rejoice the eye. But just as you are about to break the stem what do you find under your fingers? At the base of the flower and all over the branch that bears it, the superb plant is contaminated with a legion of green lice; a host of odious vermin has taken possession of it; the magnificent has associated with it the disgusting. The eye is offended; the fingers recoil before this species of animated bark which the slightest pressure turns into a sticky mush. Let us pluck the rose nevertheless, and before shaking the lice from it let us examine them a moment.

"They are light green in color, big-bellied, and wingless. With a little attention we distinguish the two minute posterior horns whence oozes the liquid on which the ants regale themselves. They have, underneath, a sucker, straight and very slender, a sort of bore which they push into the tender bark to extract from it the juices on which they live. The sucker once implanted at any convenient point, the animalcule seldom stirs from that spot. If it does decide to move a little, it is because its well has run dry and it must bore another close beside it. A promenade of merely the length of the branch is a liberty that only the most adventurous dare allow themselves. As a rule, the plant-louse sticks to the spot where it was born, to the very end."

"But how can the stem of a rose get so completely covered with those little green lice?" asked Emile.

"That is easily explained," answered his uncle. "Plant-lice multiply very rapidly, since each one, without exception, from the first to the last, whatever their number, becomes capable in a few days of procreating a family. The newly born settle down beside their mothers, and are themselves soon surrounded by their own progeny. These in turn, in a little while, have offspring of their own; and so on, indefinitely, as long as the season lasts. Thus the stem, the branch, the entire plant, become covered with lice so closely packed one against another that in places the real bark is hidden by this bark of vermin.

"Have you ever seen a garden-patch of broad beans overrun by black lice? There, better than anywhere else, may be seen the rapidity of propagation. On that green expanse appears at first a small black stain, announcing the beginning of the inva-sion. It is a family of lice installed at the top of a beanstalk, the tenderest part of the plant, where the insects' suckers can work to best advantage. The gardener, as soon as he is aware of what is going on, hastens to cut off this part of the stalk and crush it under his heel. He hopes to exorcise the evil by destroying this nest of vermin.

"His hope is short-lived. A few days later, instead of one plant invaded there are dozens. He lops off again; he turns up the remaining leaves and examines them one by one; he crushes what vermin he finds, taking all pains to make the extermination complete. Will he make an end of it this time? Not at all: the black hordes reappear in greater numbers than ever; the invaded stalks can no longer be counted. A few lice that escaped the slaughter were enough to infest the whole patch of beans. The foliage hangs down, foul and withered; the young pods, riddled with punctures and corrugated with scars, shrivel up and can grow no larger. For this ill there is no remedy; the harvest is ruined.

"The gardener pulls it all up and throws it on the dung-hill. His care and vigilance have been unable to arrest the invasion. In vain he crushed legions at a time under his angry heel: in a few days the half-dozen survivors had propagated a larger colony than ever. Man is hardly in a position to contend successfully against this lowly vermin which braves extinction by virtue of its countless numbers.

"As I told you, the plant-louse does not like to change its place. It plants its sucker on the very spot where it has just been born, and thenceforth sticks to that spot, filling its stomach with sap and surrounding itself with a family. This love of repose explains to us very well how the twig of a rosebush or the top of a beanstalk undergoes a progressive colonization; but it does not account for the distant propagation of the species.

"With its home-keeping habits the insect ought to be confined within narrow limits, on a single leaf and not on all leaves, on one rosebush and not on the neighboring rosebushes. But as a matter of fact it is disseminated everywhere. When one patch of beans becomes infested, those in the neighborhood are equally unfortunate; when one rosebush shows a colony of plant-lice, all those around it are similarly visited. No vegetable growth can defend itself from the pest. How, then, is it that this obese animalcule, which totters with fatigue after one step forward, succeeds in passing from rosebush to rosebush, from garden to garden? By what means is it able to spread in all directions without limit?

"Let us examine a number of rosebushes, and we shall have a prompt answer to our question. In addition to the wingless plant-lice, big of belly and all grouped on the tender twigs, we shall see others, green like the first ones, but more elegant in form, of greater freedom of movement, and provided with four wings, very beautiful wings too, diaphanous and gleaming with rainbow tints. These creatures are no lazy sap-bibbers forever squatting over the well their sucker has bored. They are seen to come and go, circulating briskly among the stationary herd, inspecting the foliage, passing from branch to branch, and even taking flight for some distant goal. They are the travelers of the family. Their function is to propagate the race in the surrounding district, with the aid of their wings, and even at considerable distances when a puff of wind carries them thus far.

"Two classes, then, dissimilar though related, are to be noted among the green lice of the rosebush and the black ones of the beanstalk, as also among countless others. The members of one class have no wings; they pass their lives where they were born, and multiply in serried legions. Those of the other class, which is relatively small, are equipped with wings. Confined

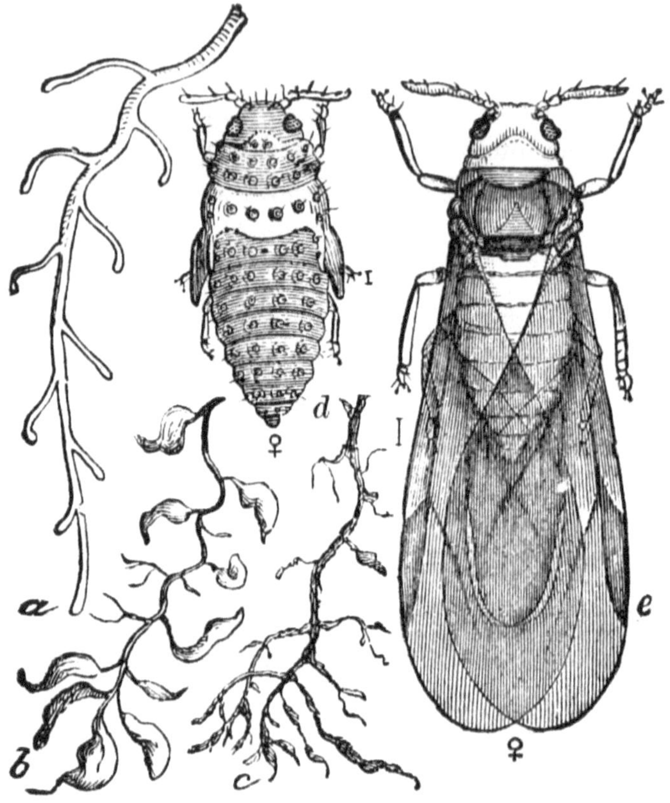

VINE-PEST (PHYLLOXERA VASTATRIX)
A, HEALTHY VINE ROOTLET; B, ROOTLET SHOWING NODOSITES;
C, ROOTLET IN DECAY; D, FEMALE PUPA; E, WINGED FEMALE, OR MIGRANT.
(HAIR LINES SHOW NATURAL SIZES.)

to no one spot, they fare forth as some passing breeze or their own strength of wing may determine, and deposit in favorable localities the germs that are to serve each as the beginning of a community of wingless plant-lice. The first kind procreate on the spot with a fecundity almost beyond belief; the second take leave of the stationary family and go out to start new centers of population in various quarters. The first propagate without limit; the second colonize.

"To soil the stem of a rose with a coating of lice is not exactly a capital offense; but to lay waste a field of beans, the hope of the farmer, is a far more serious matter. Yet even that is as nothing when compared with other depredations committed by plant-lice. There is a species of these insects that lives underground, subsisting on the roots of the grape-vine. Oh, the hateful creature! Never has agriculture known anything to equal the ravages it commits; no floods or droughts or inclement seasons have ever wrought such woes. Its terrible sucker has, up to the present time, caused us losses estimated at the fabulous sum of ten milliard francs. What a mouthful for a miserable little louse hardly visible to the naked eye! And to think that the combined efforts of nations cannot succeed in exterminating this pest! Alas, how feeble is mere force when confronted with the exceedingly minute infinitely multiplied!

"This destroyer of the vine is known as the phylloxera, a name strange to our tongue, but losing nothing of its impressiveness in translation. 'Phylloxera' means 'witherer of leaves.' The plant-louse thus denominated does indeed cause the foliage of the vine to wither up—not acting on the leaves directly, it is true, but attacking the roots. These, done to death by the insect's sucker, cease to draw from the soil the nourishment needed by the vine. The vine-stock wastes away, and with it the leaves, which become yellow and withered.

"It is not merely the foliage, then, that the phylloxera dries up; it withers and kills the whole vine. Moreover, the name it bears was not invented expressly for it, but was borne by another before the ravager of vineyards became known. The louse that was first called phylloxera lived at the expense of the oak-tree and took up its station on the leaves, sucking the sap from them. There you have the true witherer of leaves. The vineyard louse has therefore inherited an old appellation which fails to indicate fully the seriousness of the creature's depredations.

"This last-named insect is a tiny yellowish louse, plump of body, but hardly discernible to untrained eyes, its length being barely three quarters of a millimeter. It lives in clusters on the minute ramifications of the roots wherever the bark is tender enough to enable it to push in its sucker. Its ranks are so dense that the infested rootlets wear a continuous coating of vermin which stains the fingers with yellow. It lays its eggs in little heaps in the interstices that occur in the swarming colony; and these eggs are oval in shape and sulphur-yellow at first, but turn brownish as the moment for hatching approaches.

"From these eggs there come, in a few days, new layers of eggs, which settle down beside the earlier comers and add their own progeny to the already overgrown family. Thus, as long as the season continues favorable, these myriad numbers of successive generations are added to the existing myriads, until the thread-like rootlets become completely hidden by the accumulated layers of eggs and the eggs themselves.

"Riddled with punctures, the rootlets swell up at intervals and present the appearance of a string of elongated seeds. Thus deformed, fatally injured in their delicate suckers, the roots cease to imbibe the nutritive juices of the soil, the famished vine languishes for a time, putting forth only feeble shoots that are incapable of bearing fruit, and at last the whole plant dries up and dies. To secure its own prosperity the louse has killed its nurse."

CHAPTER LIII

THE PHYLLOXERA

(Continued)

"THE YELLOW plant-louse found on the roots of the grape-vine," resumed Uncle Paul, "has no bent for traveling: wingless, sluggish, and big-bellied, it is ill adapted to locomotion. Where once its sucker has implanted itself, there the creature is glad to abide as long as the place is tenable. But when the rootlet dies and begins to decay, then a new refectory must be sought out, with a better-furnished table. Accordingly the louse has to move. A persistent explorer, it knows how, with patience and in course of time, to make its way through cracks in the soil from one root to another, and dares even to climb to the surface, where, proceeding in the open air, it emigrates from the exhausted vine-stock to the neighboring one rich in sap; and there it pushes down to the roots through some fissure in the ground.

"To this slow-goer a single one of our steps would be a journey of excessive length. Therefore, to propagate its kind far and wide, it must have other and quicker means than the extremely deliberate method of locomotion just described. This other method for planting colonies at a considerable distance has already been illustrated for us by the green louse of the rosebush. Like that species, the phylloxera has a special division of winged travelers, and it is these that propagate the race throughout the grape-growing district.

"At the time of the greatest midsummer heat there make their appearance, amid the throng of yellow lice covering the roots, certain individuals with longer bodies, which soon change their skin and then bear on their sides two pairs of black stumps, the sheaths of four future wings. These are the nymphs destined for emigration. These nymphs leave their subterranean abode and climb up to the foot of the vine-stock, or sometimes even out upon the surface of the ground. There another change of skin takes place, whereupon we behold the winged insect, superior in form to its underground relatives.

"It measures a little more than a millimeter in length, not including the wings. These latter, transparent and iridescent, extend far beyond the length of the body, and the upper ones are wide, rounded, and slightly smoke-colored at the end, the lower ones narrow and shorter. They are supported by strong sinews that denote great power of flight. With its large, diaphanous wings, its broad head and big eyes, its belly ending in a blunt point, and its yellowish color, the traveling insect bears some resemblance to a very small cicada. Such, in brief, is the phylloxera commissioned to propagate the race at a distance.

"We have here no longer to do with the sluggish pot-bellied creature that needs all its strength to move from one root to the next adjoining; we behold an agile denizen of the air, capable of covering with the swiftness of an arrow a distance of several leagues, especially when aided by a favorable wind. During the warm season of July and August these winged insects take flight and settle in swarms on the vineyards not yet ravaged. They alight on the leaves, where their suckers perform their function in sober moderation.

"To stuff themselves like gluttons, after the manner of their kindred that live on the roots, is not their way. Hence their own depredations are of no importance. Unfortunately, however, it is their mission to do us a most disastrous disservice by infesting, one after another, the adjacent vineyards, peopling the still unaffected districts with underground ravagers. All take part in this; all, without exception, set to work laying eggs.

"These eggs are few in number, it is true, each insect laying at most but half a score amid the cotton-like down of the buds and young leaves. But the aggregate is none the less enormous, since in this strange family we have thus far encountered none but mothers. We have just seen that all the wingless phylloxeras on the roots lay eggs, and now we find that all their winged kindred on the leaves do likewise.

"This excessive fecundity would in the end exhaust the insect and result in its extinction if there were no seasons of quietude for renewing the vitality of the race. Yellowish in color like the eggs of the underground phylloxera, those of the winged insect are of two kinds: one of a larger size, the other only about half as large. The first produce females, the second males. Here, at last, we have the two sexes, whose coöperation will assure indefinite prosperity to the race. That is the normal order governing all animal life.

"But what queer little creatures! Yellow, wingless, stubby, they look like the lice on the roots, but even smaller. These phylloxeras of the third kind are dwarfs in a family of dwarfs. They have no stomachs for digesting, no suckers for puncturing the leaves and extracting their sap. Self-nourishment, however slight, is not at all their affair. The laying of eggs that shall renew the vigor of the race, the placing of them where they will be safe, and then a speedy death—that is the sole purpose of their brief span of life.

"For some days these dwarfs, male and female, wander over

the vines and mate, one with another; then, in the fissures of the wrinkled bark, the mothers lay each an egg, a single egg, of enormous size in comparison with the smallness of the layer, greenish in color and sprinkled with fine black spots. This egg takes the name of 'winter egg,' being destined to pass the cold season fastened by a little hook to the vine's bark. After this the layer of the egg shrivels up into a reddish point and dies."

"But how do these eggs manage to get through the winter without freezing?" asked Louis. "Hens' eggs or birds' eggs would be good for nothing after being left out-doors from autumn till spring."

"That is true," assented Uncle Paul; "nevertheless these minute germs of future insect life seldom fail to hatch when warm weather returns. From them come plant-lice like those on the roots of the vine. Each new-born louse crawls down the natal vine, hunts around on the ground until it finds a crack in the soil, and then makes its way through this fissure to settle at last on a rootlet, into which it plunges its sucker. At ease thenceforth beneath the surface of the ground and in the bosom of abundance, it does not long remain alone. Close to its fixed position it deposits its little heap of yellow eggs, whence there quickly issues a new generation. In like manner each member of the family surrounds itself with a family of its own; and so on by several successive repetitions of the process until, from having but a single occupant at first, a root speedily becomes covered with a legion of destroyers. To this population of recent origin we must not forget to add the older inhabitants that have passed the winter under ground and have only waited for the return of the warm season to resume their own laying of eggs on the roots of the vine.

"Let us recapitulate these singular ways of the phylloxera. The species comprises three forms of insects, each having its own peculiar structure, its manner of life, its separate function. The customary animal unity is here a trinity: three different insects are grouped in a single species.

"The sedentary members are wingless and live on the roots. All lay eggs and are followed by several generations likewise capable of laying eggs. Under the pricking of their collective suckers, numberless in the aggregate, vineyards are ruined. There we have the formidable foe, the ravager whose sucker, hardly visible to the naked eye, has already cost us more than ten milliard francs.

"The migrating members are furnished with large wings. They live on the leaves and lay each a small number of eggs in the down of the buds. Like their sedentary kinsfolk, they all lay eggs. Their peculiar office is to disseminate the race from one vineyard to another.

"The members endowed with sex come under the operation of the general law: they are divided into male and female. Unprovided with wings, sucker, or stomach, they wander over the vine without taking any nourishment. Each mother lays a single egg, the winter egg, whence issues in the spring a sedentary phylloxera, which makes its way down to the roots, establishes itself there, and becomes the head and center of a new colony.

"How to contend against this foe which, by reason of its numbers and its underground abode, defies our attempts to exterminate it? Three principal methods are employed. In the lowlands the vineyards are flooded and kept under a good depth of water throughout the winter. This submersion causes the death of the phylloxera at the roots of the plant. As a second method, through holes bored to the roots the soil is injected with an asphyxiating fluid called sulphur of carbon, the fumes of which instantly kill all insects that they reach. The difficulty is to do a thorough job and leave no survivors. A third device is employed by those who import from America certain wild vines much hardier than our cultivated ones, but producing inferior fruit. These American plants resist the attacks of the phylloxera, and continue to flourish where our vines would succumb. On these wild stocks, as soon as they are well rooted, are grafted our native vines, and thus is obtained a grape-vine of two-fold quality, resisting by the hardy nature of its root the phylloxera's assaults, and bearing, on its engrafted shoots, the incomparable fruit of our old vineyards."

CHAPTER LIV

NOCTURNAL BIRDS OF PREY

"THE BROWN owl, the horned owl, the barn-owl and other species of this family, are known under the name of nocturnal birds of prey. They are called birds of prey because they live on the small animals that they catch, such as rats and mice, both those that infest our houses and those that live in the fields. Owls are, among birds, what cats are among quadrupeds,—the inveterate foes of all those small rodents of which the mouse is our most familiar example.

"The French language has recognized this analogy in its term *chat-huant*[7] (hooting cat) applied to a certain kind of owl. This bird is, in some sort, a cat in its manner of living, a cat that flies and that utters a long-drawn cry like a plaintive howl. It is nocturnal; in other words, it keeps itself hidden by day in some obscure retreat, whence it comes forth only at nightfall, to hunt in the twilight and under the rays of the moon.

"Owls have eyes of remarkable size, round, and both in a frontal position instead of being placed one on each side of the head. A broad rim of fine feathers encircles each eye. The reason for their great size is found in the bird's nocturnal habits. Having to seek its food by a very feeble light, it must, in order to see with any distinctness, have eyes that admit as much light as possible; that is, eyes that open very wide.

7   The corresponding English term is "screech-owl."—*Translator.*

BARN-OWL

"But this wide-openness of the eyes, so advantageous by night, is a serious inconvenience to the owl in the bright light of day. Dazzled, blinded, by the sun's rays, the bird of darkness keeps itself in hiding and dares not venture forth; but if forced to do so, it observes the utmost circumspection, flying with cautious hesitation and by short stages. The other birds, those accustomed to broad daylight, come and insult it at will. Robin redbreast and the tomtit are the first to pay their compliments in this manner, and are followed by the chaffinch, the jay, and many others."

"And doesn't the owl do anything to get even with them?" asked Jules.

"Very little," replied his uncle. "Perched on a branch of some tree, the night bird answers its aggressors by a grotesque balancing of its body, turning its large head this way and that in a ridiculous fashion, and rolling its eyes in bewildered alarm. Its menaces are vain: the smallest and weakest birds are its boldest tormentors, pecking it and pulling its feathers without its daring to defend itself.

"Because of its wide-open eyes the nocturnal bird of prey

needs a subdued light like that of early dawn and of evening dusk. It is, therefore, at nightfall and at the first signs of daybreak that these birds leave their retreats and seek their prey. At these hours their hunt is a fruitful one, for they find the rats and mice, whether those that lurk about our houses and barns or those that live in the field, either fast asleep or on the point of going to sleep. Moonlight nights are the most favorable for the nocturnal bird's purposes. Such nights are nights of plenty, affording opportunity for protracted hunting and many captures.

"Let us follow the owl on its nocturnal expedition. The moment is propitious, the air is calm, the moon shines. The bird leaves its sylvan retreat; it skims over the open field, the meadow, the prairie; it inspects the furrows where the field-mouse lurks, the long grass where it burrows, the ruins of deserted buildings where both rats and mice scamper about.

"Its flight is noiseless, its silent wing cleaving the air without the faintest sound. It is careful not to give the alarm to its destined victims. This noiseless flight it owes to the structure of its feathers, which are silky and finely divided. Nothing betrays its sudden coming, and the prey is seized without even suspecting the enemy's presence. An extraordinarily keen sense of hearing, on the other hand, advises the bird of all that is going on in the neighborhood. Its ears, large and deep, perceive the mere rustle of a field-mouse in the grass.

"The prey is seized with two strong claws warmly clothed in feathers clear down to the very nails. Each foot has four toes, of which three ordinarily point forward, and one backward; but, by a privilege common to nocturnal birds of prey, one of the anterior toes is movable and can point backward, so that the claw becomes divided into two pairs of equally powerful grippers when the bird wishes to seize, as in a vise, the branch whereon it perches or the victim struggling to escape.

"A blow of the beak breaks the head of the captured rat. This beak is short and hooked, and the two mandibles have great mobility, which enables them, in striking against each other, to make a rapid clacking, a demonstration by which the bird expresses anger or alarm.

"The mandibles open wide in the act of swallowing, revealing a mouth of ample proportions and a throat of excessive width. The prey, which has first been well kneaded by the claws, disappears down this throat, bones and all. Nothing is left of the rat or the mouse, not even the fur.

"Digestion completed, there remains in the stomach a confused mass of skins turned inside out and still wearing their fur, and bones stripped as clean as if they had been scraped with a knife. The bird then proceeds to rid itself of this encumbrance of innutritious matter. Grotesque retchings indicate the labor of this deliverance. Something makes its way upward through the extended throat, the beak opens, and the act is accomplished. A rounded mass falls to the ground, composed of skins, bones, hair, scales—in fact, everything that has defied digestion. All nocturnal birds of prey have this ignoble manner of freeing the stomach: they vomit in globular form the residue of their prey after the latter has been swallowed whole."

CHAPTER LV

THE SMALLER BIRDS

"ALMOST ALL the smaller birds are helpful to us in protecting the fruits of the earth from the ravages of insects. Their services deserve to be recorded in a long and detailed history, but time for that is lacking and we must confine ourselves to brief mention of a few of these valiant caterpillar-destroyers.

"The titmouse, or tomtit, is a small bird full of life and showing a petulant humor. Always in action, it flits from tree to tree, examines the branches with minute particularity, perches on the swaying end of the frailest twig, where it clings persistently even though hanging head downward, accommodating itself to the oscillations of its flexible support without once relaxing its clutch or ceasing its scrutiny of the worm-infested buds, which it tears open in order to get at the enclosed vermin and insect-eggs.

"It is calculated that a tomtit rids us of three hundred thousand of these eggs every year. It has to supply the needs of a family seldom equalled in size; but the support of twenty young ones, or even more, is not too

Tufted Titmouse

heavy a burden for this active bird to bear. With this infant brood on its hands, it must give constant and careful inspection to buds and to fissures in the bark, in order to catch larvæ, spiders, caterpillars, little worms of all kinds, and thus find food for twenty beaks incessantly agape with hunger at the bottom of the nest.

"Let us suppose the mother bird to arrive with a caterpillar. The nest is immediately all in a tumult: twenty beaks are stretched wide open, but only a single one receives the morsel, while nineteen are kept waiting. The indefatigable mother flies off again, and when the twentieth beak has at last been fed, the first has long since begun again its importunate demands. What a multitude of worms such a brood must consume!

"Whole families of birds devote themselves, as does the titmouse, to this patient quest for insect eggs in the crevices of tree-trunks or concealed in rolled-up leaves, for larvæ between the scales of buds and in worm-holes in wood, and for insects hidden in cracks and crannies. In this kind of hunt the bird does not have to chase its game and catch it by superior swiftness of flight; it must simply know how to find it in its lair. To this end it needs a keen eye and a slender beak; wings play but a secondary part.

"But other species spend their energies in the free open-air chase: they pursue their game on the wing, hunting for gnats, moths, mosquitoes, and flying beetles. They must have a short beak, but one that opens wide and snaps up unerringly insects on the wing, despite the uncertainties of aërial flight; a beak in which the victim is caught and held without any retardation of the bird's swift course; in short, a beak with a sticky lining which a tiny butterfly cannot so much as graze with its wing and not become entangled. Above all, an untiring and swift wing is necessary, one that does not flag in the pursuit of game desperately putting forth its utmost efforts to escape, and one that is not baffled by the tortuous course of a moth driven to bay. A beak inordinately cleft and wings of extraordinary power—such, in a word, should be the equipment of the bird whose hunting ground is the vast expanse of the open air.

"These conditions are fulfilled in the highest degree in the swallow and the martin, both of which hunt flying insects, pursuing them this way and that, back and forth, ceaselessly and with a thousand subtle tricks. They catch them in their wide-open and viscous gullet, and continue their course without a moment's pause.

"The bird that lives on grain and seeds, the granivorous bird, as it is called, has a beak that is very wide at the base and adapted by its strength to the opening of the hardest seeds. In this class are the chaffinch, the greenfinch, the linnet, the goldfinch, and the swallow. The bird that lives on insects, or the insectivorous bird, has a beak that is fine and slender, in delicacy proportioned to the softness of its prey. To this number belong the nightingale, the warbler, the fallow-finch, and the wagtail. Agriculture has no better defenders against the ravages of worms than these little birds with slender beaks, voracious devourers as they are of larvæ and insects.

"But the granivorous birds have certain grave faults: some of them are addicted to pilfering in the grain-fields and know how to get the wheat out of the ear, and some even come boldly to the poultry-yard to share with its inmates the oats thrown to them by the farmer's wife. Others prefer the juicy flesh of fruit, and know sooner than we when the cherries are ripe and the pears mellow. Such failings, however, are amply atoned for by services rendered. The granivores pick up in the fields an infinite number of seeds of all sorts which, if left to germinate, would infest our crops with weeds.

"To this rôle of weeder they add a second not less meritorious.

Grain and seeds are, it is true, their regular diet; but insects are to few of them so despicable as to be refused when sufficiently plentiful and easy to catch. Indeed, we can go still further in our commendation of these birds: in their early days when, feeble and featherless, they receive their nourishment by the beakful from their parents, many of them are fed on insects.

"Let us take for example the house-sparrow. Here we have, it must be admitted, an inveterate devourer of grain. He robs our dove-cotes and poultry-yards, steals their food from the pigeons and the hens, and anticipates the farmer in reaping the grain-crops near his house. Many other misdeeds are to be reckoned against him. He plunders the cherry-trees, commits petty larceny in the garden, plucks up sprouting seeds, and regales himself on young lettuce and the first leaves of green peas. But as soon as the season of insect-eggs opens, this shameless pilferer becomes one of our most valuable helpers. Twenty times an hour, at least, the mother and the father take turns in bringing the beakful of food to their little ones; and each time the bill of fare consists of a caterpillar, or an insect large enough to be divided into quarters, or perhaps a fat larva, or it may be a grasshopper, or some other kind of small game.

"In one week the young brood consumes about three thousand insects, larvæ, caterpillars and worms of all species. There have been counted in the immediate vicinity of a single nest of sparrows the remains of seven hundred June-bugs, besides those of innumerable smaller insects. That is the supply of food required for rearing only one brood. Let us then, my children, wish well to all the little birds that deliver us from that formidable ravager, the insect."

CHAPTER LVI

BIRDS' NESTS

"IT IS in the building of nests destined for the rearing of a family of young ones that the bird shows in a remarkable way that wonderful faculty which enables the little creature to accomplish, without previous training, results that would seem to require the intervention of reasoned experience.

"These adepts in bird-nest architecture have talents of the most varied sort. There are diggers, who scoop out a hollow in the sand; miners, who excavate a little cell to which a long and narrow passage gives access; carpenters, who bore into the trunk of a worm-eaten tree; masons, who work with mortar made of earth tempered with saliva; basket-makers, who weave together small twigs and fine roots; tailors, who with a filament of bark for thread and the beak for needle sew a few leaves together into a cornet for holding the mattress on which the young brood will rest; workers in felt, who make a fabric of down, hair, or cotton, that rivals our own similar

AMERICAN GOLDFINCH

257

CHAFFINCH

products; and builders of fortresses, who protect their nest with an impenetrable thicket as a rampart.

"The goldfinch, that pretty little red-headed bird which feeds on the seeds of thistles, builds a wonderfully wrought nest in the fork of some flexible branch. The outside is made of moss and the silky down of thistle-seeds and dandelions, while the inside, artistically rounded, is lined with a thick cushion of horse-hair, wool, and feathers.

"The chaffinch builds its nest in nearly the same way, but, more mistrustful than the goldfinch, it covers the outside of its abode with a layer of gray lichen which, merging with the lichen growing naturally on the branch, serves to baffle the scrutiny of the bird-nest hunter.

"The window-swallow makes its nest in the corners of windows, under the eaves of roofs, and in the shelter of cornices. Its building material is fine earth, chiefly that left in little piles after its digestion by earth-worms in fields and gardens.

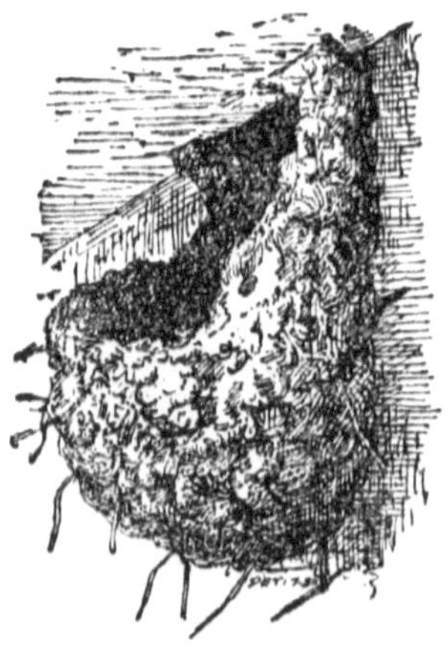

NEST OF A SWALLOW

European Oriole

The swallow fetches it, a beakful at a time, moistens it with a little viscous saliva to make it stick together, and deposits it in courses, shaping the structure into a sort of hemispherical bowl fastened to the wall and having a narrow mouth at the top to allow the bird to squeeze through. Bits of straw embedded in this masonry of earth serve to give it greater solidity. Finally, the inside is upholstered with a quantity of fine feathers.

"The chimney-swallow chooses a similar situation for its nest and uses the same building-materials, but the nest itself takes a different form. Instead of a hemispherical structure entered by a very small opening, it builds a cup-shaped nest, of no great depth and wide-open at the top.

"Swallows like to live together in large numbers, so that their nests are sometimes found touching one another in colonies of several hundreds under the same cornice. Each pair recognizes unerringly its own belongings and respects scrupulously the property of others, in return for like respect paid to its own. There is among them a deep sense of solidarity, and they render mutual aid with no less intelligence than zeal.

"Sometimes it chances that a nest has hardly been finished when it crumbles to pieces, the mortar used having been of poor quality, or else the masons, with injudicious haste, having had too little patience to let one course dry before laying another on top of it. At the news of this mishap neighbors of both sexes hasten up to console the unfortunates and to lend their aid in rebuilding. All apply themselves to the task, fetching mortar of the first quality, and straws and feathers, with such ardor and enthusiasm that in two days the nest is completely rebuilt. Left to their own unaided efforts, the afflicted pair would have needed a fortnight to repair the disaster.

"The golden oriole is one of the most beautiful birds of our clime. About as large as the blackbird, it has plumage of a superb yellow, except the wings, which are black. In building its nest it selects, in some tall tree, a long and flexible bough with a fork at the end. Between the two branches of this fork a hammock is woven for receiving the nest. Strands of fine bark that has become shredded by long exposure to wind and weather are used for this work of art. These strands or cords pass from one side of the fork to the other, enlacing them, crossing and recrossing, and thus forming a sort of pocket, firmly fixed and securely hung.

"Broad blades of grass consolidate the structure. Then in this hammock a mattress of the finest straw and having the form of an oval cup is put together. The completed work bears some resemblance to those elegant little wool-lined wicker baskets that are used as nests for caged canaries.

"The long-tailed titmouse, remarkable for its excessive caudal development, which constitutes more than half the total length of its body, lives in the woods during the summer season, and comes into our gardens and orchards only in winter. It is a small bird with a reddish back and white breast. The stomach is tinged with red; the neck and cheeks are white.

"Its nest is built sometimes in the fork of a high branch in a clump of bushes, and sometimes in the dense underwood of

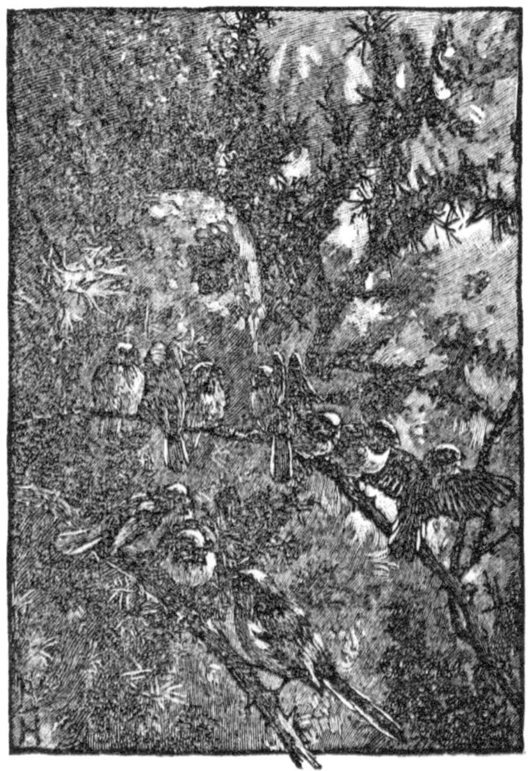

LONG-TAILED TITMOUSE

a thicket, a few feet from the ground; but it is most often attached to the trunk of a willow or a poplar tree. Its shape is that of a very large cocoon, and its entrance is at one side, about an inch from the top. On the outside it is made of lichens like those that cover the tree, in order to blend with the bark and deceive the eye of the passer-by. Fibers of wool serve to hold all the parts securely together. To make the dome of the nest rain-proof, it is formed of a sort of thick felt composed of bits of moss and cobwebs. The inside resembles an oven with cup-shaped bottom and very high top, and is furnished with a remarkably thick bed of downy feathers, whereon repose from sixteen to twenty little birds, arranged with careful order in the restricted space no larger, at the most, than the hollow of one's hand. By what miracle of parsimonious economy do these twenty little ones with their mother manage to find room for themselves in this tiny abode? And how in the world can tails ever grow to such length there?

"The nest of the swinging titmouse is still more remarkable. In our country this bird is hardly ever found except on the banks of the lower Rhone. It hangs its nest very high, on the tip-end of some swaying branch of a tree at the water-side, so that its brood is gently rocked by the breeze sweeping over the river."

"Why, I should think," put in Emile, "there would be danger of the young birds' spilling out of such a swinging nest."

"Not at all," replied his uncle. "The shape of the nest provides against that. It is a sort of oval purse about as large as a wine-bottle, with a small opening at one side, near the top. This opening is prolonged like the neck of a bottle and will at the utmost admit one's finger. To pass through so narrow an entrance, the titmouse, small as it is, must stretch the elastic wall, which yields a little and then contracts again. This purse, as I have called it, is made of the cotton-like flock that comes from the ripening seeds of poplars and willows in May. The titmouse gathers these bits of down and weaves them together with a woof of wool and hemp. The fabric thus obtained is not unlike the felt of a cheap hat.

"It would be useless to seek an explanation of the bird's astonishing success in manufacturing, with no implements but beak and claws, a textile that man's skilful hand, left to its own resources, would be unable to produce; and this success the bird achieves with no previous apprenticeship, without hesitation and without ever having seen the thing done by others. At the very first trial the titmouse surpasses in its art our weavers and fullers.

"The top of the nest includes in its thickness the end of the branch from which it hangs, with the terminal twigs of that branch, which serve as framework for the nest's vaulted roof, while the foliage projecting through the sides of the nest protects it with its shade. Finally, to secure greater firmness of support, a cordage of wool and hemp is passed around the branch and interlaced with the felt of the nest. The inside of this hanging habitation is lined with down of the finest quality from the poplar tree.

"Are you acquainted with the troglodyte or, as it is more commonly called, the wren? It is the smallest of our birds, and it too is a master in the art of nest-building. Clothed in reddish brown, with drooping wing and upturned beak and tail, it is always frisking, hopping, and twittering,—*teederee, teeree, teeree.* Every winter it comes flying about our houses, frequenting the wood-pile, inspecting holes in the wall, and prying into the densest thickets. At a distance it might be mistaken for a small rat.

"In summer it lives in the pathless woods. There, under the shelter of some big root that lies close to the ground and is covered with a thick fleece of moss, it builds a nest patterned after that of the swinging titmouse. Its materials are bits of moss, selected for the purpose of making the nest undistinguishable in appearance from that to which it is attached. The bird gathers these materials and works them into the shape of a large, hollow ball with a very small opening on one side. The interior is upholstered with feathers.

"The magpie fixes its dwelling in the top of some lofty tree whence, as from an observatory, it can spy from afar the approaching enemy. At the juncture of a number of branching twigs that offer adequate support it plants its nest, constructed of interlacing flexible sticks with a floor of tempered earth. Fine rootlets, blades of grass, and a few tufts of down form the bedding for the prospective brood.

"So far there is nothing to differentiate the structure from ordinary nests; but now we behold the exhibition of a special

TAILOR BIRD OF JAVA AND NEST

talent on the magpie's part. The entire nest, and more particularly its upper part, is surrounded by a thick rampart, a sort of fortified enclosure composed of thorny twigs securely intertwined. One would take the whole thing for a shapeless mass of brushwood. Through this rampart, on the side that is most strongly defended, an opening is left of just sufficient size to admit of the mother's entrance and exit. It is the only door to the aërial fortress.

"Let us turn now to a bird that builds upon piling. It is a warbler of large size, called the great sedge-warbler or river-thrush. It selects a cluster of four or five reeds that project above the surface of a pond, with their stalks rooted in the mud under the water and growing near together. These slender piles, the tops of which the bird brings into such proximity as may be desired and fastens with connecting strands, are made to bear an interlacing of flexible materials, such as rushes, bark-fibers, and long blades of grass. It is a basket-weaver's job, with a framework of reeds as a basis for the structure. Finally, in this basket, which is made much longer than wide, is placed the nest proper, a warm little bed of cotton-like down, spiders' webs, and wool.

"But this abode resting on piles above the water is exposed to two dangers,—the swaying of the reeds which, bent over by the wind, might incline the nest so that it would spill its contents either of eggs or of young birds; and secondly, the spring freshets, which might rise so high as to submerge the nest. These dangers, however, have been foreseen by the bird. The nest is very deep, and furthermore the edges of the opening bend inward and form a parapet. In this way is avoided the risk of a fall when the reeds that bear the nest are swayed by the wind. Finally, since the sedge-warbler is at liberty to build her nest at any desired height above the surface of the pond, she places it always high enough to be beyond the reach of the rising water, even in great floods. One suspects the bird of being able to foresee, months in advance, the coming inundation; for she builds her nest at a greater or less elevation according to the high-water mark destined later to be reached by the surface of the pond.

"The cisticola is a small warbler very common in the marshes of Camargue, at the mouth of the Rhone. Its nest is placed in the middle of a cluster of grass and rushes, and takes the form of a purse with a small round opening. Fine dry leaves form the bed on which the eggs rest, while other and larger leaves are fixed all around it to form an enclosure.

"For this work the bird turns tailor, cutting the leaves and lapping them over one another. Along the border of each leaf it punches holes with the point of its beak and through these holes it passes one or more threads made of cobwebs and the down from certain plants. Its distaff for holding the thread— namely, the beak—does not admit of using very long strands;

hence the needleful, so to speak, goes only twice or, at most, three times from one leaf to the next one. But no matter; the sewing is strong enough to fasten the whole into a sort of purse which keeps out the rain.

"The orthotomus, or grass-warbler, a small bird of India, is an even more skilful tailor, and in fact is commonly known as the tailor-bird. It selects two large leaves, still living and attached to the branch on which they grew. These are brought together, with their longer edges touching, and are sewed border to border with strong cotton thread made by the bird's beak. The seams run only half the length of the leaves, in such a manner that the two together, hanging down as they do, form a conical sac with its mouth upward. In this sac the nest is placed, hidden by its protecting envelope, which so blends with the rest of the foliage that even after a person has once found the nest he can with difficulty find it again.

"In South Africa there is a bird scarcely larger than our swallow and known as the social republican from its living in large societies with one nest in common. This nest, a sort of bird village, is shaped like an enormous mushroom, spreading out all around the trunk of a tree, which serves as its stalk, while the lower branches also furnish their support. This colossal edifice is of such bulk and weight as to make a wagon-load, and if one wishes to see the interior structure it must be chopped to pieces with an axe. It is formed wholly of dry grass arranged much like the thatch on our rustic roofs.

"Indeed, this structure, built at public expense by all the associated birds, is nothing but a roof, a dome, destined to shelter the real nests, which are attached to the inside of the thatched covering. Here are to be found a multitude of round holes presenting all together somewhat the appearance of a honeycomb. Each hole gives access to a small cell, a veritable nest and the separate work of a single pair. The grass roof, then, is built in common by the whole society, after which each family provides for its exclusive use a little apartment attached to the lower side of the roof. The number of inhabitants may reach as high as a thousand."

CHAPTER LVII

MIGRATION OF BIRDS

"A T THE approach of the cold season," Uncle Paul resumed, in his account of bird habits and bird peculiarities, "before winter clears the fields of insects, covers the ponds with a coating of ice, and whitens the landscape with snow, thus cutting off the food-supply hitherto obtainable from the earth, many birds, especially those that live on insects or frequent bodies of water and marshy meadows, take leave of their native land and direct their course southward, where they will find a warmer sun and a more assured supply of food.

"They take their departure, some in large flocks, others in small groups, or even each one separately. With no guide other than an irresistible impulse too mysterious for us to explain, they traverse by successive stages immense tracts of land, cross seas, and bend their course toward the countries of the south. Africa is the rendezvous of our birds and of European birds in general.

"After the cold season has passed, with the first fine days of spring the same birds return to the regions where they were born, making the journey this time in the opposite direction, from south to north. They take possession once more of their groves and forests, their rocks and prairies, which they know how to find with an inconceivable accuracy. There they build their nests, rear their young, and gain strength for the coming journey; and upon the return of cold weather they go back again to the lands of sunshine.

"These periodical journeys are called migrations, of which there are two each year,—that of autumn, when the birds leave us and go southward, and that of spring, when they fly northward and come back to us. These semi-annual flittings take place all over the earth.

"The various species do not all fix upon the same time for their migration, but each has its own calendar, from which it departs only very slightly. Some start well in advance of the increasing chill and the lessening abundance of food, while others do not leave their native land until driven by actual necessity, when the cold has become severe. Thus our martin flies away for Africa as early as the month of August, whereas the chimney-swallow lingers until October or even November.

"The martins forsake our turrets and old walls, our steeples and belfries, while the summer heat is still intense and the small flies on which they feed are still abundant. It is not, then, any lowering of temperature that drives them away, nor is it any lack of food that hastens their departure; but they have a secret presentiment of the change of season that is coming in a few weeks; a deep-seated unrest, which they cannot overcome, warns them that the hour for their departure is drawing near.

"If one desires to witness this anxiety that torments the bird when the time for migrating arrives, he may do so by rearing in captivity a migratory bird caught very young. The captive, though never having lived with its kind or had any knowledge of their migratory habits, and furthermore having been kept in a cage with no experience of cold or hunger, nevertheless, when the season for flitting arrives, shows agitation and mental distress, and tries to escape from its prison—after remaining so quiet and contented up to that time. Some inner voice—instinct we call it—says it is time to go, and the captive is eager to be off. If the desire is thwarted, death follows.

"To tear oneself from beloved haunts to incur the fatigues and perils of a long journey is undoubtedly a painful decision; yet the bird courageously submits to the inevitable, but in the hope of coming back again some day. The strong reassuring the weak, the older ones guiding the young, the departing flock forms itself into a caravan and takes wing for the south. The sea is crossed, the treacherous sea from which, at long intervals, rises an island as halting-place. Many perish in the crossing, many reach the goal worn with hunger and spent with fatigue.

"The day for starting on this momentous journey is decided upon in a great assembly, toward the end of August for the window-swallow, and considerably later, even as late as November, for the chimney-swallow. When once the date has been fixed, the window-swallows gather together daily for several days on the roofs of tall buildings. Every few minutes small parties detach themselves from the general conclave and circle about in the air with anxious cries, taking a parting look at their native haunts, and paying them a last farewell. Then they return to their places among their companions and join in noisy chatter on the subject of their hopes and fears, all the while preparing themselves for the distant expedition by a careful inspection of their plumage and a final touch to one lustrous feather after another.

"After several repetitions of these farewells a plaintive twittering announces the fateful hour. The moment has come, it is time to start. The flock rises, the emigrants are off for the south. If one of them has been marked with a red string around the claw in order to be recognized, you may be sure you will see it come back the next spring and take possession of its nest again with little cries of joy at finding it intact and ready for occupancy after a few repairs.

"With their vigorous wings the duck and goose, in their wild state, are ardent travelers. On a gray day in November, when there are signs of snow, it is not unusual to see passing from north to south, at a great height, birds arranged in single file, or in a double file meeting in a point, like the two branches of the letter V. These birds are a flock of either ducks or geese in the act of migrating.

"If the flock is of no great size, the birds composing it arrange themselves in one continuous file, the beak of each following bird touching the tail of the preceding, in order that the passage opened through the air may not have time to close again. But if the flock is a large one, two files of equal length are formed, which meet at an acute angle, the front of the moving mass.

"This angular arrangement, of which we find examples in the ship's prow, the plowshare, the thin edge of a wedge, and a multitude of utensils designed for cleavage, is the most favorable for pushing through the mass of the air with the least fatigue. If in marshaling their flying battalions the goose and the duck had taken counsel of the engineer's science, they could not have managed better. But they have no need of others' advice: instructed by their own instinct, they utilized long before we did the principle of the wedge.

"Moreover, to divide among all the members of the flock the excess of fatigue incurred by the file-leader in opening a passage through the air by strength of wing, each in turn takes the post of honor, the forward end of the single file or the point of the angle formed by the double file. Its term of service ended, the bird at the head retires to the rear to recuperate, and another leader takes its place. By this equitable division of labor the fatigue does not prove excessive for any one bird, and the flock leaves no stragglers behind."

CHAPTER LVIII

CARRIER-PIGEONS

RESUMING THE subject of bird instinct as illustrated by the migratory flock's unerring precision in finding its way over thousands of miles to a desired nesting-place, Uncle Paul continued as follows:

"How is it that so many thousands, even millions, of migrating birds can direct their course through trackless space each to the particular rock or tree or nest left behind six months before, when the yearly removal was decided upon to some southern region a thousand miles or more distant? How, for example, does the frail swallow manage to find again, at the return of spring, its tiny abode in the north when it retraces the long journey of the previous autumn? In order that we may be sure it is the same swallow returned to the same nest we tie a colored string, as I have said, around the bird's claw; and, lo and behold, when April comes, with it comes our swallow to its dwelling under the eaves. It is indeed our identical bird and no other; it is the very one that fashioned the nest of clay, cherished bit of private property now so eagerly taken possession of once more. The owner's demonstrations of satisfaction and delight are convincing proof, even were the bit of red thread not there to dispel all doubt.

"If the swallow is able to find its nest again upon returning in the spring from the land of the negroes, still more will it be able to find it after being removed merely from its native canton to the neighboring one.

"A mother sitting on her eggs or feeding her young is taken, let us suppose, put into a basket, and carried quickly to a spot twenty or thirty leagues distant, where she is set free again. The surrounding country is unfamiliar to her: she has never been there before. Of the road over which she has just come she has not the slightest knowledge, having traveled it in the darkness of a closed basket. No matter. With only a moment's hesitation she gets her bearings amid these strange scenes and takes flight toward her nest as unerringly as if it were possible to see the very roof under which repose her little ones. In a few hours we shall find her back again on her nest.

"A like behavior under similar conditions might be witnessed in the case of divers other birds noted for strength of wing and power of sustained flight. They would return to their domicile in spite of the distance to be traversed and the unfamiliarity of the intervening country. Maternal love can accomplish wonders. In order to save her eggs from a chill or her little ones from starving in her absence, the mother-bird exercises a geographical skill as marvelous as that displayed at the period of migration."

CARRIER PIGEON

"I have heard it said," remarked Louis, "that the pigeon is very clever at finding its way over long distances, and that it is used for carrying letters from one place to another."

"Yes," replied Uncle Paul, "this aptitude for retracing the homeward way over vast distances is shown to an extraordinary degree by some of our domestic pigeons. Economizing all their strength for purposes of sustained flight, they have retained the wild pigeon's pointed wings, sleek plumage, and symmetrical form. We call these birds carrier-pigeons, a name well earned, as you will see from what I have now to tell you.

"A pigeon having a brood of young is taken from the pigeon-house, put into a closed basket, and transported a distance of a hundred, two hundred leagues, or even further if you choose—from one end of France to the other. There it is set free. It rises in the air, circles about a few times as if to assure itself of the direction to be followed, and then starts off in impetuous flight toward the quarter where pigeon-house and young await its coming.

"Does the bird catch sight of the pigeon-house as it circles about in the upper air? By no means; the distance is too great. Even should it rise to the height of the clouds, or to still greater altitudes, where moreover its wings could not sustain it, it would be unable to see its home. On the journey to the point where it was released it has had no passing glimpse of any object, shut up as it has been in the dark basket. The region it now traverses it sees for the first time. Nothing in the surrounding landscape is familiar, and yet its flight evinces the assurance that comes from having a definite goal in view. With a speed of about twenty leagues an hour it wings its way straight to the journey's end. If the distance is too great to be covered without pause, halts are made here and there for food and rest; then the journey is resumed, swift as an arrow's flight. Finally, at the end of some hours or days, according to the distance and the duration of the halts, the bird reënters the pigeon-house with its beakful of food for the waiting little ones.

"In serious situations the carrier-pigeon is a valuable messenger. During the winter of that terrible year, 1870–71, when the German hordes besieged Paris, no communication was possible by ordinary means between the invested city and the rest of France, in arms to repel the odious invader. With Paris rendered mute by its isolation, one might have said that the heart of the country had ceased to beat. For communication between those within and friends without, recourse was had to balloons and pigeons.

"Certain persons of dauntless courage left Paris by balloon, choosing especially the night-time for their departure in order to avoid encounter by day. They carried with them despatches from Paris and a number of carrier-pigeons. Over the enemy camps they went, to alight somewhere, far or near, at the pleasure of the winds. Thus the provinces received despatches, newspapers, and private letters from Paris. The car of the balloon was loaded with all these.

"But how carry back to Paris despatches from the provinces? To leave a city by balloon in any chance direction is not so very difficult; but to return by balloon to the same city is practically impossible. The balloon goes as the wind wills, not as its passengers would like to have it go. To seek to return by the means employed in departing would be to compromise everything by incurring the risk of landing in the midst of the Prussian lines.

"The only remaining expedient was to use those incomparable aids, the pigeons, which the aëronaut had taken with him on his departure. Released, one at a time, with despatches enclosed in a quill and fastened to the bird's tail, they flew back over the German army to the pigeon-house; they reëntered Paris and brought news of what was going on in the provinces.

"Do not imagine that the winged messenger was able to transmit only a few words or at most a few lines. It was not with a pen or on ordinary paper that the despatches entrusted to the pigeons were written. By ingenious methods and with unheard-of delicacy it was found possible to obtain characters so fine and sheets of paper so thin that a roll of these sheets weighing scarcely a gram and enclosed in a quill contained as much reading matter as ten printed volumes. What a marvelous piece of work, that package of letters fastened to the pigeon's tail, that quill transformed into a library in which thousands of persons—friends, kinsfolk, statesmen—communicated their projects, their fears, their hopes! In this manner the mail service was maintained during those woeful times."

CHAPTER LIX

SOME PREHISTORIC ANIMALS

"FOSSIL REMAINS of all sorts of animals, from the largest to the smallest, are found embedded in stone. There are lizards which, if alive, would hardly find room enough to turn around in many of our public squares, so monstrous is their size; tortoises with shells as large as a small boat; fishes of strange formation; birds of a singular character such as we no longer behold; and enormous quadrupeds that would dwarf to insignificance our sturdy ox. All flying creatures of the air, all walking and creeping animals of the earth, every form of life swimming in the water, are represented in these fossil remains found in the heart of our rocks, but of a shape and often of a size very different from those of our living animals.

"These ancient creatures have never been seen alive by man, so far back in the past is their period. After inhabiting the earth for a very long time, they disappeared forever, to give place to other species. What remains of them consists chiefly of bones, which from their hardness and their mineral character offer the most resistance to the various destructive agencies. With the sole aid of these bones science succeeds in reconstructing the exact form of the animal. It also tells us what the animal fed on and what were its habits. By a miracle of sagacity it resuscitates, so to speak, the ancient, dislocated carcass, and makes it live again to the mind's eye.

"Fossil bones are commonly found embedded in stone quarried at considerable depths; it needs the work of pick and chisel and hammer to free them from the rock. How did they come to be there? In the same way as shells. If the creature lived in the waters of a lake or of the sea, the mud at the bottom covered the body after death. If it lived on land, the floods swept away its carcass and bore it to the river, which in turn carried it to lake or ocean. Later the lake dried up or the ocean receded, and the hardened clay left behind became the stone whence to-day are obtained the relics of prehistoric forms of animal life.

"What, then, were these prehistoric forms of animal life that preceded man? Regarding ourselves as related to the animals provided with bones, a sort of inner framework sustaining the corporeal edifice, we may say in a general way that there has been a gradual succession from lower to higher in structure. First appeared the fishes, then came the reptiles, next the birds, after them the quadrupeds, suckling their young, and last of all man, placed above all the rest by his incomparable endowments.

"Let us glance rapidly at some examples of the ancient denizens of land and sea. Look at this picture. The back of the creature here represented resembles a little, in its form and in its regular rows of scales, the tail of a fish; but the front—to what can that be likened? What is the meaning of those large bony plaques

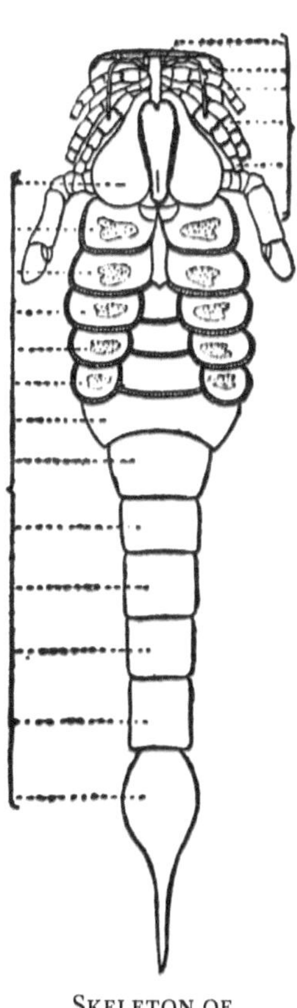

SKELETON OF
PTERICHTHYS

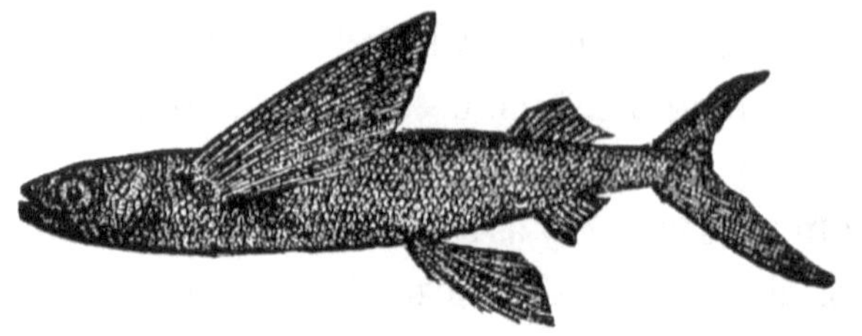

Flying Fish

arranged side by side like the squares in a tessellated pavement? The animal is armed with coat of mail, perhaps to protect itself from the bite of an enemy.

"What is the purpose of those wing-like appendages that strike the flanks? Of what use are those two short horns at the base of the forehead? What sort of a creature can it be that thus singularly combines in its structure the tail of a fish, the shell of a tortoise, the featherless wings of a bird, and the nascent horns of a ram? You will never guess the answer, so different is the creature from any that are known to you. It is a fish, but such a fish as no frying-pan of ours has ever had acquaintance with, nor does the ocean now hold any more like it.

"It goes back to the earliest ages of the world, and is called the pterichthys. Do not exclaim at this name, as strange to our ears

Pterodactyl

as the creature itself to our eyes. Translated into our tongue, it means a winged fish. But did this fish of former ages really fly? Assuredly not. It was too heavy, too massive, to admit of that. Its wings were simply admirable fins for swimming.

"In the seas of our day there live certain fishes fitted for flying. Their lateral fins, which are very long, open like large fans and enable them to sustain themselves for some time in the air. Pressed too hard by a pursuing foe, they escape by leaping out of the water and flying over the waves, clearing a certain distance before plunging again into the water, as they must when their fins begin to get dry and to lose their suppleness. They are called flying fishes. Compare these two pictures and you will see how greatly the present flying fish differs from the ancient winged fish.

"And this other creature—what wild dream could have conceived such a monstrosity? It has the head and neck of a plucked bird; and it also has a bird's beak, but an enormous one armed with pointed teeth in each mandible. Its wings are those of a bat, one talon of each claw being disproportionately elongated and serving as support to a wide membrane, much as an umbrella-rib holds the stretched fabric of the cover. Its other talons are free and are furnished with hooked nails.

"The hind legs and feet are those of the lizard. The body is covered with fine scales, is marbled with touches of a darker color, and ends in an abbreviated tail. Take away from this strange animal its bat's wings, its long neck and its bird's head, and you will have something closely resembling the lizard, the creature that basks in the sun on old walls, or that other one, larger and all green, which gives us a start when it scuttles away among the dead leaves or in the dense growth of the hedge."

"And was it a lizard, then, or a bird?" asked Emile.

"It was a reptile, certainly," was the reply, "and it might be called a sort of lizard. There were several species, varying from the size of a lark to that of a crow. Like the bat, the animal left its retreat in the hollow of rocks and came out at night to flutter awkwardly about in the air by the aid of its wings of stretched skin. With its toothed beak it snapped up in their flight immense dragon-flies, the chief insects of that time. Its hunger appeased, it took its repose on the ground, wings folded against its sides, body supported by the hind legs; or else it hung down from the rocks, suspended by its claws. Its name is pterodactyl, which means wing-fingered.

"Let us consider another of these prehistoric creatures. This time it is a bird, and what a marvelous bird, too, my friends! Its beak, no less monstrous than that of the pterodactyl, had likewise the two mandibles armed with a ferocious-looking set of teeth. Pointed teeth in the jaws of a reptile, such as a lizard, crocodile, or serpent, are nothing extraordinary; but in a bird's mouth, that is unheard-of. To-day one would search in vain all over the earth for anything like it. There are beaks of all shapes and sizes, there are short ones and long ones, straight ones and crooked ones, strong ones and weak ones; but all are toothless, as are the hen's and the sparrow's. What a singular custom in the primitive bird, to adopt for beak the toothed jaws of the reptile!

"And that is not all. This bird adopted also the reptile's tail, but covered it with feathers. Birds of the present day have a short, wide rump, from which grow a dozen coarse feathers. The first bird in the order of time had its tail composed of a long succession of little bones, each supporting two feathers. Here is a picture of that tail just as it was found in the rock where the strange creature left its remains. The bird to which the tail belonged is called by the learned an archæopteryx, or ancient winged animal.

FOSSIL REMAINS OF ARCHÆOPTERYX

"One more of these monsters, and that will suffice. The animal that you see here is the mammoth, a sort of enormous shaggy elephant, so tall that its back would have touched the ceiling in most of our great halls. Its height was as much as six meters. By its side the ordinary elephant, the largest of extant terrestrial animals, would look no larger than a sheep beside an ox.

"Its tusks, which had a pronounced backward curve, measured four meters in length and weighed as much as four hundred and eighty pounds each. What must have been the strength of a colossus carrying between its lips a weight of nine hundred pounds as easily as a cat carries the hairs of its mustaches!

"Man was already in existence at the time of the mammoth. Armed with sharp flint-stones and bone-pointed arrows, he made bold to attack the enormous animal whose weight made the earth tremble. He hunted it in the chase and feasted on its flesh. What a piece of game when the giant fell into the deep ditch masked by a light covering of boughs and foliage! The victim was then overwhelmed with masses of rock, after which there was an interminable banquet for the whole tribe.

MAMMOTH

"Let us go no further, but merely say in conclusion that the animals of to-day are not the same as those of former ages. Long before the present species on land and in the sea, there gradually made their appearance other very different forms of animal life, which have now become extinct. Nowhere on the earth are there now living any creatures like those that have left their fossil remains for our inspection."

CHAPTER LX

THE ORIGIN OF COAL

"COAL IS a fuel of inestimable value. By the heat which it develops in burning it gives movement to divers machines. It makes the locomotive move over the iron rails and the steamship traverse the ocean. With its aid metals are worked, fabrics woven, pottery is baked, glassware manufactured, newspapers and books are printed, tools are shaped, and all sorts of instruments necessary to our daily activities are produced. The arts and crafts have no more powerful auxiliary. If we had to substitute the heat of wood for that of coal, our forests would prove insufficient.

"What, then, is the origin of this combustible, which feeds an immense industry and is the source of incalculable riches? Ordinarily a piece of coal has no great interest for the eye. It is black, lustrous, formless, friable, without any definite character to afford us instruction. One can learn more from the fragments of refuse rejected by the miner as too poor in carbon, fragments in which the predominating element is a kind of dark stone that splits in sheets. In these a surprise is lurking that will tell us the secret of coal.

"These laminate blocks, stone rather than coal, show us, on the slabs that have just been separated by the blow of the hammer, various wonderful designs in which we recognize without hesitation the imprint or mold of some form of vegetation.

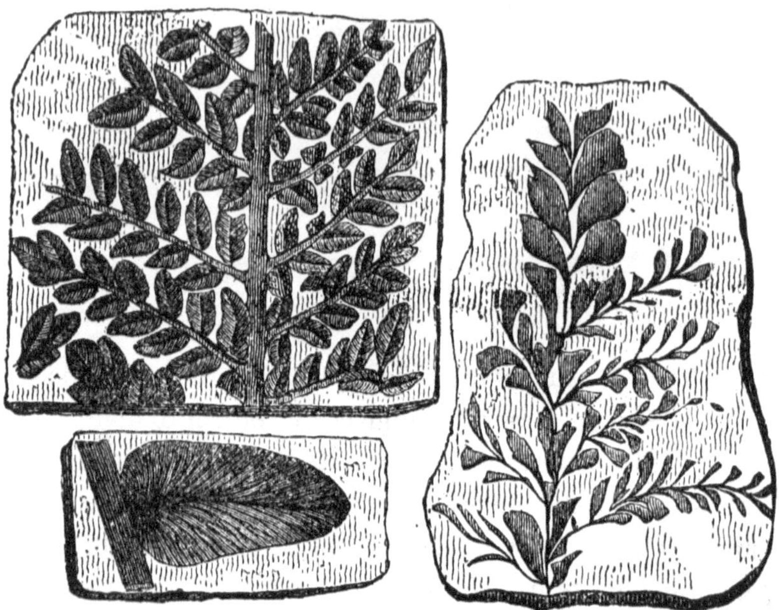

FERN IMPRINTS FROM THE COAL EPOCH

There is no mistake about it; a plant has left its remains there; we behold in very truth the leaf with its subdivisions and its veins. It is all there, even to the minutest detail. It is really the leaf minus the green color, for which is substituted the black of the coal. We should not obtain a more exact representation if we ourselves took the imprint of some sufficiently firm leaf on a soft plaque of clay.

"Pending the time when some lucky chance shall bring you into the neighborhood of a coal mine where you can obtain a laminate block that you can split into sheets and thus discover for yourselves the vegetable imprints there concealed, here is a picture that will show you what these curious markings look like.

"What do you think of it? Have we not here what seems to be actual leaves, and very elegant ones too? They are spread out with a care that would appear to indicate the work of a painstaking human hand. Yes, these are real leaves, but turned to carbon and firmly incrusted in their bed of black rock.

"Similar imprints are found in great abundance in all coal mines. Certain coal-deposits, several meters thick, are composed entirely of them, the smallest chip that one splits off bearing on each face the markings of foliage. The whole is nothing but an accumulation of leaves and broken tree-trunks. An entire forest, heaped up in one pile, would not present an equal mass. Thus it is demonstrated that in coal are preserved the remains of ancient vegetation.

"During great floods the rivers of former ages swept away in enormous masses the trees they had uprooted along the banks, together with the foliage washed into the current by the heavy rains; then all this refuse was deposited in the mud at the river's mouth, or in some lake or bay. Thus were amassed here and there, under the water, during a long series of centuries, the remains of primitive forests.

"Fine clay became packed about these masses, molding itself with delicate accuracy around even the smallest leaf; the weight of the superimposed mud crushed the softened tree-trunks; a gradual decay converted the whole into charcoal; and finally the ligneous mass became a layer of coal. Later the waters changed their bed, driven elsewhere by upheavals in the surface of the earth, and the previously inundated bottom-lands became solid ground in which to-day we find coal under massive strata of rock.

"Is it possible to distinguish the forms of plant-life whence has come our coal? Yes, it is possible, so well preserved are the details of that life in the products of our mines. Now an examination of the imprints left to us in the laminæ or leaves of our stone book shows us that the plant-life of those remote ages in which the coal was accumulated bore not the least resemblance to that of our present forests. And this difference was to be expected.

IMAGINARY VIEW OF A FOREST OF THE COAL EPOCH

The animal life has changed; why, then, should the plant-life have remained unaltered?"

"Didn't they have trees then like ours?" asked Jules.

"No," replied his uncle; "we do not find in our coal mines any signs of the existence of trees resembling those of our day. Nowhere in the world, in fact, are there now to be seen any such forms of plant-life as flourished so abundantly in those remote ages; or if any still exist that are at all analogous, they must be sought in the islands of the tropical seas. No vegetable growth of that coal epoch, whether tree or bush or simple cluster of leaves, bore flowers. The splendors of the corolla were not to appear until a later period.

"For the most part there were only tall stems or stalks, without branches, of equal size from top to bottom, and furrowed with channels or dotted with large points arranged in spiral lines. At the top a tuft of enormous leaves balanced itself, the under surface of each leaf bearing elongated or rounded swellings containing a fine brown dust, each grain of which was a seed for the propagation of the plant.

"Plants that thus bear their seeds, or spores, in powdery masses on the under side of the leaves are called ferns. A number of species flourish in our part of the world. They are unpretentious plants, fond of shade and coolness. Old damp walls, rocks that drip water drop by drop, the darkest corners of our woods—these are the customary haunts of the fern.

"A short underground stock and a sparse cluster of leaves, very elegantly shaped, it is true, constitute our native ferns. Those of the coal epoch were of a different pattern. Some of them displayed at the top of a stem as tall as our poplars a cluster of leaves five or six meters in length. They are called tree-ferns, and they contributed the greater part of the coal-forming material.

"The accompanying illustration will give you an idea of what the vegetation of that period must have looked like. What strange trees! How different from our oaks and maples and hemlocks! The soil is a liquid mud in which lie and rot the tree-trunks prostrated by the weight of years; the air is sultry, moist, heavy, strongly impregnated with a moldy smell; and the density of the foliage barely admits a few sunbeams to flicker over the surface of the stagnant pools.

"Everywhere profound silence. No song of bird bursts forth from the foliage of those tall fern-trees, for the bird is not yet in existence. No foot of quadruped treads the ground, for the quadruped with its coat of fur will not come until much later. Some lizards lurking in the rock-fissures, some large dragon-flies at the water's edge, some odious scorpions under the heaps of dead leaves—that is all the animal-life to be found in the forests that gave us our coal."

CHAPTER LXI

THE FARMER'S HELPERS

"B Y 'HELPERS' I here mean those animals and birds that come to our aid, though not subject to our care and protection, and make war on the insects and divers other devourers that would soon get complete control of our crops if we were left to our own resources for preventing their excessive multiplication. What could man do against those voracious hordes that annually propagate their kind at a rate defying calculation? Would he have the patience, the skill, the keenness of eyesight necessary for effective warfare upon the smallest of these marauders when the June-bug, despite its size, mocks at our utmost efforts to exterminate it? Would he undertake to examine all his fields, a clod at a time, to inspect his grain, ear by ear, to scrutinize his fruit trees, one leaf after another? For so prodigious a task the combined efforts of the whole human race would not suffice. The devouring hosts would eat us up, my friends, if we had no helpers to come to our rescue, helpers endowed with a patience that nothing can weary, an adroitness that baffles all wiles, a vigilance from which there is no escape. To lie in wait for the enemy, to seek him in his remotest retreats, to pursue him without pause or rest, and finally to exterminate him, that is their sole concern, their incessant preoccupation. They are implacable, pitiless; hunger urges them on, both for their own sake and in behalf of their families. They live at the expense of those that live at our expense; they are the enemies of our enemies.

"As participants in this great work must be named the bat and the hedge-hog, the owl, the martin, the swallow, and all the smaller

ADDER, OR VIPER

birds, the lizard, the adder, the frog, and the toad. Praise be to God who has given us as protectors from that glutton, the insect, such birds as the swallow and the warbler, the robin and the nightingale, the martin and the starling. And yet these invaluable creatures, guardians of earth's bounty, a delight to the eye, a solace to the ear, have their homes pillaged by the barbarous and stupid robber of birds' nests. Praise be to God who for the protection of our daily bread has given us the owl and the toad, the hedge-hog and the bat, the adder, the lizard and the mole. Nevertheless these useful creatures that come so valiantly to our aid are cursed and calumniated, and we stupidly vent upon them our loathing and hate.

"By what perversity are we, in general, impelled to destroy animals whose coöperation is so much to our advantage? Nearly all our helpers are persecuted. Their good will must be indomitable to make them bear our ill treatment and not forsake our dwellings and fields, never to return. The bat rids

GREEN LIZARD OF EUROPE

us of a host of enemies, and is nevertheless under the ban; the mole clears the soil of vermin, and is likewise proscribed; the hedge-hog wages war on vipers and cut-worms, and it too is an outlaw; the owl and various other night birds are accomplished rat-hunters, and they also are in disfavor; the adder, toad, and lizard feed on the ravagers of our crops, and all the while we hold them in abhorrence. They are ugly, we say, and without further reason we kill them. But, blind slayers, the day will come when you will perceive that you have been sacrificing your own defenders to an irrational repugnance. You complain of rats, but you nail the owl to your door and let its body dry in the sun as a hideous trophy; you cry out against cut-worms, but you crush the mole every time your spade turns one up; you disembowel the hedge-hog and set your dogs on him just for fun; you bewail the ravages of moth and worm in your granaries, but if the bat falls into your clutches it is seldom that you show him any mercy. Your complaints go up to heaven, but all these willing helpers of yours you treat as creatures accursed. Blind fools that you are, filled with an insane desire to kill!

"Insect-eating birds are of immense importance to agriculture. They divide among themselves the work to be done in field and hedge, meadow and garden, forest and orchard, and wage unceasing warfare on every species of vermin, a terrible tribe that would destroy our crops were not more vigilant guardians than we continually on the watch—guardians of far greater adroitness, of sharper eyesight, of more lasting patience in their endless quest, and having nothing else to do. I am not exaggerating, my little friends; without insect-eating birds famine would decimate us. Who then, unless he be an idiot with a mania for destruction, would dare touch the nests of birds that enliven the country with their plumage and deliver us from the devouring scourge of insects? But

B AT

there are, nevertheless, blood-thirsty gamins who, if they can manage to elude the school-master and play truant, find it a joyous pastime to climb trees and explore hedges in order to rob birds' nests and slaughter the young. These good-for-nothings are under the surveillance of the rural guard and liable to the utmost rigors of the law, to the end that our crops may still be protected by the birds and that our fields and orchards may continue to yield sheaves of grain and baskets of fruit.

"Let us add a few words on the mode of life of these indispensable collaborators. The bat feeds exclusively on insects, anything in that class serving its purpose,—beetles with hard wing-sheaths, spindle-shanked mosquitoes, graceful butterflies, plump-bellied moths of all kinds, such as make havoc of our cereals, vineyards, fruit trees and woolen stuffs, and those that come in the evening, attracted by the lamplight, and singe their wings over the flame. Who shall say how many insects are snapped up by the bats in their nightly tour of our premises? The game is so small, the hunter's appetite so insatiable!

"Note what takes place on a calm summer evening. Lured abroad by the mild temperature of the twilight hours, a swarm of insects leave their retreats and come out to play in the open air, to hunt for food, and to mate, one with another. It is then that great night-moths fly abruptly from flower to flower and plunge their long proboscis to the bottom of the corolla, where they suck up the honey; it is then that the mosquito, eager for human blood, sings its war-song in our ears and chooses our tenderest spot for the insertion of its envenomed lancet; and it is then that the June-bug quits the sheltering leaf, spreads its resounding wings, and goes booming through the air in quest of its kin. The gnats dance in joyous swarms which the least puff of wind disperses like a column of smoke; the moths, their wings powdered with silver dust and their antennæ displayed plume-fashion, indulge in frolicsome gambols or go in search of favorable places for laying their eggs; the little wood-gnawing beetles explore the wrinkled bark of old tree-trunks; the wheat-moths rise in clouds from the ravaged grain and take flight for fresh fields; and other night-flying insects flutter about, alighting on grape-vines and fruit-trees, all busily searching for food and shelter for their calamitous offspring.

"But suddenly this scene of jollity is intruded upon by a most unwelcome kill-joy. The bat, with zig-zag course, flits hither and thither, up and down, back and forth, untiring of wing, appearing and disappearing, darting its head out this way and that, and each time catching an insect in flight, which it immediately crushes and gobbles up, sending it to its doom down a throat that opens wide from ear to ear. It is famous hunting: gnats, beetles, moths, all are there in plenty, and every once in a while a little cry of joy announces the capture of an especially plump victim. As long as the fading twilight admits of it, the ardent hunter continues in this way his work of extermination. Stuffed to repletion at last, the bat regains its dark and quiet retreat; but on the morrow, and every day thereafter throughout the summer, the hunt will be resumed, always with the same ardor, always at the cost of insects only. My children, respect the bat, our helper in destroying the ravagers of our fields."

CHAPTER LXII

THE FARMER'S HELPERS

(Continued)

"THE HEDGE-HOG'S diet consists especially of insects. The lowest order of vermin is disdained by him as too small, but a June-bug larva or a fat-bellied cricket is a capital prize, and when these are not too deeply buried he burrows with claws and snout to unearth them. All night long he goes prowling around, routing out and crunching a goodly number of our enemies, without doing any appreciable harm himself.

"Listen now to what I am going to relate to you from the book of a learned observer. 'I had in a box,' he says, 'a female hedge-hog with her sucklings; and I added to the occupants of the box a vigorous viper, which coiled itself up in one corner. The hedge-hog slowly approached and smelt of the reptile, whereupon the latter raised its head and put itself on guard, showing the while its venomous fangs. For a moment the aggressor recoiled, but only to resume the offensive immediately after and with no sign of fear. The viper then bit the animal on the end of its snout. The hedge-hog licked its bleeding wound, and in doing so received a second bite on the tongue without suffering itself to be at all intimidated. Finally it seized the serpent by the middle of its body, and the two adversaries rolled together on the floor in a furious struggle, the quadruped grunting and snorting, the reptile hissing and making repeated use of its fangs. Suddenly the hedge-hog seized its antagonist's head and crunched it between its teeth, after which, without the least sign of perturbation, it proceeded to devour the forward half of the body. That done, it returned to the opposite corner of the box and, lying on its side, calmly began to suckle its young. On the morrow it ate the rest of the viper. The same experiment was several times repeated, with an interval of some days between each repetition and the next, but the issue was always the same: in spite of wounds that set its snout to bleeding, the hedge-hog invariably finished by devouring the reptile, and neither the mother nor her young showed any ill effects from the experience.'

"It is to be assumed that the hedge-hog has not received the gift of withstanding the venom of reptiles only to leave that gift unemployed. The animal is evidently intended to find its chief pleasure in haunting the places frequented by the viper; in its nightly rounds among the underbrush it must often catch the lurking serpent and make short work of the venomous creature. What valuable service it must render in regions infested by this dangerous reptile! And yet man is the hedge-hog's inveterate foe, showering it with maledictions and treating it as an unclean beast good for nothing except perhaps to arouse the fury of dogs, which have to beware of its bristling back. Do not, my children, imitate this evil example, but respect the hedge-hog for ridding you of the cut-worm and the viper.

"Now as to the mole, what does it eat? The best way to decide the question of an animal's diet is to examine the contents of its stomach. Let us, then, open the mole's stomach and see for ourselves. Sometimes it is found to contain red fragments of the common earth-worm; sometimes a hash of beetles, recognizable from the tough remains that have resisted digestion, such as bits of claws and wing-sheaths; sometimes, again, and oftener

than not, a marmalade of larvæ, especially those of the June-bug, with their distinctive signs like the mandibles and the hard casing of the head. One finds, in short, a little of every sort of game haunting the soil,—polypods and millepeds, insects and caterpillars, moths in the chrysalis, underground worms and nymphs, and so on; but the minutest scrutiny fails to discover a single particle of vegetable matter.

"The mole, then, is exclusively carnivorous, and furthermore it has a monstrous appetite, a perfectly insatiable stomach that in twelve hours demands a quantity of food equal to the animal's weight. The mole's existence is one gluttonous frenzy, ever renewing itself, never appeased; a few hours' abstinence suffices to kill the creature. To still the anguish of that stomach, which is no sooner stuffed with food than it is emptied again, what can the animal count upon? On the grubs living in the ground, and especially on those of the June-bug, tender and fat. It is a small creature for supplying the wants of such an appetite, but its numbers make up for its littleness. What a massacre of worms, then, must not the mole be credited with in the season when worms abound! Scarcely is one meal finished before another begins, and at each repast the worms must be gobbled up by the dozen. To clear a field of these formidable ravagers the farmer has no helper equal to the mole. The only regret is that to reach the vermin on which the animal lives, it has to burrow among the roots where they have their haunts. Many roots that lie in the way are necessarily ruptured in this work; plants are broken off and destroyed; and, finally, the little piles of earth, or mole-hills, heaped up by the animal in the course of its excavations, impede the reaper when harvest-time comes around. Never mind: the worms would have caused much more serious damage, and to get rid of them there is nothing like this ravenous insect-hunter. Therefore, children, never molest the mole, the protector of our crops.

"The toad is harmless, but that is not enough to commend the creature to our attention. It too is a helper of great worth, a greedy devourer of slugs, beetles, larvæ, and every sort of vermin. Discreetly withdrawn by day under the cool cover of a stone in some obscure hole, it leaves its retreat at nightfall to make its regular rounds, propelling itself, hoppity-hop, on its ample stomach. Here is a slug on its way to the lettuce-plants; yonder is a cricket chirping at the entrance to its hole; and over there a June-bug is laying its eggs in the ground. Master toad comes along in circumspect fashion, opens his cavernous mouth, and in three gulps swallows them all with a gurgle of satisfaction. Oh, but that was good! Now for some more of the same sort.

"He continues on his rounds, and when dawn begins to glimmer in the east what kind of a hodge-podge of variegated vermin must there not be in the glutton's capacious maw? Yet they kill this useful creature—stone it to death because, forsooth, it is not so handsome as it might be. My children, may you never be guilty of such cruelty, such foolish and mischievous cruelty! Never stone the toad, for in doing so you would be robbing the fields of a vigilant guardian. Let the poor creature perform in peace its appointed task as destroyer of worms and insects.

"Finally, and not least of all, must be mentioned the various birds, chiefly the little birds of our fields and farm-yards, that help the farmer by devouring harmful insects and the seeds of wild grasses and intrusive weeds. These indefatigable assistants, however, we have already discussed, and we have gratefully acknowledged our indebtedness to them. No more, then, need be said about them at present, except in the way of renewed admonition never to molest them, never to rob their nests; for they are our friends and benefactors."

FINIS

www.ingramcontent.com/pod-product-compliance
Lightning Source LLC
Chambersburg PA
CBHW050550190726
48283CB00007B/2084